BROTHERHOOD BEYOND *the* YARD

BROTHERHOOD BEYOND *the* YARD

Sally Fernandez

DUNHAM
books

This is a work of fiction. Although based on some actual events, other events, names, characters, places, and incidents either are the product of the author's imagination, or are used fictitiously. Any resemblance to actual persons, living or dead, business establishments, events, or locales is entirely coincidental.

For information on licensing, bulk sales or permissions, contact the publisher:
Dunham Books
63 Music Square East
Nashville, TN 37203
www.dunhamgroupinc.com

Cover design by Sally Fernandez
Drawings by Massimo Pivetti

Trade Paperback ISBN: 978-1-939447-03-6
Ebook ISBN: 978-1-939447-04-3

Library of Congress Cataloging-in-Publication Data has been applied for,
Library of Congress Control Number: 2011900948

Dedicated to my incredible editor, best friend, and greatest supporter—my loving husband.
Ti Amo

AUTHOR'S NOTE

This story is pure fiction. The principal characters and many of the locations are fictitious as well. On the other hand, there are numerous facts for readers to sort out for themselves. The story may also seem to have a tinge of a conspiracy theory, which it is not. It gestated solely in my vivid imagination—a story concocted in my own mind that needed to be expressed.

A few authentic locations play an integral part in the plot. The descriptions of Harvard University and of Florence, Italy, are genuine, although Banca Nazionale does not exist. Some of the characters in Florence are real, and with their permission, I have used their actual names and occupations.

Just because you do not take an interest in politics doesn't mean politics won't take an interest in you!

—Pericles, 430 BC

PART ONE

1

THE DARKEST HOUR

The ground floor of the White House was shrouded in darkness, except for the slight glow under the door of the room where the Secret Service agents relax and the illumination from the corner office on the northeast side of the building. It was the office of Hamilton Scott, director of the States Intelligence Agency, or the SIA, of the United States government.

His office was only a stairway from the president.

Director Scott began his career in 1985, in the Foreign Service, working for the U.S. Diplomatic Security Service, the DSS, headquartered in Washington, D.C. In 1987, the DSS transferred him to Rome, Italy, to manage the security detail for the American embassy. Almost a decade later, in 1996, he was transferred back to the States to work for the Central Intelligence Agency in Langley, Virginia.

In 2003, the head of the CIA appointed Director Scott to head up the SIA, an agency newly established in reaction to the September 11 terrorist attacks. The charter of this new agency was to coordinate information throughout the intelligence community and to establish priorities to ensure the protection of American citizens.

The personnel of the SIA are exceptional men and women with military and law enforcement backgrounds. They have operated in high-risk situations and carried out complex operations for both the intelligence agencies and the private sector.

The president, through his initiative, signed an executive order granting the SIA top security clearance for all aspects of domestic, foreign, and defense intelligence. It is the intelligence gathering, the assessments, and the high-risk security solutions that are paramount to achieve its goal.

—

It was April 6, 2009, at 2:10 a.m. eastern daylight time. Director Scott had been sitting for hours at his large executive desk, with file folders stacked and papers scattered on top. Behind him was a long, slender fluorescent light casting a glow over two secure computers stationed on top of the credenza.

The door to the office was locked from the inside.

The director was alone, having just finished recording the events of his last and most crucial investigation. He reconstructed those events chronologically, piecing them together from his notes along with the evidence he had gathered over the years. Most of the evidence came to him by way of his associate and the testimonies of those directly involved. He had transcribed in infinite detail as best he could the actions he had taken, using his written summation, and at times referring to his notes to guide him.

The director began by describing how the U.S. citizens were slowly coming out of one of the worst economic disasters of their time, a time when the country was still engaged in the war on terror or "man-made disasters," as referred to, incredibly, by a high-ranking official in the administration.

"I believe the administration had encouraged the use of these euphemisms, even though it put our national security at risk," he said to the computer. "However, this was not a time to engage in more adversity."

Hamilton's primary role as director had always been to protect the U.S. citizens, not only from enemies abroad but also from enemies within. For these reasons, he had chosen to take certain precautions; had he not, the security of the United States would have been in grave jeopardy.

To maintain the utmost security, he dictated directly into his computer using the latest voice recognition techniques. "After recording the details of this case I will transfer this statement and copies of the evidence to a flash drive," he voiced. "The flash drive, along with six memory sticks containing the video-recorded testimonies that support the facts, will be stored in a place of safekeeping."

Using the Department of Defense's secure delete standards, under Section 5555.2-M, Hamilton used LSoft Technologies' Hard Disk Scrubber to remove his declaration from the computer's hard drive. He then destroyed all the original evidence, including his copious notes, and the summary he created containing his talking points.

Although he had painstakingly recorded the details of his last investigation, he would not release his statement until an undetermined time in the future. "My intent is not to change the course of history, but

I am prepared to withhold these facts until the country has sufficiently healed and the American people are equipped to cope with the impact that which will surely follow."

"The time is not now," he recorded, completing his statement.

Director Scott had prepared instructions, however, and arranged with a third party to release the information sooner, should either he or his associate, the only people who knew the totality of this case, meet with an untimely death or any other suspicious events.

Or, if the president did not live up to his commitment.

Secured with the flash drive and memory sticks, containing the evidence, is a copy of a letter that reads as follows:

UNITED STATES OF AMERICA
States Intelligence Agency

April 6, 2009

News Corporation
1211 Avenue of the Americas
New York, NY 10036

Attn: Current CEO of Fox Television Stations Group

My recent disappearance or death now triggers a series of actions vital to the future of the United States.

Enclosed is a flash drive containing a detailed statement and copies of substantiated evidence, along with a set of memory sticks with video-recorded testimonies. In combination, the evidence describes the most horrific crime ever perpetrated against the American people.

I trust you will divulge this information in its entirety and in the most appropriate way.

With deep regret,

Hamilton D. Scott

Hamilton D. Scott
Director

cc: Managing Editor, Wall Street Journal
Enclosures: (1) flash drive, (6) memory sticks

Hours earlier, the director had met with the president.

The president fully comprehended what the director had done and understood the severity of the consequences if he did not follow his directives.

While speaking with the president, Director Hamilton Scott tendered his resignation, to be effective April 30, 2009.

2

LA FRATELLANZA

Nine months earlier, in August 2008, members of *La Fratellanza*, "The Brotherhood," sat around their round conference table in a small office tucked away on the South Side of Chicago. The table was similar to the one they had used in their study group years ago while attending Harvard. At this table, however, these men had spent countless hours carrying out each phase of their mission, a goal that officially started in the bitterly cold winter of 2000.

During that same period, each member of this elite group established his career. Some had met and married their mates and had begun to rear their children, and others had remained single.

All had remained devoted to La Fratellanza.

—

One prominent member was Seymour Lynx, who was the media genius and CEO of MediaLynx, Inc., located in Los Angeles. At that time, he was the creator of several political documentaries targeting various presidents; two received Academy Award nominations for Best Documentary, one rumored to be only a few votes away from carrying home the Oscar. Seymour did not start out focusing on political affairs, for his first passion was to write and produce a great epic, paying particular attention to period detail and opulent settings. Somehow, he ended up producing films more like Oliver Stone's.

Along the way, his focal point changed and he found his groove. Seymour became the man every special interest group wanted. They needed his help to get their messages across to the public, primarily to thwart the political opposition, whoever it might be at the time. He was instrumental in producing many of the 501(c)(3) "nonpolitical" political ads and highly political assault ads for 527 organizations. Interestingly, Seymour was apolitical. As a political agnostic, he didn't care about the right, left, or the middle, for that matter; he just liked spinning the truth.

Seymour was tall in a lanky sort of way, just topping six feet, with short curly black hair capping his head. If his hair were an inch higher it would qualify as an Afro, and if one looked closely enough, one would see a hint of a goatee. Moreover, he always sported a different pair of eyeglasses to coordinate with his trendy clothing. He was affable, and at first glance, one would not exactly consider him a ladies' man, but looks are deceiving. He would often boast he enjoyed many years of an active bachelorhood.

After five years of playing the field, Seymour married his childhood sweetheart. They reconnected while attending his tenth high school reunion; he was smitten the moment he laid eyes on her, and she was with him, even to this day. Seymour and his wife, along with their two girls, lived in Brentwood, just outside Hollywood, California.

Chase Worthington, the oldest member of the group, was the CFO, chief financial officer, for the National Depositors Trust Bank in New York City. At first, his climb up the corporate ladder was slow. Earning a bachelor's degree from Boston University only propelled him to a managerial position at a local community bank close to his hometown of Dorchester, near Boston, Massachusetts. It wasn't until several years later that he returned to school to earn a master's degree in finance, this time from Harvard.

Evermore serious, Chase stood six feet five inches tall with a slender build. His hair, a sandy brown color, was always slicked straight back. At all times, he donned one of hundreds of his bow ties, and with his horn-rimmed glasses, he painted the personification of a corporate banker. He was also as much a Puritan as his ancestors who first stepped on these shores. That, along with his name and mannerisms, led most to assume he came replete with a pedigree. In his case, both looks and name were deceiving.

As a single child, Chase was reared in a working-class section of Boston. His father, Henry Worthington Jr., was a mathematics teacher at the local high school, and his mother worked at the corner produce market. When he was born, it was his mother's idea to give him an affluent-sounding name. Her hope was that the name would in turn give him the respect and opportunity she and his father never had. Whether it was the name, the dress, or Chase's particularly high IQ, one could not decipher.

After Harvard, he resumed his banking career, this time at the National Depositors Trust Bank in New York, where he found himself quickly climbing the corporate ladder. During the climb, he married the public relations officer at a competing bank, whom he had been courting for a number of years. Shortly after his marriage, Chase received his promotion to CFO. The Worthingtons, finally affluent, lived in Greenwich, Connecticut, along with their four sons.

The sophisticate of the group, Paolo Salvatore, was born in Italy, but moved to the United States, with his parents, as a young boy. While Paolo was fluent in Italian, he exuded confidence with his fluency in the English language. He was capable of constructing a falsehood that would convince almost anyone, on any subject, that his premise was true. Like Seymour, he knew how to spin the truth—or rather, twist the facts.

Despite Paolo's towering height and strong physique, he possessed a surprisingly soothing manner. That, along with his dark hair and sapphire eyes, helped to open the hearts and minds of his listeners.

Early on in his career, Paolo attempted to run for the office of mayor in his hometown, but after a long, drawn-out campaign, and losing by a wide margin, he decided that side of the political sphere was not for him. Paolo determined he was better suited to placing his powerful words in the mouths of more experienced politicians. Quickly changing his focus, he started writing campaign speeches for governors and then senators from various states across the nation. However, Paolo's most prominent position was that of communications director and speechwriter for a U.S. president.

Paolo was truly in demand, and those who sought his talents had no hesitancy when engaging his services. It made no difference that he'd just written speeches for the opposition party. Those who employed him generally accepted that he had no political allegiance and was impartial.

Like Seymour, Paolo was forever the ladies' man and had remained single for many years. It was only two years ago that he decided it was time to settle down and married a law professor from Georgetown University. They had one son named Mario. At the time, the family resided in Reston, Virginia, just outside Washington, D.C., in an affluent neighborhood full of intellectuals like themselves.

Then there was Hank Kramer, the colorful character of the team. He was of average height and build, just average, including the slight paunch, but with a gift of gab that made him exceedingly popular. He effectively communicated well with people from all walks of life, and he put his talents to excellent use in the organization he built. As founder and CEO of the Chestnut Foundation, a grassroots organization committed to social justice, he would frequently rally the neighborhoods on the South Side of Chicago around any cause.

Hank married one of his organizers, divorced her, and then married another. After several affairs, and several more marriages and divorces, he was once again single. Evidently, his gift wasn't much help to him in the organization called marriage. Besides, he was more wedded to his career than to anything or anyone.

While Hank could talk a good game, he was a bit of a charlatan. He spent his days helping those less fortunate through his foundation, but at night, he hypocritically rubbed shoulders with the elite, which he preferred. On many occasions, he would share the elevator in his luxury high-rise on North Lake Shore Drive with his neighbor Oprah.

After all, he worked hard and felt he had earned the good life, a mantra he often cited.

Ah, yes, Simon Hall. He was next to the oldest in the group, a year shy of Chase Worthington. With several degrees from various universities under his belt, he often referred to himself as a "professional intellect." As brilliant as Simon was, he never fit into the corporate environment and preferred to freelance as a consultant.

Among many of his accomplishments, he was instrumental in redesigning the security software for ATMs, automated teller machines, which he downloaded to thousands of ATMs across the United States. That gave the added protection needed against the underworld of computer "hackers" who gain unauthorized access to other people's information.

Simon was undeniably a technology expert who knew his way around the world of the Internet, and there wasn't a server he couldn't breach. Of course, Simon never thought of himself as a hacker, but more of a computer junkie with extraordinary skills in the areas of technology and programming.

Of this influential group, Simon was an enigma. Describing his physical attributes was simple. He was tall, with black hair and dark eyes, almost equal in color, and olive skin. Most would consider him somewhat handsome. The character of the man, though, was more difficult to understand. Simon had an enormous amount of charisma and powers of persuasion. His magnetic appeal connected instantly with those he met. He clearly wasn't your run-of-the-mill computer geek.

The other members of the group claimed his mysterious persona and empathetic demeanor created an aura that defied description. One of the members quipped, "He is sort of a cross between Joe Black, Brad Pitt's role in *Meet Joe Black,* and Frank Abagnale Jr., played by Leonardo DiCaprio in *Catch Me If You Can.*"

Nevertheless, they all came to trust Simon in short order for reasons even they were not able to articulate.

In spite of his tremendous hypnotic appeal, he remained single, never finding the perfect mate that could match his intellect. Simon had resided alone for many years in the San Francisco area of California.

—

Knowing the players and the roles they played was crucial to understand how and why certain events transpired. Because at one o'clock that morning, in August 2008, still hot and steamy from the evening before, this eclectic group had assembled to layout the steps of the critical phase of their plan—a plan hatched over a decade ago, during their college days.

Over the past seven years, La Fratellanza had located, educated, prepared, and groomed a man for the highest office in the land. It was up to them to place him behind the desk in the Oval Office. Three years prior to that point, Abner Baari had become a member of the United States Senate, representing the state of Illinois. The time had arrived and La Fratellanza needed to ensure their newly minted Senator Baari did not lose his run for president of the United States.

There were only three months until the election.

3

THE HARVARD YARD

To grasp the enormity of how these events unfolded, one must dial back to the beginning, to October 1995, thirteen years before that crucial meeting in Chicago.

La Fratellanza then sat around a different round table, this time in Simon Hall's apartment on Irving Terrace in Cambridge, Massachusetts. It was the table where they gathered for their study group sessions. Simon was the only one at the time who could afford to live off campus, and his apartment was located just a short distance from Harvard Yard.

The Yard was located on the southern edge of "Cow-yard Row" when the land was first purchased in 1638, hence the name. The Yard now houses the buildings for the Graduate School of Arts and Sciences. The wide, grassy area surrounded by these buildings is the geographic center of the campus of Harvard University.

It was the site where the members of this diverse group would earn their various degrees.

When the group first entered apartment #2B on the second floor of Simon's three-story building, they walked into the dining room with its large picture window overlooking the street below. There was an archway on the left with an entrance to the kitchen and a sizable living room to the right. Between the living room and the dining room, on the side farthest from the street, there was a small hallway leading to two doors: one to the bathroom and the second to the only bedroom.

Modestly decorated, the apartment normally had two large sofas centered on opposite walls in the living room facing a square coffee table. No one was allowed in the bedroom, so all that remained to the eye was the round dining room table and six chairs.

But that was before.

Each of them individually had visited Simon's apartment on several occasions, but at their first official gathering, something was different. The changes Simon had made to his small one-bedroom apartment surprised them. The round dining room table was still in place, encircled by its chairs, but he had turned the living room into what resembled a computer lab.

Simon had removed one of the sofas and in its place was a long table. Alongside the adjoining wall was another table abutting at a ninety-degree angle. Three computers were set up on each table, with a large black box in the center where the tables joined.

"What's with the new decor?" Hank probed.

Simon explained that each of them would have his own computer and that all the computers had a connection to a server. As he pointed to the black box in the corner, he said, "Think of the server as a large hard drive that will contain—and more importantly, secure—your data."

Sensing they were still puzzled, he pointed out how distracting it was to work in the labs on campus, and that having to back up their data each time to floppy disks was cumbersome.

"The wired computers have unlimited access to the campus system and the Internet, and I've configured them to run much faster than the campus computers you are accustomed to using," he casually mentioned. "Most important, you won't have to back up your data every day."

Simon averred that because the other members would be spending so much of their time at his apartment for their study group, it would be advantageous for them to have the freedom to prepare for their other assignments as well. He then presented each of them with a key to his apartment, reminding them, "The bedroom is off-limits."

As they sat around the round table, Simon studied their faces intently and glowed in self-satisfaction at his choice of members. In turn, his new recruits also seemed pleased to have been included, especially with open access to his apartment and the computer lab.

The shape of the table never lent itself to recognize formally a group leader to assume the leadership role, but by consent, the others in the group elected Simon to that position. After all, Simon had established the study group and recruited each of the members. Clearly, it didn't hurt that it was also his apartment.

At that first meeting, Simon recommended some ground rules for their study sessions, "I suggest we meet every Monday, Wednesday, and Friday at five o'clock in the afternoon." Having full knowledge of their schedules, he knew there would be no conflicts. "All of us can take one hour to discuss any issues we are facing with any of our course assignments and the other team members can offer solutions," he suggested. "The timing can be flexible, and any one of us can yield his time to support the others when deemed necessary."

After some discussion of various alternatives, they collectively accepted Simon's proposal.

He then went on to propose that each of them take the opportunity to do a brief show-and-tell to become better acquainted. "Let's talk about what we've been doing for a living, what coaxed us to get another degree, and what we enjoy doing in our leisure time. Things like that," Simon put forward, "Mostly, a get-to-know-you session."

Actually, he had already acquired intimate knowledge about his fellow members and knew most of what they were about to say.

Simon, giving them no time to object, was the first to volunteer.

He began with how he grew up in San Francisco and attended the University of California, Berkeley, where he obtained a master's degree in psychology. "I was fascinated with how a person's mind operates and thought it would be helpful in whatever career I'd eventually select." He told the group that he had no desire ever to work for a corporation, or even a small business, unless it was his own. He saw himself as a freelance consultant, but was unsure in what area of business, given his wide range of interests.

Then, as one member of the group remembered, he appeared to have strayed in a moment of reverie. Several of the others believed he was referring to a romantic interlude in his life, which explained the restricted access to the bedroom. In a short time, however, they realized he was talking about the Internet. It was riveting when Simon spoke of how the Internet, and yet-to-be-discovered technology, was going to change the world forever.

He continued to elaborate on how the arrival of Microsoft Internet Explorer, a few months before, had already changed the way people gathered and utilized information. However, he thought the users of the Internet had not yet realized its full potential, and he wanted to be on the leading edge of that discovery and any other advances that followed.

Simon casually mentioned, "I also have a BS in computer science from UC Berkeley," which explained his expertise in setting up the computer lab. He then went on to clarify his approach, utilizing this new age of information management, from a different angle. He wanted to focus more on the business-related challenges of the technology.

Simon believed it was essential for him to earn a master's in science, technology, and management from Harvard, to fulfill his long-harbored dream.

"As for my spare time," he said, "I use it to hone my programming and research skills."

Simon, with a self-satisfied smile, turned to Chase Worthington, who picked up the cue.

—

Chase stated his main interest was in the world of economics and finance. His desire was to one day be the CFO for a major national bank. "Frankly, I was looking for an opportunity to leave Dorchester, my hometown, and move to the financial capital of the world, New York City," he said gleefully.

He described his work as the bank manager of a small community bank in Boston, and alluded to the fact his career had stymied. While he had a bachelor of science degree in the field of finance, Chase was convinced a graduate degree would provide him with more opportunities, and certainly, a master's degree in business economics from Harvard would provide him with a platform to advance his career.

In terms of interest, Chase was not an avid sports fan and preferred mind games over sporting events. He loved reading business books, although from time to time he would unwind with a novel. "For example, I just finished reading Ludlum's *The Scorpio Illusion*. The story line was about a beautiful terrorist determined to kill the heads of state of several major countries, including the United States. It was vintage Ludlum. I liked the fast-moving thriller elements and the international intrigue," he confessed. Chase let slip that it was so different from his life, where he tended to play it safe; occasionally he needed a vicarious "benign" pleasure. It was his fix.

"I'm single," he further acknowledged, "but hope someday that will change, although I'm not currently dating."

Simon's selection of Chase was a natural.

Their relationship started long before they arrived at Harvard, under circumstances that became a determining factor. They met several years earlier when Simon set up a sizable account at Chase's branch in Boston. Transferring upward of a million dollars was an astronomical amount in those days, and Simon immediately became one of the bank's highest net-worth clients, a relationship that Chase treasured and nurtured. For the first time in his career, it had moved him into the limelight.

Eventually Chase and Simon became trusted friends.

In their early days, Simon convinced his new friend he had a lot more to offer. He admonished Chase for having already spent so many years as the bank manager, all the while knowing there was little future in sight. Simon recognized Chase's intellect and desire for something more. He persuaded Chase to return to school to further his education.

Shortly after Harvard accepted Simon, he was able to convince Chase to apply. Simon worked hand in glove with Chase to help him complete his

Application for Admission and compose his Statement of Purpose—but two obstacles had remained.

First, Chase had already missed the deadline for taking the GRE, the Graduate Record Examination. So, with a little of his "magic," Simon entered the Harvard University computer database and recorded Chase's GRE score of eight hundred, the highest score one can receive. It was of little importance to Simon that he illegally recorded the score, but Chase was uneasy.

"If you had actually taken the test you would have attained that score," Simon offered convincingly. It would be the first of several times Simon would need to entice Chase.

The second obstacle had been Chase's inability to give up his job to return to school, so Simon agreed to loan him the necessary funds from his sizable bank account. Moreover, he wrote Chase's Statement of Financial Resources, indicating that he had the ability to pay tuition and housing for the full two years. Chase was then able to produce a bank statement from the account he set up as an educational fund, underwritten by Simon.

Chase was low-key, overly conservative, and had an impeccable record. He was a natural with numbers and understood all aspects of the banking system. So there he was, attending the Graduate School of Arts and Sciences at Harvard University, satisfying a lifelong dream, as was Simon.

Simon had his man in tow and was relieved. *Thank you, Chase, for not acknowledging our prior relationship to the group.* He was acutely aware that Chase was indebted to him and he could rely on Chase to follow the rules without challenge.

—

Paolo Salvatore picked up the nod from Simon and followed Chase by explaining that his plan was a career in some area of public service. He had earned an undergraduate degree from New York University in law and society, its pre-law program, but was uncertain as to how he would apply his knowledge. There was no doubt he loved to talk, to write, to preach, and most of all, to spin anything political.

"I'm amazed at the gullibility of people," he proclaimed. "I've witnessed firsthand how words can turn the most committed into the uncommitted, lies into truths, virtues into scandals." His belief was enough to motivate him to enroll in Harvard, to broaden his knowledge and study to attain a master's degree in political economy and government. Paolo punctuated his desire for a firmer understanding of the full impact of politics on the economy. He believed that the economy was most influential when it came time to vote, votes he hoped his words would persuade.

"After all," he boasted, "Harvard is where many lawyers turned politicians. If it was good enough for them, it certainly is good enough for me. Someday these politicians might even need my help if they want to be elected."

Paolo was a quick study with raw intelligence, but his charm alone, delivered with that sophisticated Italian accent, was almost enough to assure him a bright future. Surprisingly, Paolo had no immediate plans for any serious relationship. "There are so many women and so little time." He laughed.

His only other passion besides women and politics was calcio, which is Italian for football, but is actually the game of soccer. Paolo, like every other Italian, worshipped his football team and never missed a game. His VCR was forever recording, because unfortunately, the games were played across the pond, six hours ahead of eastern daylight time.

Simon met Paolo when they were seated next to each other at the complimentary dinner in Dudley Hall for newly admitted students. Paolo, who took enormous pleasure in conversation, would happily talk to anyone, especially about politics. He was perfectly comfortable starting a tête-à-tête, even with complete strangers, and no matter what their political bent was, he could spin either way.

It just so happened on that night he struck up a conversation with Simon, complaining, "Can you believe the problems brewing at the White House over this Lewinsky scandal? The definition of *is*, was rather a lame riposte coming from the president." There was no doubt in Paolo's mind it would have been better for the president to come clean sooner rather than later.

Simon, not caring either way, had taken the defense. He suggested it was a personal matter and should not be of any concern to the American public.

Paolo, fully prepared, utilizing the myriad of information he had acquired from the governors and the senators for whom he had written speeches, challenged Simon's premise, and their debate continued. Feeling he had sufficiently made his argument and not wanting to engage any further, Paolo diverted from the subject, shrugged, and said, "They should fire whoever is writing the president's material. I could have done so much better."

Simon loved listening to Paolo, his arguments, and his passion. Most of all, he admired his extensive knowledge of the questionable activities inside the Beltway. He had previously vetted Paolo, so sitting next to him at the dinner that night had been no coincidence. A few more planned encounters were all that were necessary before asking Paolo to join his study group.

True to form, Paolo had accepted without hesitation.

—

Hank Kramer's love was social policy. He loved pulling groups of people together to fight a cause, believing the more voices heard, the more strength would be given to the issue. It didn't matter what the rallying cry of the moment was, so long as it was tackling what he conceived to be a social injustice. He felt there were an endless number of issues to address.

"To be effective I have to be more knowledgeable than the other people in my field," he rightfully admitted.

Hank had solid experience, but needed more structured knowledge that would ideally come from a master's degree in government and social policy from Harvard, to supplement his bachelor's in sociology from the University of Illinois. He understood that credentials alone wouldn't carry all the weight, but he felt that in conjunction with his experience, it would be a formidable combination.

"While I want to fight for the poor against injustice, I'm not fighting to be poor." He smiled. He had intended to start his own foundation that would allow him to follow his vision, and at the same time provide him with a comfortable living. He spoke with such an air of confidence; the others knew it would unfold exactly the way he planned.

"I am also a member of Mensa, which in Latin means table," Hank managed to slip into the conversation. "Coincidently, it is a round-table society, specifically an international high IQ society. In order to qualify for Mensa, one must score above the ninety-eighth percentile on the standard test for intelligence."

What may have seemed like boasting to some seemed natural and innocuous to those in the room.

Hank was also proud of the fact that he was a chess master, as he made clear. "I love the strategizing, setting up the long-term goals, and then achieving them, the basic premise behind the game. The board is my mental battlefield," he boasted, and then continued to brag, "Other than chess, I don't have much time for extracurricular activities, except I can find time for an occasional rendezvous with my female acquaintances." One would hardly describe Hank as good-looking, but his gift of gab evidently attracted the opposite and attractive sex.

A week after settling into his new life on campus, Hank had met his first new friend. It was at the Widener Library. Hank had been reaching for a large book, titled *Housing Finance: Expanding Capital for Affordable Multifamily Housing,* from one of the stacks. It was a report to the congressional committees from the United States General Accounting

Office, dated October 1993. The 136-page volume slipped from his grasp, only to find Chase on the receiving end.

Chase couldn't help but notice the hefty title and thought it an odd choice. "Rather weighty, no pun intended," he said, "especially for the first week of class. What's the interest?"

Hank pontificated for several minutes about how every citizen had the right to own a home, and that the United States was failing miserably at providing that entitlement, among others.

Chase in turn had argued that it wasn't necessarily a right, but more a privilege, and a discourse followed.

Amazingly, at the end of an hour, the consummate conservative Chase and the hopelessly liberal Hank struck up a friendship that continued for years.

Chase relayed to Simon his encounter with Hank.

Actually, Simon had already checked into Hank's background and had suggested that Chase befriend him. He asked Chase to spend time with Hank and ferret out whether he would be interested in joining their study group.

Hank had proved he had the talent to be a formidable organizer, and fortunately, for Simon, he wanted to enhance his education at Harvard.

After Chase made the introduction, Simon formally invited Hank to join.

More than curious and intrigued by the whole idea, Hank accepted wholeheartedly.

—

The last member of the group to sign on was Seymour Lynx, who was majoring in film and visual studies. "My dream had always been to be the next Sir Richard Attenborough, the British filmmaker of great films like *A Bridge Too Far* and *Gandhi,* to name two," he stated with dramatic flair.

Seymour then reluctantly acknowledged that he had a bachelor's degree in Jewish studies from the University of California in Los Angeles.

At which point Simon interjected, "Why Jewish studies, if you want to be a filmmaker?"

Seymour explained he had grown up amid the filmmaking business. "I basically teethed on film strips on the cutting room floor. Oh, coincidently, my father is a top production manager for MGM Studios. Filmmaking is in my DNA. It is my calling, and I want to be the best. From here, it gets a little complicated," he admitted.

Seymour explained that his father had warned him that he was pursuing a career in a fickle business, and if he wanted to continue to work at the studio, he had to complete a formal education. "My skill level far exceeds what a formal education could possibly offer," he boasted. Then, with less gusto, he added, "Having no choice, I relented."

Therefore, Seymour enrolled in Jewish Studies, in part, to get back at his father who forced him to get a degree. In addition, having been reared an atheist; he suspected he had a lot of misinformation about religion. Surprisingly, he found that he enjoyed his religious courses. He even envisioned one day that it might present a new genre for his films.

"That wasn't the end of it." He grinned. Seymour told the group that he vividly remembered the first thing his father said to him on the day of his graduation. "Now that you have wasted the last four years of your life, plan on spending the next two years majoring in film and visual studies, and this time at Harvard." Seymour mimicked his father's edict. "I'm good, but my father is better, so here I am," he conceded.

Seymour's ego evidently complemented his appeal, so as he waxed on, the others did not find it the least bit offensive. With not much more to convey, he admitted that aside from filmmaking, he loved women, and more than women, he loved gambling. Poker was his forte.

He knew nothing of politics and was apolitical at best, which made him and Paolo decidedly strange bedfellows, one a political junkie and the other a political virgin. The two had met and had become friends during the second week of classes over a couple of brews at Jake's, the local pub on Cambridge Street. The one trait Paolo and Seymour shared was that they oozed with charm, captivating the ladies.

Simon, again in his usual manner, had previously checked out Seymour thoroughly. He knew both Paolo and Seymour hung out at Jake's, and had asked Paolo if he was of the opinion that Seymour would be a suitable fit for the study group.

Paolo said he was extremely likeable but offered to scope him out further; if he found Seymour acceptable, he'd formally introduce him to Simon. Of course, Simon already knew Paolo would be impressed, and the introduction would predictably be forthcoming.

Hence, Seymour became the fifth member of the study group.

—

Their majors were dissimilar, but their ambitions were the same. They were all overachievers who loved challenges. The fact that they all happened to become members of this study group was no coincidence. Simon had a list of potential candidates, and thus far, he had been fortunate to recruit his first choices. However, he had one more candidate he wanted to bring into the fold.

That would come later.

During the first year, the group met several times a week to discuss their various assignments. They found it invaluable to have their own personal computer lab and to be able to study freely in Simon's apartment. They also managed regular time-out sessions at Jake's Pub to chow down and relax.

Jake's had a mezzanine level with a row of booths that overlooked the long bar below, and within a short time, most of the patrons were aware of a tacit understanding that the last booth was permanently reserved. It was where this group of eclectic students gathered regularly. Their subjects of conversation embraced a vast assortment of topics, usually outside the realm of their particular studies, tapping away at each other's emotional, as well as their intellectual quotient.

It was also the place where these intellectuals came to know and admire each other, on a different, more personal level.

It was the place where they bonded.

4

TRUTH OR DARE

Throughout the first year of adjustment to academic life, some members of the group were fraught with personal dilemmas. Some brought on by themselves; some introduced by others. It was also a time when the group exhausted many hours studying together, coaching each other when necessary, and spending many evenings at Jake's Pub.

Eventually, during the time spent at the apartment and their jamborees at Jake's, this group of men began to feel more like brothers than schoolmates. To outsiders they seemed inseparable, and they were. It was also toward the end of that first year that they began to be more open and personal with each other and the group as a whole.

As for Chase, he was not normally prone to working in such proximity with others, so his desire to be part of this group was atypical. However, years before, Simon had instilled in him the confidence he needed, producing a burning ambition Chase had not previously experienced. His loyalty to Simon was for instilling in him a new desire of wanting to belong.

Similar to Chase, Hank felt a kindred spirit with Simon and the others as well, but on a different level. He sensed they all understood his personal quest, but it was Simon's knowledge of the Internet that provided him access to an entirely new medium for getting out his message.

Seymour's motivation was a little more complicated. With his father's accomplishments overshadowing his own, he always strived to compete, and while the film industry was all he knew, he was becoming more restless about his future. He'd swing from genre to genre, his lust for the epic film being subdued. It wasn't until listening to Paolo ad nauseam that politics crept into his psyche. Along with Simon's understanding of the Internet, Seymour had found his true calling. He felt indebted to the group for his awakening.

Paolo's reason was simpler: he loved being in the group. Maybe it was an Italian "guy" thing. It certainly provided him with a built-in audience that liked listening to what he had to say. Surprisingly, he liked to listen to them as well.

It was one of those nights at Jake's, after they professed their gratitude for being part of the group, that they committed their allegiance to the fraternity.

From the sidelines, Simon concluded the time was ripe. Until that moment, he'd had many opportunities to test their talents. Now, the time had arrived—for the final and most crucial test—their loyalty.

Simon took the opportunity to suggest they engage in a high-stakes version of truth-or-dare, that seemingly innocuous game of placing an opponent in a situation with potentially embarrassing consequences. The high stakes are borne out of the depth of questioning. "It would be an opportunity to cement our relationships further, sharing on an even deeper level some of our secrets," he said, encouraging them.

But it would also be his way to evaluate privately their level of devotion.

It was nearing eight o'clock on a Saturday night after several rounds of beer. So it was clear at that moment why they toasted each other with the words, "Why not!"

Jake's became the scene of their truth-or-dare game where they would divulge some of their inner thoughts and learn some surprising details about one another, but only after they had taken a pledge to maintain total secrecy.

—

Sitting in their booth, Simon spun his empty beer bottle. With the neck of the bottle pointing to Chase, the game began.

Chase opted to turn to Hank, and asked, "Truth or dare?"

"Truth," he responded with a smile.

Chase then posed the question, "Were you aware that the information about the dean was false?"

Hank, the consummate organizer, was surprised that Chase even knew about his ordeal. He explained how he had planned to pull a group together to demonstrate against the administration for its minority scholarship selection process, at which time he was going to implicate the dean of the Graduate School of Arts and Science.

"I received an e-mail with shocking information pertaining to the awards allegedly granted to several of the selection committee's family members, including the dean's," he reported. "Admittedly, I reacted hastily and broke one of my cardinal rules to validate all information."

Unfortunately, by a strange coincidence, the dean's office discovered Hank was the organizer of the protest. The dean, feeling Hank had impugned his reputation, was considering having him stand before the student ethics committee and face the possibility of expulsion.

Actually, Hank was aware that the e-mail was from Simon, who provided the information as a "private" dare, challenging Hank to dispute the administration's actions. All along Simon had known the information was false, but did not enlighten Hank at the time. Brazen as usual, Hank had believed Simon not only could, but also should, help him out of the mess. He knew that Simon was one of the dean's favorites and had asked him to intervene on his behalf. On several occasions, Simon had helped the dean with some crucial problems. Coincidently, they involved efforts to thwart a computer hacker who wreaked havoc with the campus database.

Hank's misguided position was set straight when Simon appealed to the dean with a passionate defense. He was able to convince the dean it would not happen again, and assured him that Hank would correct the record regarding the authenticity and merits of the minority scholarship program. It was a close call.

"I promised Simon I wouldn't engage directly in controversial issues, a difficult commitment for a dedicated activist." He smirked. He consoled himself by rationalizing the concession was justified by his feeling of indebtedness toward Simon for bailing him out of a jam.

Although, after the episode, Hank did challenge Simon and asked him if he knew that the information was false.

Simon had matter-of-factly responded, "Yes, but you didn't know that at the time, and that was the point. You rallied around a cause, and you've demonstrated once again your ability as a great organizer."

Hank suspected from the beginning that it was a test, an initiation rite of some kind. He admitted to himself that he foolishly went along, thinking it was worth the risk. He wanted to become part of this exceptional group, with members he admired and had become fond of, including Simon.

Hank took the "truth" option, but with a slight variation—he omitted the part Simon had played.

In Simon's mind, Hank had proven his ability by rallying the troops around a cause, and had proven his loyalty by not implicating him in his "private" dare. He admired Hank's passion and fiery determination to fight injustice, but thought it best not to encourage him further and put the group potentially at risk. Those vital gifts and skills that he recognized in Hank were essential to the study group.

—

It was Hank's turn to spin the bottle, and that time the neck pointed in Paolo's direction.

Paolo turned to Seymour, "Truth or dare?"

Seymour, ready to take him on and with nothing to fear, said, "Truth."

Paolo asked straight out, "Do you have a serious gambling addiction?"

Clearly, the questions were becoming a bit more personal.

Seymour, with full confidence, responded, "No more!" He went on to explain that several months ago he was at an after-hours club, in the posh neighborhood of Beacon Hill, participating in an illegal high-stakes poker game. He admitted he didn't even have sufficient funds beyond the opening ante. True to form, he believed he was unbeatable.

Seymour, looking around at the others, said, "Then there was a police raid and they arrested me." He bragged that he was ahead at the time, but as luck would have it, his winnings were confiscated. Then, in a slight whisper, he said, "I had no recourse so I reached out to Simon and asked him for help." He had needed Simon to bail him out, which he did the next day. Seymour quite humbly admitted, "I can't remember a time when I was so terrified. Spending the night in police lockup; being in a cage with real sleazy types was more than I could bear."

Then, he continued on an even more personal level, saying, "I also have a confession. I'm broke." He said he knew they all thought he was some rich kid from Beverly Hills, but the fact was his father had him tethered to an exceedingly tight financial leash. Since the stunt he played at UCLA, his father paid the tuition directly to the university and parceled out a measly allowance to him, which was in part why he continued to gamble.

Looking directly at Simon, he said, "The reason I don't gamble anymore is that Simon has been functioning as my informal sponsor for Gamblers Anonymous." It was clear that he was grateful to Simon for his friendship.

Seymour was happy to unleash a personal burden to a group of people he felt he could trust. He took the "truth" option without reluctance. It didn't negate the fact that, at the time, he had a suspicion that Simon had something to do with the raid. Actually, the night of the game, he had invited Simon to join him, only to have him reply that he might meet up with him later and asked for the address where they were holding the game. The day after the arrest, Seymour asked Simon if he was involved, and he admitted that he had alerted the police.

Simon quipped, "Think of it as shock therapy." Actually, Simon knew a police officer in the Beacon Hill precinct. He told him he would provide him with information on the after-hours club's activities, if he would agree to arrest Seymour and keep him overnight but not charge him, and the police officer agreed.

"I did it for your own good," Simon insisted, "and I was only trying to help you overcome your addiction."

Seymour was angry beneath the surface, for several weeks, but eventually he appreciated Simon's intervention. He never divulged to the group Simon's involvement in the raid, only about the bail.

Perhaps this time, Simon's motives were altruistic.

In any case, Simon didn't need to test Seymour's proven talents in the filmmaking industry. What was more imperative was that he passed the loyalty test. He worked closely with Seymour to calm his wild streak and redirect his creativity to more worthwhile activities, those directed specifically toward the group.

—

Unfortunately, for Paolo, Seymour spun the bottle and the neck pointed to Simon. As Simon adjusted his seat to face Paolo, he had already surmised the question Simon would pose, and there was no way Paolo would risk taking a dare from him. He planned to respond with an emphatic "Truth."

As predicted, Simon, in a jocular way, asked, "With all your dalliances, have you ever gotten a girl pregnant?"

The others in the group were somewhat aghast at how personal the questions actually had become, but Paolo knew Simon was just setting him up, again.

Paolo's predicament had required money and smooth talking. He could handle the latter, but he had needed Simon for the other. He revealed to the group that he had a friend who was pregnant and seeking to have an abortion immediately. He discovered the procedure was expensive, costing upward of $500, money he didn't have because all his savings had gone to his tuition.

Looking in Simon's direction, he said, "I trusted Simon would lend me the money if he thought a loan would resolve my dilemma."

Never one to miss an opportunity, Simon had loaned Paolo the money.

Simon grinned as he looked at Paolo, and interjected, "I know you're a ladies' man and always assumed one day it would lead to complications of one kind or another." Simon held that he was pleased to support one of his brothers, and of course, money was not an issue.

Paolo, ignoring Simon's boast, continued. "As it developed, I had a friend who was indeed pregnant, but not by me," he assured. A minor detail he had left out when asking Simon for the money. While he felt a trifle dishonest for deceiving Simon, he felt the end justified the means. He glanced at Simon for his reaction; there was none.

"I won't tell you her real name, but let's call her Alicia."

Paolo explained the father of the child was her boyfriend, Josh, the son of a U.S. senator. Josh, evidently a pathetic person, was deathly afraid of being disowned by his father if he ever discovered the pregnancy. Josh had begged Paolo for his help to make the problem "go away," something to which Alicia reluctantly agreed. Paolo didn't respect Josh, who he considered rather spineless. The request for money further sanctified his feeling toward Josh.

After receiving the money from Simon, the solution proved to be more complicated. Paolo knew it could be a high-risk game for all of them, especially Alicia. It was 1996, and the reported level of violence and public disruption against abortion providers had elevated in terms of protests, hate mail, bomb threats, and, up to that time, eighteen murders, as reported by the National Abortion Federation.

Danger aside, the following day, Alicia entered a clinic on the other side of town to meet with an abortion doctor, escorted by Josh and her faithful friend Paolo. Shortly after Alicia was ushered into the treatment room, Paolo became extremely distressed.

"I had to prevent Alicia from making an irreversible mistake, but, not wanting to intrude further, I didn't act because it was Josh's responsibility." Paolo, however, was able to convince Josh to retrieve Alicia and stop her from going forward with the procedure, after assuring Josh that he would help them find a solution to their problem.

"Fortunately, Josh was able to intervene in time," he said with relief.

However, just as they were about to leave the building, the senator arrived in a rage and headed straight for Josh. Alicia, still shaken from what had almost occurred, was then facing an entirely new trauma.

Happily, for all concerned, Paolo used his charm and persuasive manner to slice through the anger, and was finally able to appeal to the senator's sense of duty as a father and soon-to-be grandfather. "Ultimately, Alicia decided to have the baby, Josh agreed to marry her after graduation, and the senator was looking forward to welcoming his new grandchild. It was the most exhausting emotional encounter I've ever experienced." Paolo let out a deep sigh of relief.

The consummate ladies' man proved to be decent to the core. Paolo's version of the truth was substantially accurate, although he had left out the actual names of the parties involved and he downplayed his ability to resolve the situation. There was one thing that plagued him, though, and that was the arrival of the senator at the clinic. The only other person who had known the time and the location of the clinic was Simon. Paolo never challenged Simon, partly because he was guilt-ridden for misleading him in the beginning, and in the end, with a successful conclusion, it seemed pointless. Paolo liked to think Simon's motives were honorable, but his doubts didn't leave him immediately.

Simon, on the other hand, was immensely pleased. Paolo proved not only worthy of his reputation but also for his loyalty. His seductive nature and artful persuasion were skills Simon had prized and particularly needed in the group.

—

Hours had gone by, and there were empty beer bottles to spare, one of which was pointing directly at Seymour. Steering away from Simon, his Gamblers Anonymous sponsor, he posed the option to Chase. He logically assumed Chase would choose truth; a dare would have been too risky, and out of character.

Seymour asked his straight-laced brother, "Did you ever commit an unethical act at the bank where you formerly worked?"

The only incident Chase had to offer was a bank account he had established for himself without following the proper banking regulations. He explained it was an education fund he'd set up to store the money he had taken out as a loan to pay for his expenses at Harvard.

It seemed rather mundane, compared to the other confessions, but that was Chase—loveable, but perhaps a bit dull.

Simon had no need to test his abilities. However, Chase once again validated his loyalty.

—

Simon was pleased and proud of the group of scholarly brothers he had personally assembled, so he took the opportunity to offer his own sort of "dare."

As they sat in their booth, both private and quiet, away from the lively crowd below, Simon expressed his views to the others. He praised them for their honesty and the trust they showed by sharing their experiences. Most of all, he said he was most honored by their loyalty, adding, "Each of you understand my meaning."

Then, following a sip of his beer, the moment came when he suggested they cement their friendship, formalizing their commitment to each other. He suggested they form a secret society similar to those that already existed on campus.

It was an eerie few seconds for the others, who were somewhat struck by his statement about loyalty, but also because they had reached the same conclusion individually, about formalizing the group by various routes. It was as if Simon had psychic powers.

However, before anyone had any opportunity to endorse his proposal,

Hank chimed in with, “Simon, you were never presented the challenge; truth or dare?”

Simon grinned as he pronounced, “Truth, of course; it is so much more interesting.”

Hank, quite straightforward, asked, “Have you ever hacked a computer?”

Simon proceeded to stun the group, announcing, “I never formally applied to Harvard.”

Watching their expressions carefully, he could see they were astounded. “A conventional entrance was much too simple,” he bragged. “It was more challenging to break into the campus computer system and manipulate the records.” Simon explained, “I was able to create a record with all my pertinent personal information, indicating I’d completed the acceptance process, and with flying colors, of course,” he admitted with a half smirk. He proudly announced that he was also able to enroll in all his courses at that same time.

Each of them was in a state of shock and disbelief, but then it was a moment of truth, culminating in a sense of relief. Simon was an exceptional person in many ways, and this was just one more aspect of his puzzling character.

When the aftershock ultimately subsided, and after a long pause, Paolo was the first to speak. “If we’re going to be part of a clandestine group, we most certainly need a name.” As the name rolled smoothly across his Italian tongue, the others smiled with implied acceptance.

They swore it would be their own private fraternity.

With a clink of their beer bottles, the group officially became La Fratellanza.

5

THE SIXTH BROTHER

There would have been six members in this extraordinary group had Simon's plan succeeded perfectly.

Amazingly, the members of La Fratellanza never thought to ask why there were six chairs around their study group table. Perhaps because Simon always loaded it with his books—his prerogative, as it was his apartment—but "Why are there six computers?" was a common query.

Much later, they learned Simon had reserved the sixth chair and computer for Lordy. He was the only other candidate on campus that could match or perhaps outshine Simon's intellect, especially in the world of information technology. Simon himself respected his superior intellectual ability and desperately wanted him to join the group.

Lordy was to play an essential role, eventually.

He was a fellow classmate of Simon's who attended most of his computer science classes, but unlike the rest of the group, he was a loner. Lordy's intellect, accompanied by an aloof personality, caused many to consider him a geek. Early in his life, he had been the subject of derision, which carried on to some degree in college. He had learned to keep his distance, more out of self-preservation, and he learned to thrive in solitude.

Lordy was the ideal candidate for the group and Simon tried to entice him at every opportunity, only to have Lordy respectfully decline. Simon, never one to tolerate rejection, spent the first semester creating somewhat difficult situations for Lordy, and then would swoop in to save him in an effort to win his loyalty, as he did the others.

His first attempt was to hack into Lordy's computer, located in Dudley House's computer lab. He erased an unusual assignment Lordy had been working on tirelessly. The next day, after perpetrating his hoax, Simon noticed that Lordy was predictably distraught.

Cleverly masking his insincerity, he inquired, "Hey, Lordy, what's with the downcast look?"

Simon didn't need to pry further; Lordy gave a full explanation of his predicament. Ironically, Lordy was in the process of designing a foolproof computer program to prevent access to individual computers by hackers.

"I believe I know exactly how to solve your problem," Simon crowed, *generously* offering to help.

During 1996, the technology was still rather raw, and few understood how to erase a hard drive totally. However, this was an area of Simon's expertise.

"I don't see how it is possible. The program is completely wiped out. It's gone," Lordy lamented.

"Have a little faith. I still have a few tricks up my sleeve."

Lordy may have had a higher IQ, but this was uncharted territory, and Simon had made it his specialty. They worked together for several hours and eventually were able to retrieve the program.

"Unbelievable! Simon, you are a miracle worker. How can I ever thank you?"

Waving off his gratitude, Simon replied, "I'm glad I was able to help."

His first attempt to win Lordy's confidence appeared to be working.

Weeks later, Lordy was crossing the Yard one evening when, as defined in those days, a "lady of the night" propositioned him. While Lordy was in the process of rejecting her blandishments, the campus police arrived. It was an odd situation because the campus police had been extremely successful at keeping these "ladies" away from the Yard. Besides, their preferred hangouts were near Broadway and Hampshire, lined with some of the students' favorite watering holes.

Once again, Simon had miraculously appeared on the scene while the fiasco was under way and vouched for Lordy's reputation with a litany of facts defending his character. The campus police escorted the woman off Harvard Yard while Simon walked in the opposite direction with a slightly embarrassed but grateful Lordy, who had naively paved the way for Simon's intervention.

"That's twice you've bailed me out of trouble. How can I repay you?"

Simon offered a huge smile, and Lordy knew the answer.

"You know how I feel about this group thing. I just prefer to work alone!" Toning it down a notch, Lordy offered, "Let's just be friends."

Simon, confident he would win in the end, offered a high-five and dropped the subject.

Unlike some of the members of La Fratellanza whose troubles were self-imposed, Lordy was always Simon's unwitting victim. Throughout the next several months, other minor incidents occurred and Simon always appeared in a timely manner to lend a hand, directly or indirectly. After those torturous months and a string of episodes, Lordy finally warmed up to Simon and considered him a true friend, agreeing to socialize occasionally.

Still, not even Simon's "goodwill" had been enough for him to become part of the group. Notwithstanding the fact that it was a group of intellectuals he admired and respected. Lordy had come to know the other members, first by reputation and then on an individual basis. He liked them all, but he was a consummate loner and liked that even more.

—

Then, tragedy struck in a devastating way. Two weeks before the second semester was to end, the dean's office had called Lordy. The office had just received a phone call from Lordy's sister, Natalie, who had been trying to reach him. The dean had to break the news to Lordy's that his parents had died in a terrible automobile accident and his sister needed him to return home at once.

While crossing the Yard shortly after he received the terrible blow, he happened upon Simon.

"Lordy, my God! What is wrong?" he asked with unusual sincerity.

In a monotone, Lordy replied, "I have to go home. My parents are dead."

Simon escorted his friend back to the dorm, all the while attempting to offer comforting words. Apparently, Simon's initial effort to console Lordy had been fruitless, but he wasn't about to give up. While Lordy prepared for his trip home, Simon slipped out to make a few calls from the communal phone down the hall. When he returned to Lordy's room, he informed him, "I have arranged for a car to take you to the airport, and there is a ticket at the American Airlines departure desk waiting for you as well."

Still in shock, and not taking in the fullness of the generosity of his friend, he distractedly offered, "Thank you, Simon," and headed to the limo parked out front.

"I found Lordy somewhat dazed," Simon explained later to the group, "moving like a zombie with a face so ashen it resembled death."

The group had thought it was quite melodramatic coming from Simon, but he said he had comforted his friend and encouraged him to call upon them should he need anything.

—

Lordy spent several weeks in his hometown of Independence, Kansas, settling his parents' affairs. Natalie worked closely by his side, for which he was eternally grateful. Nonetheless, he knew, as the head of the family, his sister must be the one to return to college and complete her education. Given the limited resources, there wasn't enough money for both tuitions, so Lordy pooled all his savings for her expenses for the next semester. However, she, being as independent and strong willed as he, refused his help.

At the end of the second week, Natalie, with tears in her eyes, hugged her brother and reluctantly returned to school. Lordy returned to Harvard, but this time only to pack up his belongings, with plans to return home and find a job.

—

Unexpectedly, La Fratellanza was there to greet him the day he returned. It was actually late in the day, so they invited Lordy to join them at Jake's for a beer. At first, he refused, but they insisted, telling him that they had something vital to share with him.

Sitting in their booth, this time six of them, Simon informed Lordy, "While you were away, all of us worked together to complete your assignments. I was able to convince each of your professors that I would personally fax the course work to you and then arrange to have the assignments returned for credit."

The others admitted that most of the work ended up in Simon's lap, especially those assignments from his technology classes.

In an attempt to add levity to the conversation, Seymour admitted, "When we turned in the course work, many of your professors expressed an opinion that your work was not up to its usual standard."

"That also included the assignments I completed for your tech classes," Simon offered with slight embarrassment.

"At least we were able to convince each of the professors to take into account how the death of your parents had affected you," Paolo said, in an attempt to console him.

Lordy expressed his gratitude, then with anguish in his voice said, "It was all for nothing because I won't be staying at Harvard."

Simon chose that moment to excuse himself and asked Lordy to join him in the hallway near the men's room. Alone with Lordy, he announced, "I would like to advance you a loan to pay your tuition." Sensing rejection on Lordy's part, he quickly added, "Hear me out. My late Uncle Rob was wealthy and generously left me a sizable trust fund at the time of his death."

"I'm truly thankful for the incredible offer, but I must refuse," Lordy rejected vehemently.

"It is not an imposition," Simon responded.

After much persuasion, Lordy accepted Simon's offer, with a promise to repay. When they returned to their booth, the other members of the group noticed that Simon seemed pleased and Lordy appeared more relaxed. They assumed it was a private matter and did not intrude.

Chase had suspected the conversation had something to do with Uncle Rob, and if true, it would have been a kind gesture on Simon's part. He was aware he could well afford to help Lordy.

It was obvious that the outpouring of support Lordy received from a group of chaps he had earlier shunned heartened him. Although this episode did cement their friendship, incredibly it still was not enough to entice Lordy to join La Fratellanza. Nonetheless, Lordy broke from his self-imposed solitude, mostly out of gratitude, to join the group for a few beers and occasional dinners. In a way, he considered La Fratellanza his brothers, and he felt indebted to them.

The feeling had been reciprocal, although initially the others were sympathetic toward Lordy and resented the tricks Simon had played on him. Those views, however, were quickly erased from their minds when they remembered Simon's enormous generosity to Lordy in the end.

What they didn't contemplate was Simon's ulterior motive for such generosity.

As with the others, Simon had a backup candidate for Lordy waiting in the wings. He had been so confident that he wouldn't need a backup for Chase, and was so full of himself believing he'd have no trouble co-opting his other top candidates for the group. In fact, apart from Chase, the other three members of La Fratellanza were his first choices.

However, Lordy was a tremendous setback, one that cost Simon a devastating three months. He had spent days on end courting Lordy; there was no more time left to co-opt his backup candidate. Simon had to accept the fact that he would have to carry the bulk of the technology assignments he had planned to delegate to his latest recruit.

That would be his first serious mistake.

6

THE FINAL ANALYSIS

In the course of their final year, La Fratellanza had agreed to formulate their senior theses topics early. It was months before they needed to submit their proposals for approval, but each of them thought getting a head start would give them more time to frame, massage, and test their theories in the group, before presenting them to their respective academic advisors. They all admitted their course work was rather mundane, and they had plenty of time left to forge ahead with weightier assignments—an advantage their intellectual superiority allowed.

Over the next several months, they took turns presenting the basic concept of their theories, along with their problem statement and methodology. Simon, who generally assumed the part of devil's advocate, would challenge the basis of their arguments, and in most cases, his points found their way into their theses. Almost subliminally, the others leaned toward his inferences and conclusions, each seeing his own thesis take on a new shape as the discussion sessions progressed.

After endless hours of shaping, reshaping, and fine-tuning, they were ready to present their final renditions.

—

It was on a Thursday when they began to debate their theses topics, and Hank, as expected, was the first to volunteer.

"I am going to construct a national campaign for social justice using the Internet to advocate, organize, campaign, and recruit." He had dubbed the Internet "The New Wave." "My thesis topic is 'Internet Activism: Campaigning for Social Justice.'"

Hank confirmed that he would need to establish a means of funding to support this endeavor and had planned to use the Internet to solicit donations as well.

It didn't take long before Chase unleashed the urge to show off his economic prowess and interjected, "Soliciting donations via the Internet becomes a sticky wicket, especially when there is a need to file documents with the IRS. How do you plan to manage the regulations regarding those donations?"

Hank appeared to be slightly irked at the interruption, but under the surface was delighted to answer. "I will actually be addressing that very issue in a moment, if you'll be patient." Hank, readdressing the group, explained, "In the future, I hope to have the opportunity to organize community-based projects under one umbrella, depending on the success of my model. My umbrella will be the 'National Campaign for Social Justice.' The larger the community, the greater the power, and that power would allow me to influence established lobbyists."

In turn, he believed the lobbyists would join in the fight for safe neighborhoods, health care, affordable housing, and other social injustices. Hank proffered that his model would follow the precepts of the famed architect of community organizing, Saul Alinsky.

"In 1940, Alinsky first created the Industrial Areas Foundation and authored *Rules for Radicals*, which I consider my bible." Hank conveyed that many of the grassroots organizing efforts built models based on the work of Saul Alinsky, and he wanted to create a grassroots organization that would promote community organizing throughout the nation with the use of the Internet.

"I believe people need to become aware of the grassroots issues that face the disadvantaged and need to become more involved in the election of leaders that would align with those causes. My 'National Campaign' will provide an opportunity to strengthen the compassion of the haves for the have-nots by getting my message out using the power of the Web."

Hank often cited his favorite mantra and took every opportunity to repeat it. "It is everyone's obligation to fight for better housing, better schools, and higher wages for the poor."

While he acknowledged that he would become embroiled in the political infighting for his causes, he also knew the Internet was becoming more of a key resource for activists, especially when challenging the status quo.

After clarifying his basic theory, he looked over to Chase and said, "Now, to address your question."

Hank made it clear he would first need to establish an organization that could reap the tax-exemption benefits available for charitable acts, and a second organization, sort of a silent partner, which would devote its efforts to the political process.

"It is important to penetrate the leadership in Washington, so I needed to figure out how to integrate both. After investigating several options," he explained, "I will establish a 501(c)(3) nonprofit organization, to promote social welfare to educate the public, and to lobby for specific legislation. This will allow me to advocate for community organizations legally, along with get-out-the-vote campaigns, recognizing the organization cannot endorse specific candidates."

Keeping his eye on Chase, Hank continued, "My second organization will be classified as a 501(c)(4) organization. It can operate under less-strict IRS regulations and have greater flexibility in electoral advocacy, whereby the organization can involve itself more directly with voter registration and endorse specific candidates. I strongly believe that conducting door-to-door political campaigns focused on voter identification and turnout is a community-organizing effort at its best."

Hank continued to expound that he would use the 501(c)(4) organization to solicit the donations for both his political and social agendas. "The expansion of power and influence is the key aim of community organizing. The Internet will be my tool to generate this collective power for the powerless."

"Isn't that illegal?" Chase chided.

"For years there has been a blurred line between community organizing and electoral advocacy. I am only using the tax code as intended," Hank refuted.

In his closing statement, he quoted the words of his guru, Alinsky. "The first rule of power tactics is that power is not only what you have but what the enemy thinks you have."

Hank astounded Simon with his understanding of the use of the Internet. The others were equally overwhelmed, although Chase was a bit uncomfortable with Hank's earlier retort. They had nothing to ask or suggest, except for Simon.

He volunteered that Hank's approach should also target the young first-time voters, those most likely to support the liberal candidates. "Liberal candidates are more willing to spend taxpayer dollars for social causes, which appeal to this age group. The young are also more likely to be the largest users of the Internet, as first experienced to any extent in the Clinton versus Dole campaign of 1996."

Hank seemingly accepted Simon's suggestions.

Everyone was impressed with Hank's presentation, and while it was an extremely compelling argument, it was a lot to digest. The discussion had been going on for over two hours and they needed something else to digest, like food. They took a break, ordered in a couple of pizzas, and continued after being sated.

—

It was Seymour's turn to present.

Seymour backed into his thesis topic by first explaining, "As you are aware, I originally set out to produce a mini-documentary on the war that had been raging in the Gulf."

He had planned to explore the elements that led up to January 1991, when the United States started its air campaign on the Iraqi army, the official beginning of Desert Storm. Seymour had hoped to challenge the United States on whether it had legal grounds for the invasion. Part of his desire, he admitted, was that he 'wanted to' produce a film that would goad the White House and the Pentagon to dispute my right to air the content in a public medium."

Most interestingly, he confessed, "I welcomed the challenge, knowing it would come dangerously close to the line between freedom of speech and constitutional authority." He paused. "Then it all changed."

Seymour admitted he had altered his entire thought process after listening to Paolo and Hank over the past several months as they prepared their theses. He thought it best to start with a bit of history before naming his topic, which certainly piqued the interest of the others. He went on to explain that the year before, in 1995, the Republicans had taken control of Congress, both the House and Senate. That event followed by President Clinton winning a second term in office, in spite of the numerous scandals—the dalliances, Travelgate, and the FBI file controversy, to name a few that plagued his first term—set a new precedent.

"It was also a time when the World Wide Web functioned as a medium for political debate, specifically for campaigning." At this point, he referred to Hank's earlier remarks. "A few years before in 1994, President Clinton launched the first White House Web page, and the Media Study Center had just taken a poll showing the enormous impact it had on presidential politics."

Seymour agreed it was certainly going to be a new, exciting medium that would reach more of the general population, far beyond the traditional outlets such as newspapers, magazines, and television. With a huge grin, he admitted, "And of course my film." Seymour continued to explain, "As I watched the presidential wannabes line up, I noticed more and more use of the Web. It was Robert Dole who first said, 'If you really want to get involved, just tap into my home page: "www.dolekemp96.org." Emphasizing the point he added, "By then most Republican candidates in the race had Web sites."

He further held that it was during all the election fervor that he decided it was going to be his medium of choice. "I changed my thesis from an examination of the war abroad to the political war brewing within."

"At first," Simon interjected, "I was more interested in your original tack and its outcome. However, I'm suddenly very interested in your latest topic and how it has been altered."

The others knew the Gulf War was Simon's favorite subject, but now he was looking forward to Seymour's conclusion. His enthusiasm for the change surprised them. Seymour naturally appreciated his eagerness to learn more. Thus, he continued to clarify how he discovered the new medium, along with a new venue to exercise his freedom of speech.

"My new thesis title is 'The Effects of Political Campaigning on the Web.' I am planning to document the development of a political *blog* from beginning to end." He stopped to explain blog being the contraction of "Web log," which was an online diary. Seymour explained this use of the Internet had been around over a year, since early 1994, but his blog was going to be different.

"I am going to create short film clips with campaign messages for or against a candidate, but I have yet to decide which candidate to 'align or malign' in my sound bites. I am also going to create a survey inviting all viewers to participate. This will allow me to quantify the success of the message as well as the use of the medium." With the potential of attracting hundreds of thousands of people, he felt the results would revolutionize current practices. Ultimately, Seymour believed it would create a model for future political campaigns.

"This is right up my alley!" Hank exclaimed. "I'd be more than interested in your results."

"I second that," added Paolo.

Chase remained silent.

Simon evidently liked his idea, but felt he could construct a slightly more challenging theory by delving into the effects of negative campaigning. By way of example, he reminded Seymour, and the rest of the group, of the "Willie Horton" advertisement on TV during George H. W. Bush's campaign against the then Governor Michael Dukakis of Massachusetts.

"It was in 1988, during a political debate, when Al Gore asked a question about the 'Weekend Furlough' program for convicted felons. Governor Dukakis had just signed off on the program, and Gore took issue."

He continued to recap how the Bush campaign picked up on the question, knowing that in 1986 Willie Horton, a convicted murder with a life sentence, was released on a weekend furlough never to return. In 1987, Horton raped a woman, beat her fiancé, and stole their car. Shortly thereafter, he was captured in Maryland and received an eighty-five-year prison sentence. The judge at the time publicly stated he would not extradite him to Massachusetts. If the Commonwealth released Horton on another weekend furlough, the judge feared he might kill again.

Simon persisted. "The Bush campaign referred constantly to the Willie Horton story, but was reluctant to air a negative ad directly targeting Dukakis, so they didn't."

"I remember the incident, but what is the point?" Seymour probed.

"The point is that while the Bush campaign was unwilling, George Walker Bush, the son, was."

Simon, with his famous smirk, submitted how Bush Jr. established a group named the National Security Political Action Committee, seemingly independent of the Bush campaign. The PAC sponsored the television spot showing a mug shot, with the caption "Weekend Passes." Bush, the forty-first president, ushering in four more years following the eight years of the Reagan presidency, defeated Dukakis.

"It was extremely negative and effective," Simon concluded. Facing Seymour, he suggested, "You might find it more interesting and challenging to determine the 'tipping point' of negative ads. How far could the ad go without creating sympathy votes for the opponent?"

He urged Seymour to work with Hank to establish two 527 organizations, slightly dissimilar from the classic 501 organizations. "Typically, the 527 group's main objective is to influence the election or to defeat a candidate. Illogically, the Federal Election Commission does not regulate the activities of these organizations."

Chase, showing a mild grasp of the subject, questioned its validity. "How is this all possible?"

Simon, eyeing Chase, responded, "Lighten up," and continued. "The purpose of setting up two separate organizations, is one would be to support a candidate, and at the same time the sister organization would oppose the same candidate."

He suggested Seymour establish several negative ads for one of the organizations, each ad notching up on the negativity scale. "In this way," Simon explained, "you could determine through your surveys when the negative ad turned off the voter and caused the voter to cast a ballot for the opposition. It was this vital point that held the answer."

All of them, admittedly even Chase, found the whole concept intriguing.

Simon offered to work with both Hank and Seymour to help set up the Web sites.

The group agreed its session was productive, with a lot of new information surfacing, but it was also past midnight, and they decided to call it quits. La Fratellanza had consumed all that remained of the pizza and they were exhausted. They agreed to forgo Jake's and head to their respective dorms.

—

The next evening they reconvened.

After settling into their usual seats around their round table, Paolo took the floor. He started the discussion by presenting the title of his thesis, "Political Speech: Creator or Interpreter of Ideology."

Paolo submitted that many scholars, including political analysts, believe that by using cyclical data they could predict the political party that would likely reign in the White House.

"However, I believe they create a false assumption. What is a more relevant fact is that the party most accurate in sensing the mood of the people is the party that will win." Excitedly, he pointed out that thus far, no one had taken it to that level, and explained that campaigning has always been reactive, not proactive.

"That is the crux of my theory," Paolo said. "If you can gauge the pulse of the people through computer analysis you could begin to construct the campaign speeches; essentially you could craft a campaign strategy. In essence, get ahead of the game and adopt strategies to shape the ideology of the electorate toward or against a specific party or candidate. To put it in plain words, it is a sure way to back the winner."

Naturally, such a statement caught everyone's attention.

Paolo emphasized that he strongly believed words shape ideology. "People want to be led, they want to be told what to believe," he pontificated. "My challenge is to develop a model to predict future sentiment, but I believe it is essential first to understand how sentiment affected past elections." He felt it was necessary to study past elections to identify predictive factors that had a profound effect on election outcomes and provide a foundation to formulate his model for future predictions.

He pulled back from his thundering tone and patiently explained how he had arrived at his theory. "I originally began my research starting with Ulysses S. Grant in 1869, until the embattled Harry S. Truman chose not to run for a second term in 1952. I discovered there were various entrenched interests within a particular party; attempting to uncover public sentiment for those eras was difficult at best. Therefore, I dismissed analyzing the political shifts before 1953."

Paolo held that after the 1940s, there was a paradigm shift, and it became remarkably easier to measure the sentiment of the populace. First, more households began to own televisions, and then years later, with the advent of the Internet, the information highway began to play a significant part in getting out the message. "Improved communications brought about a sea change," he asserted.

"Both the research conducted by Hank and Seymour, and the contributions the Internet had played in the political process, helped to point me in the right direction." Paolo acknowledged. Consequently, he felt he could get a clearer picture of the voter mind-set by concentrating on the past forty years.

He decided first to study the past presidential nomination speeches. He began with the 1952 speeches of Dwight Eisenhower and Adlai Stevenson and continued to Bill Clinton's and Robert Dole's August 1996 speeches. He dissected the ideas that had the highest impact on the election by carefully distilling the essence used in the speeches. From there, he believed he could establish effective correlations. Paolo said he also identified patterns relating to the concerns of the American people that drove their election results.

"Eventually I will classify the key underlying issues that influenced voters. Then I will construct hypothetical campaign platforms based on my research."

He considered the issues to be precursors of future behavior. In an attempt to classify the key issues, he scoured news events using various sources and then created a scale from one to three—one being extremely discouraged, two for confident, and three meaning extremely confident—and then he ranked the mood of the country at that particular time.

"The challenge of measuring American sentiment became even easier after 1945, during Franklin Roosevelt's unprecedented third term in the White House," he acknowledged. He explained that, at that time, the Gallup organization first started polling Americans on how they rated the president's performance, providing him with the data he sought. Later, after 1984, when Zogby International was founded, he was able to see how their polls fared against Gallup's, giving him an even better understanding. He analyzed how the presidents performed and obtained a deeper insight into the attitudes of Americans. When he examined the current Clinton administration, he was able to verify his conclusions with the added aid of a third polling company, GrassRoots Research, founded in 1995 by Scott Rasmussen.

"This provided me with yet another vehicle for comparison," Paolo asserted, "giving me a more precise indication of the voters' outlook on their country and their personal futures."

For example, Paolo theorized that when he looked at the Reagan/Bush era, a twelve-year Republican stronghold, he found it posed its own set of circumstances attributable to several factors. He reasoned it was worth looking at those factors, because they served as clear indicators and explained the changes in the political climate. Paolo believed all these dimensions fit comfortably in his theory.

"By way of illustration," he stated, "the Democratic president, Jimmy Carter, had only served one term because the majority of Americans, having originally given their support as a reaction to the Nixon administration and the Watergate scandal, had switched parties." To bring home his point, Paolo asserted, "The Carter administration engendered a desire by the American people for a stronger, more effusive president who could handle not only the economic woes but also national security fears."

At that moment, Hank raised an objection to Paolo's last statement, insisting, "Carter accomplished a lot in his term, especially in the area of human rights. It was the international stagflation that ultimately brought him down, through no fault of his own."

Paolo scoffed. "I know this will seem like an odd statement, but let's keep politics out of this."

Chase, feeling he was back in the game, chimed in with, "The conflux of high inflation and high unemployment, the stagflation Hank alluded to, cannot be blamed on the Carter administration. The stagflation actually started in 1965 and had snowballed for the following fifteen years, and neither the Carter nor Reagan administrations can be faulted," he offered smugly.

Paolo shrugged and looked in Simon's direction.

Simon took his cue and said, "Boys, let Paolo continue."

Paolo, unrelenting, resumed. "As I was saying, the man elected to fill that role was Republican candidate Ronald Reagan, who served two terms, followed by Republican President George Herbert Walker Bush, serving one term that ended a twelve-year reign. Then a new era ushered in a new face. The obscure Democratic governor from Arkansas, William Jefferson Clinton, became the forty-second president of the United States. Once again, the Republicans passed the baton."

Paolo continued passionately. "When certain events are foreseeable, I will have the ability to design, with a modicum of predictability, effective speeches that are responsive to the national psyche. The net result would be that I could author campaign speeches to sway the voters before they commit to a party, and steer them toward a candidate."

At that point in the discussion, Simon stepped in and summarized Paolo's pitch, stating, "If you really could measure the current status and extrapolate future trends in areas such as economics and national security, then presumably you could write the campaign speeches, including an acceptance speech, today."

"Exactly!" Paolo proclaimed.

Simon agreed with his prior statement about backing the winner.

"That's where the power lies." He then approached Paolo's theory taking a different tack. He asked Paolo, "If it is all about the words, then why do you need to predict? Can't you just write the speech around major issues and push the cause?"

Paolo, after a slight pause, agreed. "It is possible, absent an unforeseen major event, a force majeure that could change the metrics." He also admitted that he could instantly tweak the words at any time to adapt to a shift in sentiment, without changing the tenor of the message. "Either party can own the national security or economic debate based on the strength of the message," he declared.

As a follow-up, Simon asked, "For example, could you write the campaign speeches for an unknown candidate who would run years from now, let's say, 2008?"

Paolo's inner challenge kicked in, and with great enthusiasm he asserted, "With Hank's 'Internet Activism' and Seymour's 'Media Blitz,' along with my words in the campaign speeches, I seriously believe we would have the power to steer the course of history. With that scenario, we wouldn't be backing the winner—we'd be creating the winner."

It was a boffo ending for Paolo, especially considering he'd had a rather dubious beginning.

At that moment, La Fratellanza was in high spirits and their juices were flowing.

—

Chase's emotions were working in overdrive. He was all set to rock, so the others sat back comfortably and let him roll. Certainly after all the "liberal speak," the reserved Chase was ready to lay out the details of his theory. He used the back door approach, as Seymour had, before he described his thesis topic.

"Originally, my interest was to study the long-term effects of U.S. banking deregulation on the world economy. Conversely, after a spirited conversation with Hank during the first week of class and continuing conversations on the same subject, my focus changed slightly."

Following the episode of rescuing Hank's book, *Housing Finance: Expanding Capital for Affordable Multifamily Housing,* from spiraling off the bookshelf, and after listening to his argument as to why all people were entitled to own a home, his thesis morphed into "U.S. Banking Deregulation: The Catalyst for a Housing Crisis."

Chase gave details on the enactment of the Glass-Steagall Act of 1933, named after Carter Glass and Henry B. Steagall, which established the FDIC, the Federal Deposit Insurance Corporation, and introduced banking reforms in the form of controls. "Legislators have been trying to deregulate those imposed regulations ever since, and beginning in the early eighties, the debates became ferocious." He winced.

"Banking institutions found their way around the federal laws and aggressively expanded into new lines of business. Banks began to relax their lending practices, lending to less credit-worthy clients, and at the same time increasing their interest rates on those loans," he presumed.

Chase further established that during the same period, organizations such as the Association of Community Organization for Reform Now, known as ACORN, founded in 1970 and today the nation's largest grassroots community organization, targeted the banks and challenged their alleged predatory lending practices.

Chase, referring to Hank's earlier explanation of his thesis, looked directly at him and apologized, "Forgive me, for I am about to step on your toes."

Hank took the opportunity to retort. "Don't worry, you've already stepped on my toes, twice," he said, following with a wink.

Returning the wink, Chase continued to explain that one of ACORN's tactics to battle social injustice was to acquire low-cost housing loans for the low-to-moderate-income people they support. In 1977, he explained, there was a housing crisis and, as a "Band-Aid," the Carter administration passed the Community Investment Act, forcing banks to provide subprime mortgages, fulfilling Hank's belief that all people were entitled to own a home.

"I disagreed with the concept that housing was an entitlement, which had been the mainstay of my debates with Hank," he clarified. Getting back on point, and in an excitedly higher pitch, he said, "I believe a 'perfect storm' is in the making. One that will not only create another housing crisis, but one where banks and the financial market as a whole will fail—sending shock waves around the world!"

Chase wasn't prone to histrionics, but he animatedly professed that the government had learned nothing from the savings and loan crisis of the 1970s and 1980s. The thrifts, as they were called, acquired savings deposits and then provided mortgages, car loans, and personal loans, all of which became unsustainable, so loans naturally defaulted.

"Ultimately, the government bailed them out using taxpayers' dollars, to the estimated tune of one-hundred-sixty-point-one billion dollars," he complained.

Chase had been studying the congressional records and found that as early as 1988, in the midst of the S&L crisis, the financial sector placed severe pressure on legislators to deregulate the banking industry further He explained that there are those who judge the Glass-Steagall Act of 1 which introduced the FDIC in an effort to reform the banks, as being a contributor to the S&L failures.

"I believe it created an environment where the S-and-Ls became more willing to take on additional risk," Chase declared. "While I suppose the FDIC had a causal effect, I feel the Tax Reform Act of 1986 produced a more devastating result." President Reagan signed the act into law as an attempt to simplify the tax code, and at the same time put a cap on the notorious tax shelters of the 1980s. However, many of the tax shelters were real estate investments.

"It was the countless number of investors, no longer able to take the tax advantages, who defaulted on their loans that caused the S-and-Ls holding those loans also to default," he alleged. "Within the next few years, possibly as early as 1999, another sweeping bill will pass. I predict it will be a bill that will allow the mortgage industry to offer mortgages to those who do not meet the customary credit criteria and whose income levels are below standard. Like the savings and loan crisis," he contended heatedly, "these practices will also become unsustainable."

Chase closed his argument by stressing that he was searching for compelling data to support his own beliefs, data necessary to jostle Congress and alert its members to the impending "perfect storm."

Concluding his presentation, he waited for a spirited critique as he looked in Hank's direction, but none came, except for, "Well done," followed by a big smile.

Paolo and Seymour, feeling the area of finance was out of their league and having no questions, congratulated Chase with a celebratory high-five.

During the jubilation, Simon signaled from across the table that they hadn't quite finished. Once he regained their attention, he asked Chase, "Can you predict, assuming no one heeded your warnings, as to when the storm might hit? And, can you specifically predict what the impact would be on the U.S. economy? Finally, would you be able to identify what solutions the government could provide to prevent a total financial collapse?" This was what he believed Chase was inferring.

To those questions, Chase responded, "Possibly, probably, and maybe."

Simon would be the last to explain his thesis topic, but the hour was late and he believed "The mind can only comprehend what the seat can endure," as someone once quoted. "The only preview of coming attractions," he said, "is that I have a lot to explain and it will be rather technical."

He thought it best that they call it a night and resume on Monday at their usual time.

They all agreed.

As it was nearing 11:30 p.m., the group was famished as usual. The time had slipped away from them, and they had forgotten to eat, so La

Fratellanza headed for Jake's.

While seated in their private booth in the corner, each of them tried prodding Simon to give a hint as to his topic, but he was too cagey for that. He directed the conversation back to his favorite subject, the legitimacy of Desert Storm.

7

THE SHADOW THESIS

After engaging in their weekend amusements, they reconvened at Simon's apartment and picked up where they had left off on Friday night.

As it was Simon's turn, he restated that his topic was about Internet security and submitted his title, "The Pandora's Box of the New Millennium."

"I believe it will be virtually impossible to protect data on the Internet in general," he stressed, "and most important, personal data." Underscoring his belief, he asserted, "All of us are at great risk. Not only are our identities in jeopardy, but more vitally, our national security."

Simon, the Internet guru, continued to provide some history regarding the first real use of the Internet in the 1960s, when the United States funded research projects for its military agencies. "By the early nineties," he noted, "the Internet turned out to be so popular that programmers began to design applications that became useful to virtually every aspect of one's life."

"When Seymour discussed the World Wide Web, he was referring to only one aspect of the Internet," Simon stressed. He clarified, stating, "There are multitudes of services interconnected to resources other than the Web." He pointed out that when he referred to the Internet he included the totality of hardware and software that allow computers to communicate with each other. "I feel it is necessary to make that distinction because the risk I cited earlier is the access to those computers and their data. It is the computer hackers who circumvent the system through illegal access."

Simon continued to explain that in the beginning, it was more of a challenge and there was no intent to commit harm, but then it deteriorated until it finally fell into the hands of criminals. He cited several cases. Starting in 1981, groups of hackers were forming with names such as the Warlords. In 1982, a group calling themselves the 414s broke into sixty computer systems at institutions such as Manhattan's Memorial Sloan-

Kettering Cancer Center and the Los Alamos Laboratories in New Mexico.

"This continued every year with more and more hackers. Then in 1986, Congress passed the Computer Fraud and Abuse Act, making it a crime to break into computer systems. That didn't stop the hackers, for each year the illegal access increased exponentially and became more insidious. For example, in 1994, a Russian hacker siphoned ten million dollars from Citibank and transferred the money to bank accounts around the world. The authorities recovered all but four hundred thousand."

As the security systems protecting these computers and programs became more sophisticated, so did the hackers. Simon stated emphatically, "There is virtually no system that can't be penetrated."

The other members of La Fratellanza looked at each other inquiringly, remembering Simon's own hacking episodes, and were curious to know where he was leading.

Then it all unfolded.

The time had come for Simon to present them with his "shadow" thesis.

While still holding the floor and with their full attention, Simon announced, "I have a way to make our projects even more exciting, a project we can work on together, shake it up a bit," as he put it.

Before delving into the details, he first used his persuasive skills, and complimented them for their intriguing proposals. Pointing to each of them, he acknowledged the fact that they had completed most of the research necessary to prove their hypotheses. In his view, his brothers had succeeded in their mission.

They acknowledged that each would undoubtedly ace his thesis, and agreed that in some cases they actually had to dumb down the information slightly for their respective academic advisors.

With great anticipation, La Fratellanza waited for Simon to continue.

This time Simon spoke deliberately, pacing his words as he explained, "Collectively, we can devise a theoretical plot, a sort of a *Manchurian Candidate II*, ultimately giving us control of the office of the president of the United States." He glanced at their faces and then quickly added, "Not really, but in theory." Noticing Chase's expression, Simon said, "Or, if that offends your sensibilities, you can think of it as Rudyard Kipling's *The Man Who Would Be King*. Or could be king, with our help," he cajoled.

Continuing to ignore their shocked stares, Simon went on to explain how each of them could incorporate one aspect of the plot, as it pertained to their topic, and cleverly tuck it deep inside the pages of their convincing arguments. "In essence, each individual thesis in combination would create the proposed 'shadow' thesis."

Simon, feeling he now had more than just their attention, continued to lay out the details of his conspiratorial game. "We should start by assuming we already have a candidate, a man not born in this country, with no traceable history, and, to make it even more challenging, a minority. We should also assume that the candidate possesses the level of intellect required to fill the role."

He explained that, as a team, they would need to create a new identity, construct a training curriculum, and groom the "Chosen One" to win the Oval Office. "It is obvious," he said, "we would also need to plan carefully every step necessary to enter the world of politics."

Simon reminded his brothers that they would be able to utilize some aspects of their own theories, which they had already confirmed in their theses. At the same time, he prodded them to recognize that it would require the concentrated efforts of everyone. Then, with his wry smile, he said, "That would be the easy part. Then we have to get him elected." He paused for a moment to get their reaction as they sat around their round table.

The silence in the room was overwhelming.

The members of La Fratellanza looked at one another with disbelief. However, as the clock ticked, a smattering of interest crept back into the room. The group refocused on Simon. They were curious where this would lead, but primarily, they were dubious about the level of seriousness.

Simon continued to let the silence permeate the room for a short time; then, he regained his role as self-anointed leader. "It is only a game, like war exercises, and would make the writing of our theses more interesting," he emphasized.

He allowed that the plot itself must remain a secret, for obvious reasons, pointing out that should anyone discover it, the "shadow" thesis, as he liked to call it, would be misunderstood. Simon reminded them that their only personal exposure would be if one person were to read each of the five theses. "Of course, the reader would have to know specifically what he or she was looking for to connect all the dots." He shrugged.

He then reiterated his earlier comment. "It is only a game, an academic exercise to stimulate our intellects. Since each of us has completed his thesis, we have the luxury of free time that we can use to our full advantage. This a rare intellectual challenge on which we must capitalize. It will give us a real sense of the potential of our efforts."

Simon stopped pontificating—the others began contemplating.

All agreed, except for Simon, that they needed time to dwell on it. That night they did not go to Jake's, but returned directly to their dorms.

—

The next day they gathered for their scheduled study session, but this session was different from all others. After digesting Simon's riveting plea for a little excitement, they all agreed to what they considered a harmless intellectual diversion, something to satisfy their love of a challenge.

Paolo was the only one to raise an issue. "What about the legitimacy of a non-U.S. citizen running for the office of the president?" He referred to the U.S. Constitution stating, "In order to hold that office the person must be a natural-born U.S. citizen.'"

Simon let him rattle on for a moment, and then reminded him, and the rest of them, "We will be creating a new identity, one of a natural-born U.S. citizen." He volunteered to assume the responsibility of taking all the necessary steps to validate the Chosen One, including a birth certificate, college records, and all other documents to authenticate his persona, as part of the project.

After a lengthy discussion, Paolo and the others relented and accepted Simon's logic.

Simon was more than pleased. He had been confident from the start that his proposal would intrigue them. He had planned it carefully—and thus far—perfectly.

Simon again stressed the importance of secrecy, reminding the group that if anyone were to discover the "shadow" thesis, it would surely be misconstrued. He then turned and pointed to their computer lab. A second black box stood out prominently, something they had overlooked while enthralled by Simon's presentation.

"First," Simon explained, "I installed a backup hard drive that is programmed to copy all the files from the primary drive nightly. Should anything happen to one of the hard drives there will always be a copy on record. Second, I added security software on each of our computers, and when we first turn them on, we will be asked to enter a password. The password is *Fratellanza*. Third, but equally important, we will need to restrict access to our theses once they are published and placed in the Archives in the Pusey Library."

Simon went on to describe what he said was a straightforward process. They needed to write a letter requesting the restriction. Then they needed to ask the chair of their respective departments to write a letter as well, supporting their request. The letters should be addressed to the University Archivist, Harvard University Archives, Pusey Library, Cambridge, MA 02138.

He counseled them that they would need to negotiate a second agreement with ProQuest/UMI, the company that Harvard contracts to publish theses and dissertations in book form, as well as in digital form.

Simon quoted directly from the ProQuest/UMI Publishing Agreement, as the others listened intently. "ProQuest/UMI may elect not to distribute the Work, if it believes that not all necessary rights of third parties have been secured. If Author's degree is rescinded, and the degree-granting institution so directs, ProQuest/UMI will expunge the Work from its publishing program in accordance with its then current publishing policies."

Simon held it was his understanding that they would accept a letter from the department chair and expunge all work other than the original publication archived in the Pusey Library. He again stressed, "These are just precautions."

Then Simon distributed to each of them an outline of their respective roles in the master plan to use as a guide.

Chase was slated to incorporate instructions on how to set up untraceable bank accounts utilizing the loopholes in the banking deregulations, those he had referred to earlier in his thesis.

Simon playfully remarked, "If this game were for real, we would surely need lots of money."

"I will investigate the various offshore banking practices, and I assume I will need to construct the financial course work for our candidate," Chase offered. "As long as it is only a game, I guess it will be fun to explore," he muttered.

Paolo was assigned the writing of all campaign speeches to support the mood of the people and the issues of the day, as predicted in his thesis model.

Simon observed that it would be prudent to project out to the 2004 election, and then to 2008.

"What is with the arbitrary dates?" Paolo inquired.

"It was the basis of your own thesis," Simon responded, "when you stated that scholars, using cyclical data, can predict an eight-year cycle." He reminded Paolo that Clinton was currently in his second term, which would comprise eight consecutive years for the Democrats. In theory the opposing party, the Republicans, would win the next election in 2000. "Assuming your theory has merit," Simon teased. "Following through on the theory, the Republicans would hold office for the next eight years." Obviously pleased with the tenor of the conversation, he continued. "So, it should be based on the 2008 presidential election. The precursor would be a senatorial race in 2004."

He repeated to all of them, "It is simply a baseline from which to operate. Paolo in particular would need to know what years to operate within to determine the variables that would influence the election. Certainly using current issues would be ill timed."

"Paolo Salvatore, speechwriter for the president of the United States. I like the sound of it," Paolo quipped.

"It is nice to see that you are getting into the role," Simon jested. "But you will also need to design a comprehensive curriculum with programmed tutorials for the Chosen One."

"I assume the assignments should embrace the role of government, interworkings of the Beltway, and the official roles within the White House, along with the nuances they hold?" inquired Paolo.

"Precisely," replied Simon.

Seymour's role was to design a brand for the new president, the campaign mantra: a consistent and timely message that would move the masses.

"It is essential that the brand be in step with current events, within the time frame stipulated, to ensure its appeal," Seymour insisted.

Simon suggested he work hand in glove with Paolo for that reason. He also urged Seymour to conduct a dry run when he tested his "tipping point" theory and actually create a 527 organization to market the nonexistent candidate.

Seymour liked the idea, but asked, "Can I have more specifics on the vision of this person you have in mind for our imaginary contender? It would actually make my job more precise if you would compress all the vital elements for this person. It would help to create a mental picture."

"As soon as I create the identity you'll be the first to know, but based on our conversations, each of us can contribute to the formation of the perfect candidate," replied Simon.

Seymour offered to design assignments and actually provide training exercises in the form of "acting" to prepare the candidate for the sound bites he would be filming. "Mr. President, please stand tall behind the podium and wait for my cue. And you can call me Director Lynx," Seymour joked with a smile.

The others, obviously enjoying Seymour's own acting performance, listened as Simon suggested he also construct some course work to capitalize on the religious tensions, both within the United States and throughout the Middle East that would be useful. Seymour agreed to work with Paolo when delving into church versus state issues as well.

Hank accurately predicted what Simon was going to assign him and was already preparing to create the model for a grassroots movement. During the design of his plan, he was intoxicated by the prospect of theoretically electing the first minority president. Working closely with Paolo and Seymour, he knew he could rally the troops to "Get out the Vote," specifically for their fictional candidate. Hank was also to create course assignments on the dynamics and techniques of community organizing, a cinch in his mind.

"You guys are real funny, but imagine me in a position to ask the president for millions of dollars of federal funding for my foundation. That is real power!" Hank exclaimed.

"Isn't it interesting to see each of you slipping into your roles so easily," Chase said, mocking them.

Seymour, ignoring Chase, turned to Simon and asked, "I assume once we deal with the creation of a total new identity, complete with history and detailed background, you will then decide on the best databases in which to insert all the pertinent information?"

"Yes. It will be up to me, once I have perfected the documents and determined the most logical way to penetrate the various computer systems." Simon also volunteered to work with Chase to find the best process to move money in and out of various banking systems.

While the discussion was enough to excite them, they found themselves genuinely looking forward to getting started. Moreover, to their surprise, they each had the same thought—*if it were real and not just a game; imagine the power I would have.*

—

Every week thereafter, one member presented arguments to support his thesis, including his aspect of the master plan, and the other four presented their challenges.

While their individual challenge was to stretch their imaginations, the "shadow" assignments became the most intriguing part of the project. However, as time went on it started to morph into its own reality and was becoming less of a "game."

For the rest of the year, they constructed their study sessions using a slightly different approach. Hank would challenge the presenter as to the impact his theory would have on society. Chase directed his challenges from a financial perspective, and Seymour focused on the impact of the media. When it was Paolo's turn, perpetually neutral, he played the devil's advocate. As always, Simon's arguments seemed more agnostic than Paolo's.

None of the others ever understood exactly the direction Simon was taking, as he never made it clear where he stood on any one issue. His neutral demeanor allowed him to slip in points to support his ultimate aim. As if by osmosis, once again those points made their way into each thesis.

Simon chose his brothers well, not just for their high IQs but also for their knowledge and successful experience in their various disciplines. The added bonus was that they all had respectable positions waiting for them when they returned to their former professions. He admired their desire to further those careers by returning to academia.

It was 1997, and La Fratellanza's theories were still just theories, yet to be tested. Nevertheless, Simon needed their extraordinary talents and invaluable insights—they were vital assets that would become irreplaceable.

8

THE GRADUATE DEPARTURE

The time was rapidly approaching, and in a few days, they would earn their master's degrees and become Harvard graduates. Shortly thereafter, they would go their separate ways and immerse themselves in their new lives and respective careers.

To no one's surprise, the members of La Fratellanza had completed all their exams and aced the presentations of their senior theses. Certainly, there was never any doubt in their minds. They also took comfort knowing that because they had majored in different disciplines, with different academic advisors, it was highly unlikely anyone could ever connect their theses. Most important, they had taken all the precautions Simon recommended. They were confident no one would uncover their hypothetical conspiracy buried within its pages—if one did—the brothers were confident that it would be viewed as an intellectual exercise.

As Simon often liked to remind them, "We are probably the most unique group of intellectuals Harvard has ever entertained." He was careful to omit Lordy, who he knew surpassed them all by far.

—

Finally, the day of graduation arrived, and after the Commencement Day ceremonies ended, La Fratellanza went to Jake's to celebrate. It was an occasion of overindulgence, and the group drank late into the night. As the clock approached 2:00 a.m., Simon announced, "I have a surprise."

He convinced them that before they left Harvard and went their separate ways, they should have something to remember how they bonded as brothers. "Of course," he exclaimed, "we must not forget the astounding theories we proved, at least on paper."

Simon persuaded them, as only he could, to follow him out of the pub and down a few blocks to see a friend, a local tattoo artist frequented by students from the various universities. The storefront was still open and the artist was waiting. When they arrived, Simon sprang his idea. "It is a memento! I've created a tattoo just for us, a tattoo that would signify our brotherhood. It will be our special symbol, designed only for La Fratellanza."

Then the artist handed Simon a piece of paper, which he showed his brothers. It was a sketch of their new tattoo: it was ***LF***, which was exclusive and would be unobtrusive.

Initially they squirmed at the idea. But after a night of heavy imbibing, they were in no condition to refuse, or even to figure out why to refuse. No one was aware that Simon was perfectly sober, despite his time in the pub.

—

Early the next morning, Hank and Chase were in the student cafeteria in Dudley House, downing several cups of *welcomed* black coffee. Moments later, they heard sirens blaring across the Yard.

"It sounds as though it is coming from the Widener Library," Hank blurted out.

Running out to the Yard, they saw flames shooting up in the sky, but not from the Widener Library—from the Pusey Library.

As the sirens continued to blare, Seymour and Paolo began to come out of their alcohol-induced sleep. They both could smell the strong odor of smoke that wafted in the air, which didn't comport well with their hangovers. Independently, they sprang out of their beds in their adjoining dorms, threw on their clothes, and ran to the source of excitement.

"Wait up!" Paolo shouted, as he headed in Seymour's direction.

Seymour was running toward the fire. "I see Chase and Hank standing over there. Maybe they know what's happening. Given last night, I'm surprised I can even see," Seymour added.

Somehow, in all the confusion the four managed to find one another. Together they looked on in horror as the flames engulfed the Pusey Library. After a suspenseful time, it appeared that only part of the library had suffered any damage. However, it was the wing where the Harvard University Archives were located and where it housed the graduate's theses. Each envisioned his richly leather-bound thesis going up in flames, until Hank reminded them, "Simon has the only other copies on the backup server in our computer lab." The others breathed a sigh of relief as they continued to watch the fire department in action.

During all the excitement, Paolo had been conscious of rubbing his wrist while watching the inferno. When he looked down, he had vague recollections of the night before, a night when they were not only drunk, but also tattooed. *I abhor tattoos* he thought, but was thankful that his watchband hid the artful display. He knew he could never bring himself to remove it, which would have been disloyal to their "brotherhood," and all it meant to him.

Paolo glanced at his watch to note the time. They had been witnessing the events taking place in the Yard for several hours. It was then a quarter to twelve.

"Hey, guys, we are supposed to meet at Simon's apartment at noon. Let's go," he urged.

—

Back in Simon's apartment, they sat around their study table and recounted the morning's events.

Simon seemed only mildly interested. He swiftly changed the subject and began to reminisce about their study discussions, their personal struggles, and how it would be the last time they would sit around their round table.

The others joined in, echoing similar sentiments, which eventually led them to reflect on how the five of them came together and planned an ingenious plot. They spoke about the challenges they had met, the excitement they had felt, and all they had accomplished. Mostly they spoke about the admiration and respect they felt for each other. They vowed to stay in touch and continue their friendship as they embarked on their new careers. Those two years had changed their lives in many ways, but nothing more than the intellectual fraternity they had created.

Seymour raised his hand as if he were about to ask a question, but instead flashed his new tattoo. "Thanks, Simon, for the lovely gift," he quipped.

It was at that moment that Simon chose to present them with another graduation gift. He handed each of them a small square green box, with the name and logo of Rolex in the lower-left-hand corner. Inside the box, each member found a gold watch bearing the same logo as on the cover. Their eyes widened in disbelief.

Chase was the first to protest the extravagance. "This is an amazing gift, but it is way too lavish." Even knowing that Simon could afford it, it was a heartfelt comment.

The others followed with similar objections.

Simon waved off their gratitude and instructed, "Turn over the watch face."

On the back of the watch, in the center, they noticed the engraved initials ***LF***. There was no need to verbalize their thanks. This time it came from their sincere expressions.

Simon sensed the sheer emotion his brothers felt. Leaving no time for their expressions to subside, he announced, "I have one more surprise in store. Inside the watch I placed a microchip that contains copies of our theses, the only copies with evidence of our 'intellectual diversion.'"

At Simon's mention of the "only copies," their heads all turned in the direction of the living room window, and then they realized the true value of their new watches. They were so overwhelmed by the events that had taken place in the last few hours, starting with the tattoo, the fire, and then the gifts, to notice that the computer lab was gone and the vanishing sofa had returned.

With uncharacteristic emotion, they once again reflected on how fortunate they were to become part of La Fratellanza, how they truly had grown to become brothers. They expressed their thanks to Simon for helping them out of terrible personal dilemmas, supporting their studies, and presenting them with a precious gift. Each accepted the watch as a true sign of devotion.

Arm in arm, the five brothers headed to Jake's to down a few beers one last time.

9

THE REAL DEAL

It was the year 2000, three years since La Fratellanza had left Harvard University.

After graduation, they had scattered across the country. Seymour moved back to Los Angeles, Simon returned to San Francisco, and Hank went back to Chicago. Paolo relocated to Georgetown, and Chase, finally getting his wish, moved to the financial capital of the world, New York City.

Their lives had taken off in different directions; however, the camaraderie of La Fratellanza never waned, and they stayed in touch on a regular basis. Two or three members of the group would get together for dinner occasionally, or invite another brother to a special event. When traveling for business to each other's city they would hook up, if only for a quick drink.

They always stayed close.

Although their careers and families primarily took precedence, they never missed their annual weekend reunion in May, with all in attendance. Each member of La Fratellanza would take turns to select a different venue, but it would always be a typical "guy's retreat," replete with wine, cigars, and foie gras, compliments of Simon. Normally, the weekend would commence with swapping stories about their families and their careers. Ultimately, it led to their "shadow" thesis and many "what-if" questions permeated their conversations.

When they received a letter asking them to attend a reunion in Chicago, four months early, it captured their attention. Especially, because the invitation included airline tickets for each of them; with the exception of Hank, of course, who was already living in the Windy City.

The invitation was from Simon.

Soon after they received the letter, the phones rang almost instantly, as Chase called Hank, who had just called Paolo, with Paolo agreeing to call Seymour. They all agreed to be in Chicago the following week, their universal response being, "Let's see what Simon has dreamed up now."

They all recognized it must have been important for him to go to the trouble and expense.

The intrigue was irresistible.

—

The members of La Fratellanza managed to find their way to the reserved conference room at the Hilton located just outside O'Hare Airport. It was February and freezing outside, but the warm air from the radiators along the windows removed the chill. Seeing one another also added to their warmth. As they embraced and ran the gamut of small talk, they waited for one more of the members. While absorbed in their conversations, the sound of the door closing echoed over the din of their chatter and abruptly caught their attention.

The last member had arrived, and all eyes were now on Simon.

He went around the room shaking their hands at first, followed by an embrace, all the while maintaining a serious expression, which kept the others a little on edge. After their brief exchanges, Simon asked them to be seated and, oddly, began speaking of his time in Italy during the late eighties. It was peculiar because during those years at Harvard he had never broached the subject.

He revealed that he had taken a year off after receiving his master's degree in psychology from UC Berkeley to travel around Europe. He eventually decided to live in Florence, Italy, primarily to learn the language he had always found so enchanting. While there he had met a young woman, equally enchanting, and one year became two, and then three.

"You can fill in the blanks," he invited, with a hint of a smile.

Returning to his prior demeanor, he described his one-room apartment on Canto de Nelli overlooking the steps on the north side of the Basilica di San Lorenzo. "I mention the apartment because it was where I became fascinated by the chatter of the street hawkers outside my window, when not in the company of my paramour, of course."

It was on those steps that the African street vendors would gather daily to discuss various issues, anything from personal problems, to hawking their wares, to wages. Usually on top of the list was how to avoid the *Carabinieri*, the military police, and the *Guardia di Finanza*, the police who monitor the financial, drug trafficking, and immigration crimes.

Simon explained that by the late 1980s, the Florence population was approximately four hundred thirty thousand and ten thousand of them were illegal immigrants. Most of these immigrants were Arab-speaking North Africans or French-speaking West Africans, with the majority from Senegal. While shopkeepers complained that the street vendors lured away the tourist dollars, the police attached the increase in crime to them.

"What drew my attention to these daily gatherings was a young man who appeared to be the leader of one of the groups." He further explained how this young man always stood on the top step, switching between Italian, French, and English as he lectured the vendors on various methods of selling while avoiding the police forces. "This man had an incredible flair about him, not only his articulate manner of speech and his brilliance but also the passion he showed. For those reasons," Simon asserted, "I kept my sights on this young activist."

Admittedly, he never met him directly but in speaking with other street vendors, he was able to discover a number of intriguing facts.

"First, he was born in Libya, and his name is Hussein Tarishi."

He assumed Hussein's grasp of several languages might have been compliments of his country's European occupiers, with Libya first gaining its independence from Italy in 1947, and then again from the United Kingdom and France in 1951. Simon also derived from a few discreet inquiries that, "In the 1980s, Hussein and his family lived in Benghazi, east of Tripoli, on the Gulf of Sidra. Interestingly, Hussein was also some sort of child prodigy the government apparently wanted to control, and most certainly wanted to keep in the country." He said that he heard rumors that Hussein received a full scholarship to a university in exchange for working for the Libyan government.

"Beyond that, the details were rather sketchy. Sadly, for Hussein, his family died in an aerial bombing attack in 1986. The United States launched the attack against Colonel Qaddafi, the Libyan leader. It was in retaliation for the Berlin discotheque terrorist bombing that killed two American servicemen in April of the same year." Simon acknowledged that, without knowing the full details surrounding the bombing, he presumed Hussein had taken advantage of the opportunity to escape Libya and illegally emigrated to Italy.

Until that moment, Simon's speech had been slow and deliberate. Suddenly, he elevated his tone significantly, which caused the others to pay particular attention.

"What we do know is that this young man, an illegal immigrant with no family, has all the attributes we seek." Then, for the first time, a real smile appeared on Simon's face, and he declared, "Hussein Tarishi could be our Chosen One."

Many times in the past, the group had tried to follow Simon's words. This time, they were trying to figure out where he was heading with them. Still, after his long-winded explanation, they looked on in total bewilderment.

"Il punto é?" Paolo blurted out. "Loosely translated, what is your point?" When agitated, Paolo often would revert to his native tongue. This time he was more than agitated.

Simon could see the others were anxious as well, yet also curious. He believed they were connecting the dots, but sensed they were also wrestling with the reality of what he had proposed.

"Surely you remember our shadow thesis?" he inquired with a raised brow. Being reasonably confident they would come on board, Simon ignored their apprehensive stares. He said, "Hank, I want you to fly to Florence. I've confirmed that Hussein is still living there."

"What!" Hank exclaimed.

"Hear me out! I want you to find this young man, befriend him, and confirm that he is the perfect candidate for our mission."

To the others in stunned silence, Simon's request sounded more like a command.

Simon sensed it was necessary to remind them of the decisions they had made during their "planning sessions" at Harvard. "We all agreed that Hank would be the person to administer the assignments and training exercises, and prepare the candidate to run for the Senate and then the presidency. That is the main reason why Chicago will become our home base of operation. It is where Hank lives and works. Hank will also be the only link between La Fratellanza and the future president of the United States." It was a crucial point he felt needed repeating. With even more emphasis, Simon said, "If this young activist truly is the Chosen One, then the game will start. If he isn't, then we'll find another, but eventually the game will begin for real."

Abruptly, the others broke their shock-induced silence. This time, in a fevered pitch they began to protest, punctuating that the "game" was never supposed to be for real. Following their eruptions, an odd queasiness settled in the pits of their stomachs as they realized Simon was serious, and surmised that he might have planned this outcome long before he ever met them.

They now faced harsh reality.

During those years at Harvard, he had manipulated and cajoled them into what ultimately became an intense friendship, all in preparation for the ultimate execution of his plan. They sensed their brother Simon may have taken advantage of them, and they took turns coolly expressing their resentment.

"Our 'shadow' thesis was only supposed to be an intellectual diversion, remember!" barked Chase. "It was not about committing a crime!"

Simon, not responding to Chase's outcry, allowed the others to air their protestations. Then, after respectfully giving them sufficient time to vent, he parried their objections and resentments, and continued with his pitch. This time his voice was strong and clinical.

"Now, to address Chase's overreaction and, I suspect, everyone else's concern. What we are about to embark upon isn't a crime. Actually, it is commonplace, at least in the world of politics."

Simon spoke of the politicians and about how they reinvent themselves several times over. He reminded them that the statisticians write the questions in a way to manipulate the polls, and the pollsters manipulate the numbers, which manipulate the people. He continued with how the media manipulate everything, and the capitalists who own the media manipulate them. Simon persisted with his argument, saying that congresspersons manipulate the constituents that reelect them, and special interest groups manipulate the delegates that cast the votes.

"Ultimately, it is the people who cast their vote for the person they want in the White House," he affirmed. In what appeared to be his ringing summation, he declared, "We can deliver on our shared belief that it's time for a minority to lead in the White House. All La Fratellanza would do is give them that person!"

Simon took a deep breath and then, changing tactics slightly, he began to appeal to their egos, and this time he showed a bit of compassion. He recalled why he chose them in the first place, explaining that in the beginning, he was attracted to their high level of intelligence and vast knowledge of their respective fields. However, as time went by, he said he witnessed their enormous drive to achieve, and it reinforced his opinion of them and his decision to want them as part of his group.

"Lastly, and equally important," he asserted, "it was the amazing bond that developed between us, and I knew then that I had made the right choices." Reverting to his serious demeanor once again, he reminded them, "If we actually pull it off, imagine what incredible power we will have. I recall each of you relishing the thought at Harvard, when you assumed it was just a game. And every year after that, at our annual reunions we always brought up the subject of 'What if?'"

Simon looked directly at Hank, and said, "I remember how you wanted to shape and control the social policies for the administration using the influence you would have over the president." Then he reminded Paolo, "You've always dreamed of obtaining the position as speechwriter for the president. Just think how your words could have more power than ever." To Seymour, he pointed out, "I recall how you wanted to have exclusive rights to a documentary on the president and the opportunity to use your model for political campaigning, a model you had devised only in theory. In fact, it is an opportunity for all of us to prove our theories, not just Seymour." He glanced at the others.

Simon then turned his attention to Chase. "And you, my friend, with the help from the others in the group, you would have inside information as to what position the administration, the Federal Reserve, and the Treasury would take with regard to economic and fiscal policy. Chase, you always wanted to be a huge success at some major bank. Think how you could utilize that information to manage your bank's investments."

Softening his approach, Simon admitted, "It is important for all of you to understand that it will take many years to execute, and along the way we may have to trigger certain events to accomplish our ultimate goal, placing a man in the Oval Office." Finally, he maintained, "Uncle Rob will pay for all expenses and compensate you for any loss of income."

"Just how much money did Uncle Rob leave you?" questioned Paolo.

"I've been extremely fortunate in the way I have invested the money. Does anyone else have a question?" he queried with slight annoyance.

Receiving none, and having exhausted all arguments, Simon rested his case.

They took a break, although the discussions continued. This time the issues were bantered about one-on-one. Three-quarters of an hour later, La Fratellanza reconvened.

After having spent five hours in intense analysis, discussion, and debate, they agreed—with some trepidation—to let the game begin.

The vote was unanimous.

The game was real.

However, there were a few caveats that surfaced from their discussions.

They all agreed to start the game, but if along the way anyone wanted to withdraw, for any reason, that person would have the opportunity to state his reservations. The group members would then recast their votes and at least three members of the group would have to vote to continue, or they would all walk away. In any event, confidentiality would always be preserved.

The basic ground rules were accepted, but naturally, Simon had some specific thoughts of his own. First, he handed each of them a flash drive attached to a key chain with the initials ***LF***. "You must use the flash drive to store any and all information, including your e-mails. Any information, as it relates to La Fratellanza, must not be transcribed on a hard drive. All transmissions must be sent and received on computers located in Internet cafés. You should never use the computers in your homes and workplaces."

Simon explained he had already set up an untraceable Web site with e-mail accounts for each of them. They would find their individual e-mail addresses inscribed on the back of their flash drive. He further instructed,

"When you first insert the flash drive into the USB port on a computer, it will automatically connect to the Web site. The password is *Fratellanza*, the same password we used in our computer lab at Harvard." He stressed that communications must be limited to e-mail only, with one exception.

Then Simon presented each of them with a pager. He demonstrated that when any brother activated the pager with the special code ***LF***, the pager sent a signal displaying the code to the other four, indicating a meeting was automatically set for one week from the day of the page—same time and same place.

"We will only assemble when it is necessary to take the next step or to change a step in our strategy. When it is important to gather, I will send airline tickets to your personal P.O. boxes, which you should arrange to set up as soon as you return home."

He then asked Hank to rent an office on the South Side, a place to hold their strategy meetings. "It should be out of the way and in an obscure location. Sign a five-year lease under the name of Simon Ventures, Inc., and I will arrange for a wire transfer to the management company on a quarterly basis."

Simon cautioned that they were never to enter the building together and should always protect its whereabouts. He restated his reasons for choosing Chicago as their home base, saying it was because it would also become the Chosen One's base of operation while under the tutelage of Hank.

"Also, I believe the political machine in Chicago will prove to be most useful to us."

—

La Fratellanza had a lot to think about, at least three of them, as they boarded their respective planes to return home. Hank headed to North Lake Shore Drive to prepare for his trip to Italy.

Simon understood entirely what the other members hadn't yet comprehended, the full impact of the project they were about to launch, but he felt he could resolve any issues that might arise as time went by.

Without a doubt, four members of the group fully comprehended that the commitment would be great, and hopefully within their control. However, they had yet to grasp the fact that their careers had become only a means to an end. It was no longer a game, but an affair that would dominate their lives, taking precedence over everything.

As they were leaving the Hilton, they each remembered how Simon's ideas had insidiously crept into their theses, but never imagined those ideas would ever creep into their everyday lives. Later, they would rationalize that his thoughts had also undoubtedly crept into their subconscious.

—

Simon returned to San Francisco to resume his consulting career, or so the others thought. From his home, he would conduct many of the activities for La Fratellanza, an effort that commenced immediately.

Chase arrived home to comfort his wife, who was concerned with his abrupt departure, and told her it was simply a business trip to Chicago. He explained that one of the bank branches had a serious problem while attempting to install a new computer accounting system. He wasn't happy with his deception, but knew there would be many more such trips. So he paved the way to make it clear that periodically he would have to travel for business to various locations. Then, making a passing comment, he mentioned his new pager was a way for the branch managers to contact him directly. In hopes that there would be no further questioning on the subject, he resumed his position as CFO for the National Depositors Trust Bank in New York, and waited for the pager to vibrate.

Paolo returned to his empty apartment in Georgetown, knowing that the next day he would finish writing speeches for a junior senator he didn't respect. After which, he would begin to write speeches for a junior senator he didn't know, La Fratellanza's Chosen One. Simon had "hypothetically" laid out in the "shadow" thesis that 2004 would be the year their candidate would be elected senator, and Paolo had already predetermined the pulse of the people. He could use much of what he had concluded in his thesis, although some tweaking had to take place. Paolo decided there was no need to sit by idly waiting for the pager. He would begin the political speeches immediately.

Seymour had recently married. His loving, trusting wife simply accepted that he was on an excursion to research a documentary he had been contemplating. Truly, she was a wife perfect for him in every way, including her total lack of interest in his work. He felt blessed. Over the past few years, Seymour had expanded his company, MediaLynx, to include over 130 highly competent employees. This allowed him to be less hands-on, other than to grant final approval for all new projects. The timing was perfect for him to take on The Brotherhood's ambitious new project. Seymour decided to spend his time tossing around ideas for different mantras in his head, searching for the best brand for the new senator-in-waiting, while he waited for his marching orders.

Hank gladly accepted his mission. His love life was in the off position for the moment, and he had no partner to mislead, for which he was thankful. He wasn't sure how Chase and Seymour were dealing with their women, but he was glad he wasn't facing that predicament. The Chestnut Foundation he established was self-sufficient. His primary function was to stand ready to settle the legal disputes that continually plagued his organization. At that moment, the usual attacks from various sources happened to be in a relatively calm state. The timing was ideal.

Now, Hank was to embark on a new quest, one that would start in Florence, Italy. He was thrilled at his paid vacation that landed him in the midst of wine and pasta.

It also was where he hoped to meet a young man named Hussein.

10

A FLORENTINE ENCOUNTER

After a sound sleep, preceded by a bottle of Chianti and a sizable wedge of pecorino cheese, Hank left his room at the Hotel Lungarno on Borgo San Jacopo. He was invigorated, not just because of the crisp morning air, typical for March, but because of the adventure he was about to undertake.

He crossed the renowned bridge, the Ponte Vecchio, wandered past the Duomo, the towering cathedral in the center of Florence, and up a narrow street leading to the famous Mercato Centrale, Florence's central market. It was there he noticed a crowd gathering in the Piazza San Lorenzo, directly ahead of him. It appeared to be a group of African street vendors, and precisely the place Simon had told him to start looking for their Chosen One.

Hank searched the crowd, singling out several of the street vendors, inquiring as to the whereabouts of a young Libyan named Hussein Tarishi. After his fifth inquiry, he found someone who fortunately spoke English. Equally as fortunate, the vendor was able to give him an exact description of Hussein, and easy directions to where he might find him. Hank found his way to the small café behind the Central Market on Via Taddea, and as the street vendor had accurately predicted, Hussein was there, enjoying his morning espresso.

Hussein, even from his sitting position, appeared to be lanky, with a relaxed face portraying a touch of innocence. Innocent, although he was now several years older than when Simon first discovered him. Hank guessed he was in his late twenties. His physical features defied the colorful rhetoric that Simon had heard over a decade ago. Hank had difficulty imagining that level of oratory coming from this gentle soul.

Hank, before having set eyes on Hussein, decided he would first observe him from a distance over the course of a few days. Then, when he felt the time was right, he would introduce himself. To avoid staring in the café, Hank sat off to the side as he enjoyed his first real Italian coffee and *cornetto*, the Italian version of a croissant.

In the space of an hour, Hussein left the café and wandered back toward the Central Market, with Hank following not far behind. He watched as Hussein approached the steps on the north side of the Basilica di San Lorenzo, just as Simon described. Minutes later, standing tall on the top step, Hussein gathered a sizeable crowd. Hank counted about forty in the group all looking quite similar but in different sizes, shapes, and shades.

In the moments that followed, Hank finally witnessed the seductive language Simon promised. *It is as if Hussein is standing on his own pulpit, and perhaps he is,* Hank thought.

Anxious to hear what Hussein was saying, and obviously not versed in Italian, Hank managed to overhear one of the onlookers who was fluent in English. Hank asked him if he would give a loose translation of what the man on the top step was saying. The onlooker was happy to oblige. The equally curious observer informed him that the issue of the day was how to cope with the Carabinieri that continued to hassle the street vendors.

After an hour of Hussein parceling out helpful tips, the crowd began to disperse.

Once again, Hank wended his way through the crowd to follow Hussein, staying at a safe distance and out of view. This became his modus operandi for the next several days, until he decided the time was right to approach Hussein directly.

It wasn't difficult for Hank to go unnoticed in the busy streets of Florence and he quite enjoyed his undercover role. Actually, during his bobbing and weaving in an attempt to be unobserved, he witnessed one of the supposed raids Hussein had described earlier in his speech. Upon seeing the Carabinieri, the vendors scooped up their goods in their white sheets and ran to the nearest street, dashed around the corner, and hid in the doorways of various palazzos and shops. Minutes later, after the Carabinieri drove by or walked away, the vendors would set up shop in the former location, open for business with a smile.

Hank looked on as one daring African placed his wares, specifically his counterfeit Gucci bags, next to a large tent sign. The sign, written in English, warned tourists not to buy counterfeit goods or they would be heavily fined. At first, he wondered whether it was unintentional or simply a farce, however, after observing it on several other occasions, Hank concluded it was the latter.

On the second day, Hank returned to San Lorenzo and saw Hussein again on the steps, but this time he wasn't standing before a crowd. He was perched on the top step, sitting cross-legged, with an assembled group seated below him. It appeared he was conducting some sort of training session. Unable to find an interpreter, Hank focused on Hussein's body language and the tone of his speech. He found that he was as impressed as he had been the previous day.

Then, on the third day, at the small café on Via Taddea, Hank took the opportunity to make his introduction.

—

Hussein was sitting alone at his usual table in the corner, when Hank approached.

Squinting, Hank mumbled, "*Mi scusi che non parlo l'italiano.*" He had been studying his *Say It in Italian; Phrase Book for Travelers* on his flight over, and Paolo had taught him the value of using various Italian facial expressions and hand gestures; a way of communicating in its own right. Hank didn't want Hussein to assume he knew anything about him, so he thought the evasive approach was best.

Hussein looked up, and in perfect English with a pleasant Italian accent, said, "It's not a problem. May I help you?"

It worked like a charm.

Hank proceeded to compliment Hussein on his command of the English language and apologized for the interruption. "I noticed you here the day before, and I saw you again in the Piazza San Lorenzo speaking to the crowd. While I didn't understand what you were saying to the men you had assembled, I was extremely impressed with your delivery."

Hank then asked if he could join him at his table, and Hussein invited him to sit down.

"Thank you. I'm on vacation and visiting Florence for the first time, and I didn't know a soul, until now." He smiled.

Hussein took the cue and asked, "Where do you come from?"

Hank was more than pleased to respond to the question. He said he lived in Chicago and shared a little about the Windy City.

"I read about your Chicago, and one time I saw some photos of the city. It looks like a nice place to live. What kind of work do you do?" Hussein queried.

Hank, happy to give him just enough detail to stimulate his interest, described the Chestnut Foundation. Hussein seemed most interested in the community organizing aspects, asking a series of questions. Hank was forthcoming with his answers.

During the short time they spent together conversing, Hank felt comfortable enough to ask, "Would you like to join me for lunch later in the day?"

"I'd be delighted," Hussein responded, and then suggested a time and place to meet.

—

At 1:00 p.m., they met at the Antico Ristorante il Sasso di Dante, a small restaurant across from the Piazza del Duomo that Hussein had recommended.

At first, they engaged in small talk about Florence, graduating to Hussein's own community organizing activities. He explained to Hank that when he first came to Florence, the street vendors were loosely assembled factions, usually by country of origin, competing against one another, which often led to violence.

"I fought hard to organize the street vendors into one cohesive group that can work together. I knew this was the only way the vendors could become more profitable." He was also quite proud of the fact that his efforts contributed to holding down the violence and made it easier for them to deal with the Carabinieri. "Specifically, I taught them how to work the tourist, by one vendor selling high and the other vendor selling low, ultimately striking a middle number, which produced a profit."

Hussein explained how he assigned a team leader for each group of twenty-five vendors. Currently, his group consisted of 250 vendors, and it was growing. He went on to describe how, at the end of each day, each vendor would turn in the money he had earned to his respective leader. Then the group leaders would meet with him in the evening and deposit their day's take. At the end of each week, he would pay out the vendors' salaries in equal shares, minus his ten percent cut.

"Out of the ten percent, I pay myself five and the rest goes into a reserve, as an aid fund in case of medical and or legal needs the street vendors may incur." He admitted that out of his percentage he paid a meager portion to the Carabinieri. Hussein told Hank that the raids he had witnessed were just a pretense to make it look like the Carabinieri were doing its job. "As long as I'm able to keep the violence down, everyone stays happy. Naturally, the vendors are satisfied with the structure since their earnings had increased and a collective aid fund provided a safety net."

Hank was impressed with all Hussein had accomplished, and it was obvious that Hussein himself was pleased.

At the close of an enjoyable and informative lunch, Hank gave Hussein a book and asked him if he would read it. "I would be very interested in knowing your thoughts, both about the subject matter and about its author."

Hussein happily agreed. He promised to read the book that night, and then they could discuss it in the morning, at the café on Via Taddea over their morning espresso.

—

The next day Hank waited in the café for Hussein with great anticipation, continuously checking his watch. As he confirmed the hour for the tenth time, he looked up to see Hussein approaching, with his face aglow and a smile that stretched from ear to ear.

Before the customary greeting, *buongiorno,* Hussein immediately began to sing the praises of the book Hank had given him. It was music to Hank's ears as Hussein quoted various passages verbatim. It was clear Hussein was mesmerized.

If Hank didn't know better, he would have sworn he was listening to Saul himself. Saul Alinsky's book, *Rules for Radicals*, was Hank's bible, and told him everything he needed to know about how to organize the have-nots to achieve real political power. He believed it was a must-read for all to understand radicalism and how to achieve its goals.

As if his speechifying weren't enough, Hussein also had a photographic memory and was a remarkably quick study. "Alinsky has provided the basis and the structure for true community organizing. I was unaware of many things, and I desperately want to know more!" Hussein exclaimed.

Hank thought it was beautiful—Hussein had found his voice—Hank had found his man.

—

Within days, Hussein was reciting Alinsky's message in several languages to the crowds, as they gathered on the steps of the Basilica di San Lorenzo. Sometimes he spoke in Arabic, his native tongue, to the Sudanese and Moroccans; other times, it was in French to the Senegalese or English to the Kenyans. Always he would switch back to Italian in an effort to help the other street vendors improve their facility for the local language.

Hank assumed Hussein had learned Italian in his own country, recalling Simon had mentioned that Libya was an Italian colony from 1912 to 1939. In fact, when he spoke in Arabic, his words tended to flow with the hint of an Italian accent, and when he spoke to Hank in English the accent was ever-present. Whatever language Hussein was weaving in and out of, Hank sat back in sheer amazement and admiration.

Within days, Hussein and Hank had established a routine as Hussein carried out his daily schedule. Hank would eavesdrop on his morning oratory, and when he was unable to find an interpreter or understand his words, he focused on his gestures and the faces of his audience. Then Hank and Hussein would meet for lunch at one of the various restaurants and cafés lining the Borgo San Lorenzo near the church. While they consumed pasta or a pizza, Hussein would reconstruct the general idea of his message for that day. Hank, now with permission, would follow Hussein around during the afternoons observing him performing various duties. For the most part, they would wrap up the day continuing their conversations over dinner.

After several days of following this routine, Hank added something new to the mix.

Hank and Hussein would end their evenings squaring off over a game of chess. Hank, the chess master, prided himself on his ability to strategize and ultimately win. However, with Hussein, he had lost more games than he had won. It was a first for him. While Hussein alleged that he had only played once or maybe twice, Hank wasn't so sure, but he did admire his shrewdness. *Checkmate* evidently was not a new word in Hussein's vocabulary.

After several more encounters, they were becoming fast friends.

Each day Hank discovered facts more interesting than the last about Hussein, which certainly gave him more insight into this amazing man. Hussein, unaware that Hank had any prior knowledge, described his home in Libya, and the loss of his family in the bombing that took place in 1986. Hank learned that before arriving in Florence, Hussein was a senior attending the University of Garyounis in Benghazi, majoring in political science.

"I'm guessing you are in your late twenties, which would mean that you were quite young as a senior in college," Hank said.

"Yes I was sixteen, and considered a genius. My government called me a child prodigy." After a slight pause, he added, "That explains the rest of my story." He continued to describe his home life and the extreme poverty he and his family endured. "However, my intelligence was recognized by the government, and Colonel Qaddafi wanted—or rather insisted—that I work for the government in exchange for a full scholarship to the university. I despise my government!" he exclaimed. "The government restricts many human rights—freedom of speech, freedom of assembly, and freedom of the press. Worse, the government controls the court system." With his facial expression softening slightly, he said, "Still, the one thing I loved most was to learn, to capture all the knowledge I could, and accepting Qaddafi's offer was my only opportunity to get a formal education and take care of my family."

Hank took notice when Hussein lowered his head slightly, looking down, and in a hushed voice said, "The real reason I accepted the offer was because it included a home for my family." Slightly more emotional, he recalled that after the bombing there were many newspapers reporting the entire Tarishi family had died in the attack. "It was a devastating moment, but it provided me the only opportunity to leave my country, never to return." He sighed.

Looking up at Hank, he described how he fled Libya as a stowaway on a boat heading for Sicily. He explained that was where he first learned Italian, not in the schools of Benghazi but in the streets of Palermo. Over the years, he managed to wend his way along the coast of Italy, picking up odd jobs until he finally reached Florence, where he decided to stay.

Suddenly, Hussein changed his demeanor and the subject, as he started to talk about his passion for social reform.

As he continued to express his views, it was not only the words, but also the power of his oratory, which confirmed in Hank's mind—he had found the Chosen One.

—

Several weeks had passed, and Hank was scheduled to fly back to Chicago the next day. La Fratellanza had made plans to assemble, and were anxiously waiting to hear what Hank had discovered about Hussein Tarishi.

It was to be their last evening together and Hank knew it would be his final opportunity to make an impassioned plea and to raise the ultimate question: Would Hussein be interested in going to the United States to work for him at the Chestnut Foundation?

First, he needed to lay the groundwork.

Hank invited Hussein to join him for dinner at their favorite Antico Ristorante il Sasso di Dante near the Duomo. While they waited for their antipasti, he reminded Hussein of their discussions when he indicated an interest in a career in politics.

"I remember when you explained how some people who hold a political office use their political power to support efforts to effect social change," Hussein said. "It is a position I had never considered for myself, but I find the idea intriguing."

"Yes, but before entering a political career it is best first to involve yourself directly with those activities that effect social change," Hank advised.

Hank then went on to describe some of his organization's "effective" organizing activities, as he liked to call them, as a means to increase their power base. By way of example, he explained, one of the neighborhoods outside Chicago had become infested with drug dealers. So he arranged for the pastors in seven of the churches in the neighborhood to preach a sermon, all on the same Sunday. Each pastor was instructed to admonish the actions of the drug dealers and urge the congregation members to band together in a fight to rid their neighborhood of these undesirables. Hank had also arranged for members of his organization to attend the sermons and then take to the pulpit. Speaking on behalf of the Chestnut Foundation, these members informed the parishioners that they would support their efforts and would provide the support to neutralize the drug dealers. Some of the Chestnut Foundation members were former convicts, well versed in the ways of the street and in enacting their own sort of justice. It was quite "effective," but these were details, Hank thought best not to mention. But he did say that the drug dealers relocated, leaving the neighborhood once again safe.

"So, the members of the community were beholden to the Chestnut Foundation and provided an abundance of volunteers for many of your organizing drives," Hussein surmised.

"Exactly!" Hank exclaimed, still amazed at Hussein's quick grasp of the issues.

Citing another example, Hank spoke about a series of convenience stores vandalized in a neighborhood by one of the local gangs. He again dispatched members of his organization to solicit support from the local community for a joint effort to clean up the damage inflicted on the stores. The Chestnut Foundation donated funds, and the storeowners were able to restock their shelves. Through the foundation's efforts, the individual communities were empowered, and with the support of the foundation, were able to keep their streets safe and the criminal elements at bay.

"More important, you had yet another source of volunteers." Hussein smirked.

"Yes. Then other times, the foundation would use the volunteers for different purposes. Case in point, they would picket banks and other lending organizations in an attempt to force them to provide low-cost mortgages."

Hank cited a few more instances, each time pointing out how the volunteers played a key role. He counseled Hussein that building a base of support, one neighborhood at a time, provided the power to effect the social change he desired. The volunteers also became an invaluable resource during election campaigns to encourage voters to go to the polls and cast their ballots for Chestnut's preferred political candidates.

"At times, our methods might have been in question, but the ends always justified the means," he added proudly.

As Hank was finishing his sentence, a peculiar expression appeared on Hussein face, and he quickly responded. "If you have organized a vast, mass-based peoples' organization, you can flaunt it visibly before the target to show your power openly."

Astonishingly, he was quoting Saul Alinsky verbatim.

Again, amazed by Hussein's quick grasp, Hank stopped citing examples. The time was right to pose the question.

In response, Hank saw a different expression on Hussein's face. The ear-to-ear smile returned as he expressed his desire to see the United States for himself. Then he said, "It would be my privilege to work for you, my friend. I have harbored plans to leave my current situation, which has its limitations, to go on to something bigger and better." He confessed that he felt he had accomplished a great deal in the organization of the street vendors, and believed he had sufficiently trained the group leaders to take over and appoint someone in his place.

"Florence initially provided me with the means to expand my horizons, though, after spending time with you, I realized there is so much more that I can attain. Perhaps it is time to move on. I understand now there's nothing more for me here." Hussein also confessed that, after reading a plethora of information about America, "It would be a great opportunity for me to see firsthand how a person can speak out and say anything without fear for his life or the lives of his family. Tell me what I must do to join your organization."

"Leave all of the strategy and tactics to me. I will elaborate on the plan without delay." Hank knew Hussein would be ideal, not only to accomplish the goals of La Fratellanza but also to help him accomplish his own personal goals as well.

It was a productive dinner, although a disappointing chess match for Hank.

With some sadness at leaving, Hank bade his new friend farewell with a traditional two-sided Italian hug, and promised to be in touch very soon.

Exhilaration set in over his burgeoning partnership, and he knew he had just aced his first assignment. That night, back in his hotel room, Hank assembled his notes, and then went to look for an Internet café to fire off an e-mail to La Fratellanza.

11

THE ACTION PLAN

Hank arrived home the following day, jubilant and eager to share his experience. Fortunately, preparations were already in place for La Fratellanza to assemble two days after his arrival, and he was feeling antsy. Over the weekend, Hank did his best to busy himself, planning what he thought should be the next steps before Hussein's arrival. He recognized that he needed the other members' approval; however, he had determined in his own mind that Hussein was their Chosen One.

—

Monday morning finally arrived, and the members of the group anxiously gathered in their new office on the South Side of Chicago.

Before leaving for Florence, Hank had made the necessary preparations to lease the office space, along with ordering the furnishings. During his absence, Simon took care of setting up a "quasi" computer lab. As the others scoped out their new, innovative base of operation, they noticed various computers, along with several pieces of exotic equipment, some of which they had difficulty identifying.

After welcoming Hank, they settled into their chairs around the round conference table. Minutes later, Hank opened his briefcase and removed from a plastic bag, a glass with Hussein's fingerprints on it, along with the additional data he had collected.

In that instant, this illustrious group confronted the realization that it was no longer a game.

The defining moment had arrived.

As Hank handed the glass to Simon, the others immediately noticed his reaction. Never excessively emotional except for the occasional rant, he became euphoric, blurting out, "Fantastic!" Then, in his usual mode of multiprocessing, Simon listened to Hank fill in the details of his trip while he began to process the fingerprints from the glass with the precision of a crime scene investigator.

All ears were on Hank, but all eyes were on Simon. The never-ending, hidden talents of their fellow brother continually astonished the other members of La Fratellanza.

First, he dusted the fingerprint with a fine black carbon powder and carefully placed a piece of tape over the print. They later discovered that he used something called Diff Lift tape, a soft substance with a surface density extremely low that goes into the bumps and valleys of the surface it covers. He was able to lift off a perfect thumbprint from Hussein Tarishi. He then placed the tape over a microscope slide preserving the print. Then using a digital microscope, he was able to transfer the thumbprint to his laptop.

Simon, who was not short on talent and certainly had no lack of *cojones*, ran the print through Interpol, the world's largest international police organization, which, of course, he hacked. While waiting for a response, he tapped his fingers rapidly on the keyboard on the second laptop, periodically pressing the enter key and mumbling, "Nothing."

Suddenly the tapping stopped, and for the first time since they convened, there was complete silence. Even Hank stopped in mid-sentence.

Simon turned around with an enormous smile and announced, "We have found our Chosen One."

Out of Libya and onto the streets of Florence, Italy, Hussein Tarishi had no history. In fact, he didn't even exist. "I discovered something I had overlooked before, as I was listening to Hank speak about the death of Hussein's family in 1986," Simon admitted. "I had missed the newspaper reports that all members of the Tarishi family had died, including their sixteen-year-old son Hussein. Obviously, it was misreported, but no one believes he is alive. I also checked the immigration records, both in Libya and Italy, and there is no record of Hussein leaving or entering either country."

"Evidently, Hussein is as capable of producing false IDs as you are, Simon," Hank snickered.

Aside from Hank's attempt at humor, the members of La Fratellanza realized that they had plucked this activist off the streets of a city almost five thousand miles away, and they alone would land him on the world stage.

As four of the members where taking in the enormity of what they were about to launch, Simon asserted, "Let's get to work, this time for real."

They agreed on a timetable—they had one month to get the plan in place.

"Before Hussein arrives in the U.S., we need to craft a new identity, and when he arrives we need to rid him of his charming accent," Hank remarked.

"The foremost priority, however, will be to create his new identity," Simon countered.

First, they had to agree on the name.

Initially, Seymour came up with Abdul, as his first name. "Abdul is the Islamic name that means 'Servant of the Creator.' I feel it is more than appropriate, given the circumstances." He boasted that he had taken a few Islamic courses during his undergraduate studies, to piss off his father and his neighborhood rabbi.

"Don't you think getting an African elected president will be difficult enough?" Paolo chided. "An African with a Muslim-sounding name would be impossible."

The others agreed.

Seymour, anticipating their rebuke, lined up his second choice. "How about Abner? He was the first cousin to Saul, in the book of Samuel, and the commander-in-chief of Saul's army?" Seymour loved the symbolism.

So Hussein became Abner.

Unbeknownst to the others, Simon had crafted the new identity years before, only waiting to plug in the name—an identity, totally dissimilar from the one the group had crafted and concealed in the pages of their theses, at Harvard.

Confidently, Simon took to the stage, and offered to read his shrewdly prepared bio.

Taking a deep breath, he started to read the story of Abner, filling in the blanks as he went along.

"Abner Baari's father," he began.

"Baari!" Seymour blurted out as he winced.

Simon slightly perturbed, continued, "As I was saying, Abner Baari's father, Yosif Tarishi, was born in Libya and his mother, Katherine Baari, of Irish descent, was reared in Independence, Kansas. His mother met his father in 1970 while working in Libya for the Peace Corps. After returning to the U.S., she discovered she was pregnant, and sadly she died in her hometown, while giving birth to Abner."

Paolo interrupted and questioned, "Isn't Independence, Kansas, where Lordy was from?"

Simon looked up from his script and flashed his sinister smile, as if that were a sufficient answer to Paolo's question.

As he was about to continue with the bio he was interrupted once again.

"Won't the fact that his mother was a Caucasian present a problem?"

Hank asked.

Annoyed at the interruptions, he raised his tone noticeably and stated, "The facial characteristics of the Libyan people are different from other African countries. Their eyes are sharper, their lips are thicker, and their hair tends to be less curly," Simon pointed out. "More important, the females tend to be lighter and have more graceful features. By making Abner half Caucasian, it makes his new identity an easier sell."

"Politically, it neutralizes him with the electorate, with both sides claiming he's theirs," Paolo added sarcastically. "It will certainly make the campaign interesting."

Thus far, the other members liked the way Abner's fictional biography was shaping up.

"Let me sketch in more details for our hero." Simon continued with Katherine Baari's parents. "John and Sarah Baari, not knowing how or where to locate Abner's father, reared him in Independence."

Seymour approved. "I like it! Midwestern values will make for great vignettes when I develop the sound bites."

Simon smiled as he proceeded. "In 1994, a month before Northwestern University accepted Abner for his undergraduate studies, heartbreak befell him again. Tragically, his grandparents died in an automobile accident."

"This puts Abner truly alone in the world." Hank emphasized.

"Precisely!" Simon retorted.

"Abner graduated from Northwestern University in 1998, where he obtained a BS in political science. The following year he was hired by the Chestnut Foundation and currently works as an organizer, conducting drives."

"I trust we can't say Uncle Rob paid for his education, so what's the story line there?" Chase asked.

"Abner paid for his education at Northwestern with the money left to him in a trust fund, after the death of his grandparents. He supplemented his income with odd jobs he acquired on campus, which takes me to another point," Simon noted. "Due to his work schedule at Northwestern, he was unable to join many extracurricular campus activities, which would explain why many people do not remember him." Simon smiled. "You know I pride myself on discerning human nature, and I believed if anyone were to interview any member of the administration at the university, that person would claim to remember the senator or president, honored that he is an alumnus."

Simon proudly looked up from his paper and noted that the members of La Fratellanza appeared to be in agreement with Abner Baari's life history. "Remember this is a fictional biography, but everything from this point on in Abner's life will be real," Simon stressed.

After hours of discussion, they had finally concocted a new persona for Hussein Tarishi. Abner Baari was alone in the world, with a clean slate waiting for any additional information they deemed necessary. La Fratellanza knew it would be guiding the rest of his life going forward, at least into the White House.

"What I didn't mention before is that Abner Baari will need to apply and be accepted to the University of Chicago Law School, in an accelerated two-year JD program."

All of them agreed it was necessary for Abner to earn a law degree to be able to compete successfully against other candidates, both in the senate and presidential races.

Simon confirmed that he had checked the various law schools in the Chicago area, and the University of Chicago was the only campus with an accelerated program. Given their time frame, he felt it was essential to expedite his education. "I have a list of the core curriculum from Northwestern that I'll pass out to each of you. It may be helpful when you design the specific tutorials for Abner."

"When he graduates in August of 2002, I think the Chestnut Foundation should hire him as its legal counsel," Hank suggested. "I trust that's not a problem with anyone. It will allow me to manage him more closely."

"I assume you can also adjust the records to reflect his employment since 1998, when he graduated from Northwestern?" Simon inquired.

"With an organization my size, fabricating an employment record for one person will be easy," Hank asserted. "In fact, I can include in his record that the Chestnut Foundation awarded Abner a full scholarship to law school, based on his outstanding work for the foundation."

"Nice addition," Chase complimented.

"Great, we now have one year to get him ready to apply to law school," Simon added.

With Hussein's new identity complete, Simon would manufacture all the documents, replete with diplomas and photos that Hank had taken of him while in Florence, and place Abner Baari's identity in all the appropriate databases. Creating fake passports was easy for Simon, having started out with phony driver's licenses at the mere age of twelve.

"At the time, it was highly profitable and made me extremely popular, as you can imagine," Simon bragged. "Hacking Northwestern University's computer database will also be a walk in the park when I add Abner's records, giving him a bachelor's degree in political science—with honors, of course."

Chase continually raised the question of the legality of what they were doing. "I bought your argument as to how the world of politics manages its affairs, but clearly, Simon, some of your acts are crossing the line and you are committing criminal offenses."

"I will never ask any of you to commit a crime!" Simon snapped. "As for hacking and creating false identities, I will ensure my involvement is never linked back to any of you," Simon insisted, with more apparent sincerity than any of them had witnessed for some time.

Satisfied, they agreed to move the discussion forward.

Hank was responsible for locating a rental apartment for Abner, with sufficient living space equipped for his homeschooling needs. The apartment was to be located out of the neighborhoods where the Chestnut Foundation operated and where Abner would eventually become well known. In addition, as Hank suggested, the accent had to go, along with learning proper etiquette and fine-tuning his public speaking ability. Hank's task was to manage it overall.

For the time being, each of the other members of La Fratellanza was responsible for putting together tutorial assignments that Hank would administer, which they had begun while Hank was in Florence.

"I have pulled together several documentaries of past presidents," Seymour announced, "along with biographies by the well-known presidential historian Doris Kearns Goodwin. I believe it would give Abner a firsthand view of the interworkings of Washington."

"Remember, Abner is not to be told at first about his being groomed for the presidency, so that information may seem a little obvious, or may raise suspicion," Simon argued.

They all agreed.

Hank added, "Books like *Chicago Politics Ward by Ward* by David Fremon and *Don't Make No Waves…Don't Back No Losers: An Insiders' Analysis of the Daley Machine* by Milton L. Rakove might be a better place to start."

Seymour concurred and said he would hold off and prepare assignments around books pertaining to the Illinois government and senatorial politics.

Paolo presented a copy of *Political Campaign Communication: Principles and Practices* by Judith S. Trent and Robert V. Friedenberg, published a few years prior, along with Gary C. Jacobson's book *The Politics of Congressional Elections*. "I've also designed lesson plans to test Abner's understanding of the concepts, and when it comes time, I will include information on foreign policy."

"Paolo, it would be extremely helpful if you would also design some course material for pre-law. We'll need to get him ready to apply for graduate school," Hank suggested.

"Not a problem."

"As of yet I haven't designed his course material," Chase admitted, "but I will focus on the financial system and the economy, both domestically and globally."

"Needless to say, I have social policy covered," Hank boasted, "and will teach him about Internet activism and the use of the Internet."

Simon confirmed that he would begin to make the necessary arrangements to bring Hussein to Chicago. "It will be necessary to create two U.S. passports. One passport will be under a different name, which will only be necessary for his entry to the United States and for purchasing an airline ticket to Chicago. We don't want any record of Abner Baari arriving in the States," he added.

"Once Abner arrives, I will get him ready to join the ranks of the Chestnut Foundation and begin to establish his reputation, not as an organizer but as a recent graduate of Northwestern University, and of course, a fighter for social justice," Hank asserted.

Simon asked the others to give some thought as to how to plan a senatorial campaign, in addition to spending their time to prepare the assignments.

They needed to begin preparations for the U.S. Senate race in Illinois in 2004.

12

THE GROOMING YEARS

On a Monday morning at O'Hare Airport, a relatively peaceful travel day with a modicum of passengers floating about the terminal, Hussein Tarishi arrived.

Hank's face beamed as he saw Hussein walk briskly through the doors, after declaring nothing, as instructed, when he passed by the customs officials. He was carrying only a single green, army-issue duffel bag over his right shoulder, where he had tucked all his personal treasures.

Both were tremendously thrilled, acting as though they were meeting a long-lost family member or a dear old friend. They embraced with a two-sided Italian hug and a kiss on each cheek as Hank welcomed Hussein to Chicago.

Hussein chatted excitedly, especially about how easy it was to go through immigration with his new U.S. passport. "It's already starting to feel like home!" he exclaimed.

Simon had specifically arranged for the direct Delta Airline flight from Rome to Chicago, bypassing New York. He knew the U.S. Immigration and Customs officials at O'Hare had a reputation for being less restrictive than the point of entries on the East Coast, not that he had any concerns. He knew Hussein's documentation was flawless.

Hussein, unaware of the existence of La Fratellanza, never thought to question his new passport. He trusted and admired Hank, and it was of no importance, as long as he was able to come to America.

—

Hussein's new home consisted of a small one-bedroom apartment on the South Side near La Fratellanza's office, and away from the neighborhoods organized by the Chestnut Foundation. An apartment Hussein assumed Hank was paying for as well. They walked up the three stories and Hank extended to Hussein the pleasure of opening the door to his new home.

They entered a rectangular living space where directly ahead was a sofa and a small coffee table stationed in front. On the left of the room were two side-by-side bookcases and a large desk with a laptop and printer situated on top. At the far end of the room was a small round dining table with two chairs. The kitchenette took up the remaining wall space. The one door led to the bedroom, with a double bed, dresser, and bathroom. The only windows were over the dining room table and the dresser in the bedroom. Both overlooked the alley below.

By U.S. standards, it was modest; by Hussein's it was luxurious.

—

During the first few weeks, Hank encouraged Hussein to tour the streets of Chicago to get a feel for the city. The first few days Hank accompanied Hussein, to orient him to the different neighborhoods in and around Chicago, and to explain how to best utilize the public transportation system. However, Hank first decided to show him the best Chicago had to offer and started with downtown, aptly named the Gold Coast. Hussein, dazzled by the tall buildings, also marveled at the opulence of Chicago's "Magnificent Mile," the famed street that runs the length of Michigan Avenue from Lake Shore Drive to the Chicago River. Moreover, he was in awe of the people who paraded the streets.

"This is what power can bring you," Hank assured Hussein, as he watched Hussein's eyes darting about.

"You really believe one day I could live like this?"

"With a lot of hard work and effort on your part, you could."

The next day Hank introduced Hussein to other neighborhoods nearby on the South Side. It was no coincidence that Hussein's apartment was located on Fifty-Second Street, in Hyde Park, near not only the University of Chicago, but also only a few neighborhoods away from some of the most impoverished. Hussein liked what the Gold Coast had to offer, but now, wandering about on his own, he spent most of his days roaming the streets of Englewood and New City, referred to as "Back of the Yards." Hank thought it beneficial for Hussein to see firsthand the neighborhoods and the people he would one day be working with to help improve their lot. In those areas, many projects were under way, directed by the Chestnut Foundation.

"When you venture out on your own, please wear a baseball cap and sunglasses, and speak to no one," Hank cautioned.

"Why all the undercover stuff?"

"It will make sense to you soon, I promise. Just trust me for now."

"For now." Hussein smiled.

Those first few weeks Hank and Hussein occupied their days with various activities, and in the evenings they would entertain each other with lively discussions, mostly about community organizing. Naturally, they were still chess rivals. After many nights, countless discussions, and numerous games, both in Florence and in Chicago, the level of trust and friendship had heightened between them.

Almost two months to the day of their first introduction, Hussein confirmed his desire to remain in Chicago and work for Hank's organization. That night, Hank e-mailed La Fratellanza and informed the group that he was ready to move Hussein to the introductory phase.

—

The following day, Hank, believing Hussein was ready to hear the partial truth, sat down with him and explained that a group of wealthy executives was aware of his incredible accomplishments in Florence.

"Actually these men sent me to Florence to meet you and evaluate your potential. They also provided you with the U.S. passport, airline ticket, and the apartment," Hank explained. "I didn't set out to deceive you, and during the time we had spent together in Florence, I truly felt we had become friends," he offered apologetically.

In the back of Hank's mind, he recalled how upset he was when he discovered Simon's deceit, and hoped Hussein did not share those feelings.

"I am extremely grateful, first that my talents are recognized and, second, for the opportunity to be in America," Hussein insisted, adding, "and for your friendship, of course."

Hank smiled with immense relief, and continued, "These powerful men would like you to learn about the political, social, and inner workings of the U.S., and possibly one day run for political office." Watching Hussein's expression, he carefully explained, "These men believe the American people are desperate for a new face among their politicians, a person with the talent to make real changes in our social policy. They deemed that you can bring about the kind of transformation the voters are looking for in their government."

Hank then took that opportunity to jog Hussein's memory. He reminded him about their nightly discussions in Florence and how, at times, he showed a desire to run for political office one day. Inwardly, he also took pride in knowing those thoughts were the result of the seeds he had planted in Hussein's mind during their time together. He informed

Hussein that his supporters also believed a law degree was an essential qualification for any political office he might want to hold, and they would pay his full tuition when he was ready.

"For that reason, you will need to study the personalized course work that will be constructed to prepare you for acceptance to law school. And at the appropriate time, I will also involve you in some of the activities at the Chestnut Foundation." Hank urged him to take sufficient time to absorb the enormity of the situation. He told him there would be time later to sketch in all the pertinent information.

Hussein staring in disbelief, paralyzed by the depth and magnitude of how quickly his life was changing, murmured, almost in a trancelike state, "I can't believe all this is really happening! Is all this possible, or am I dreaming?"

"Yes, it is possible, highly probable, but you'll have to be fully dedicated. We have only one year to prepare. There is no doubt in my mind that you are not only up to the task, but you will also make us proud!"

"You've seen how fast I can read and absorb the information. All you need to do is teach me what I need to know and how to use what I've learned." Hussein assured with the utmost seriousness.

"It will be hard work and will require you to study day and night."

"Who are these men? Why are they doing this?" he asked, still trying to grasp the situation.

"They wish to be anonymous, and their motives are not your concern. Just accept that they want to give you an opportunity to make a major contribution to society. Hussein, you must not question our methods, only trust that we are looking out for your best interests," Hank affirmed.

Thus far, Hank was pleased as to how the conversation had progressed, but he had another difficult obstacle to overcome. He now had to convince Hussein that for him to carry out the strategy and one day run for elective office, he'd need a new identity. Hank encouraged him not only to accept a new persona, but also to take the opportunity to embrace a totally new way of life.

Somewhat surprisingly, it wasn't a difficult sell.

Hussein's short time in Chicago had given him an insatiable thirst for the opportunities available to him, and he wanted to drink in all it had to offer.

"I have no problem changing my name, if it means I'll become an American."

"Great! Because the new name selected for you is Abner Baari. It was our first choice after much contemplation."

Hussein grimaced slightly, but Hank thought it was a natural reaction.

"How did they choose the name?" he asked curiously.

"Abner was the first cousin of Saul in the book of Samuel and the commander-in-chief of Saul's army. One member of the group was into religious studies and thought the name conveys power and leadership, something a person looks for in a politician. Your surname came from John and Sara Baari, who were real people. Unfortunately, they died in an automobile accident."

Hussein repeated the name several times, letting it roll over his tongue. Moments later he asked, "It suits me, no?"

"Yes, it suits you." Although, Hank thought, *It does suit him, but with the accent, no.*

The time had arrived, now that they had settled the issue of the name, to fill Hussein in on his new family history and his life up to the point of his graduation from Northwestern. Hank slowly delivered the bio, and after careful thought, Hussein accepted not only his name but also his family history, educational background, and new life, with all that it offered.

"I desperately want to live in this country, and one day I want to achieve real power," Hussein said with total confidence. "Hank, I see what you have accomplished and I want the same and more."

Hank smiled—there was no more to say.

—

Abner spent a considerable amount of his time in his three-story walk-up studying the course material supplied by La Fratellanza and instructed by Hank, but the second priority, the removal of his foreign accent, was more difficult to manage. He needed to replace his accent with a nondescript manner of pronunciation, and he'd need to develop a slight Kansas twang for good measure.

Abner would also need to learn American mannerisms, business etiquette, and the core essentials to become a suitable political candidate. While his oratory skills were exceptional, they still required a bit of refining, especially when working with a teleprompter.

The risk of bringing in outsiders was great, but in this instance, La Fratellanza had no alternative. None of the group members were skilled in speech-language pathology. Moreover, all agreed that none of them had the skills of an etiquette coach. Most important, aside from Hank, none of them were to meet Abner, certainly not during the grooming stage.

Therefore, Simon arranged for two coaches to work with Abner on a daily basis, but they were not in Illinois, where Abner would eventually run for public office. He had to cross state lines and take his weekly sessions in Milwaukee, Wisconsin.

The next obstacle was to change his appearance with a disguise that wouldn't raise suspicion.

When Hank met Abner at the airport a month earlier, he had looked like many of the student radicals of the sixties Hank had seen, and had been a part of, on campus. His Afro and menacing goatee gave him the appearance of a campus radical, so one of Hank's first acts was to have his hair cut and his goatee shaved.

However, for the purpose of Abner's elocution and etiquette lessons, he disguised himself again to look like a student. He put on the Afro wig over his closely cropped hair and added a pair of thick black-rimmed glasses. However, this time he was clean-shaven. The glasses gave Abner a rather studious look, and sufficiently disguised his gentle face. Hank thought it was necessary to conceal his identity and prevent any of the tutors from making a connection between Abner and the future senator.

"I look like a guy named Hussein," Abner smirked.

"Well, for the purpose of introduction to your new tutors, your name is Kenyth."

"Hank, I'm starting to feel like I'm in a witness protection program. It will be my fourth name this month, including the name on my passport!"

"Remember, you agreed to trust me!"

"Say no more." Abner surrendered.

—

Abner worked diligently for three months, studying constantly and practicing what he had learned with Hank. He not only managed to drop his foreign accent, but also became comfortable in the ways of an American "gentleman." He was an excellent student in every way. His mind was like a sponge, absorbing the words and concepts from his lessons and from the pages of his books. He was always standing by waiting anxiously for the next influx of information.

Occasionally, Hank would test him in others ways and call him Hussein, only to be quickly rebuked, "My name is Abner Baari."

Hank believed Abner was now ready to perform some fundamental organizing activities for his foundation by day, as part of his training, and continue to be homeschooled at night. La Fratellanza agreed and Hank proceeded to the next step.

He continued to work closely with Abner, teaching him all aspects of community organizing, and eventually allowed him to apply what he had learned by giving him special projects to work on, on his own.

Hank revealed that two years earlier the Chicago mayor announced a $256 million revitalization plan to improve the infrastructure of the South Side neighborhood of Englewood. It was where the most impoverished live, was predominantly African American, and it had suffered from chronic high unemployment and an elevated crime rate. Since the mayor's pronouncement, there had been little progress, and it was clear that it would be up to those affected to find a solution that would force the elected officials to make good on their promises.

"Unfortunately, the residents and groups within the community have no history of effecting social change through community organizing. This is where you come in. I want you to work with the community leaders and teach them the tools of the trade."

"Thanks, Hank. I've been waiting months for an opportunity," Abner replied. "I promise I won't disappoint you."

Within four months, Hank was able to report to the other members of the group with pride that Abner had aced his assignment, as well as all the other organizing activities he had thrown his way.

Abner was more than meeting their expectations.

—

Hank saw firsthand what he already knew. Abner was a natural and learned how to run community organizing drives with better skill than himself, which he reluctantly admitted to the others. He was feeling like a proud father, and focused on the day when Abner would become president, and the dutiful son would ensure Hank's social agenda became the major plank in the president's platform. He personally felt the current administration was off course and needed a more liberal social strategy, and Abner, the Chosen One, was needed to bring about the necessary changes.

While Hank continued to spend days with Abner on the streets, he spent evenings grilling him on the endless lessons prepared by La Fratellanza. Actually, it became quite a pleasant routine for both of them. Hank simply had to direct the lessons. Abner absorbed the information from his books and tutorials, and Hank corrected his tests and challenged him orally. Most satisfying were the discussion sessions on each of the subjects. Hank grasped most of the concepts—Abner grasped them all.

As promised, Chase prepared lessons on finance, global economic theories, and the banking industry, following the course structure from the Northwestern syllabus for political science majors.

Seymour held back on the presidential documentaries, but did include a course on the presidency, one of the requirements at Northwestern. His primary focus, though, was on the media, polling, and senatorial races, garnishing most of his knowledge from his research conducted while producing his 501(c)(3) "nonpolitical" political ads.

Paolo passed along lessons on geopolitical foreign policy derived from the many speeches he had penned, along with political theory, American government, and constitutional law courses, all of which he had taken himself.

Hank constructed the sociology course, and the race, ethnicity, and public policy course, adding them to the lesson plan, along with the on-the-job experience at the foundation.

Abner had been working fervently on his studies, all of which he mastered. His diction was free of accent, his oratory was erudite, and he had earned an outstanding reputation for his competence at the Chestnut Foundation and in the communities it served.

Abner was also accepted at the University of Chicago Law School, to commence in the spring semester of 2001.

At the end of the year, Hank felt like Henry Higgins of *My Fair Lady*, giving him a sense of empowerment. In his mind, he was becoming the creator of one of the most powerful men in the world.

13

THE MAKING OF A SENATOR

The next two years were grueling for both Abner and La Fratellanza.

Abner sailed through the accelerated JD program at the university, while still performing some duties at the Chestnut Foundation and cramming for the bar exam. Amazingly, nothing seemed to faze him. He moved ahead effortlessly as though he were in a race for his life, and perhaps he was. As the second year came to a close, Abner had graduated summa cum laude, passed the bar, and began working full-time for the Chestnut Foundation. After mastering all his assigned activities within the foundation, Abner then worked his magic defending Hank's organization against legal challenges.

Despite the pressures the members of La Fratellanza were under, everyone was resilient and responded well to the demands it placed on their lives. Initially, the members of the group, except for Simon, were reluctant participants in the game—though as it became more real—they became more obsessed with achieving their goal.

Hank's reservations were short-lived. He presumed from the start, before the "game" had become the "real deal," that he would play a dominant role that would benefit him the most. He deluded himself to believe he simply was mentoring a superior human being who was destined for greatness. He did not consider any of the other aspects of the plot. He worked tirelessly by Abner's side, directly reaping the rewards of his demanding efforts.

Meanwhile, Paolo and Seymour had serious concerns, due mostly to Simon's machinations. They feared if anyone discovered that Abner was a fraud, it would lead a trail back to them. Nevertheless, visions of their power in the White House reigned over their misgivings and eventually outweighed their fears. They both worked furiously to provide the educational material, while working together to plan a senatorial campaign.

Chase, the worrywart of the group, had the most apprehension, and although he'd repaid his financial debt to Simon, his loyalty still ran deep. He met La Fratellanza demands, while simultaneously trying to balance his time between his responsibilities at the bank and his obligations to his family.

Several years had elapsed, countless days had been stripped from their personal lives, and now, as they were about to turn the page on yet another year, they were all finally and totally committed.

The commitment was irreversible.

—

It was that pivotal moment, in September 2001, that strengthened La Fratellanza's resolve to see its plot play out in full.

Six months after Abner entered law school; nineteen Muslim hijackers were responsible for crashing planes into the World Trade Center and the Pentagon and the crashing of another plane heading for the nation's capital. These events not only shattered the buildings but also shattered thousands of lives. It abruptly awakened a complacent American public that was now in a frenzy.

It unnerved La Fratellanza as well, and was equally upsetting to their student, Abner Baari, but on a different level.

As Hank watched the events unfold on television, he knew Abner would be doing the same. After prying his eyes away from the horrific event, Hank went to Abner's apartment and found him in a state of panic.

"How fortuitous it was of my supporters to have changed my name. Now there will surely be a heightened sensitivity to Muslims!" Abner fumed. As he continued his rant, it became more political, and reverting to form, he defended his birthright and those of other Muslims. "How do they know it is al-Qaeda? Why do they always blame the Muslims?"

At which point Hank interrupted him. "Abner, remember that you are an American, a U.S. citizen with no religious ties. You know nothing about Muslims or about the Islamic culture," Hank said, admonishing Abner. "All you know is what you've read and heard. The only information you have is that your Muslim father, a father you never met, was from Libya, and you discovered later in newspaper clippings that he had been killed in his home during a bombing attack." Hank reprimanded him once more for bringing up the subject, and reminded him again, "Your name is Abner Baari. Hussein Tarishi no longer exists."

Abner never broached the subject again, at least not to Hank.

Following September 11, La Fratellanza was even more resolute to achieve its ultimate goal. The members were convinced that their Chosen

One would offer hope and bring about the needed change. Hank could sense the power he'd have within the White House. Paolo and Seymour were starting to feel a slight tug on their apolitical heartstrings. Even Chase was beginning to conjure up negative thoughts toward his own political party.

Ever focused, Simon's thoughts were only on the end game.

While the subject of Muslim hijackers may have been off-limits for Abner, La Fratellanza discussed the events relentlessly. It had shaken up Washington and politics was not as usual. Soon after the attacks, the president sent troops to Afghanistan to dispose of the Taliban, who had harbored the al-Qaeda terrorists, and proudly claimed victory for the attacks. In January 2003, the same president was in the process of gathering support from Congress and the United Nations to invade Iraq, also considered to have aided and abetted al-Qaeda. National security would now become the battle cry on the campaign trail. Seymour and Paolo were franticly revamping their materials as the sea change they feared actually occurred.

Abner, at his peak, was standing by, waiting to take on whatever his supporters had in store for him. His growing ambition for power was becoming stratospheric and totally focused.

Hank watched Abner closely.

—

Hank joined Abner in his apartment, not for the usual lesson or game of chess, but for something more critical. This time it was to inform Abner that his supporters had been keeping up to date on his progress. "They are extremely impressed with how quickly you have morphed into an American, and all you have achieved in an amazingly short time. Now they want to offer you an unheard-of opportunity, one that will change your life dramatically."

Easing slowly into the conversation, Hank reminded Abner how extraordinary he was and how effective he could be in helping those less fortunate. "This group of wealthy executives has the power and resources to help you run for the U.S. Senate, representing the state of Illinois."

Hank sat back, studying Abner's face.

Abner was speechless, but when he finally recovered, all he could muster to say was, "It wasn't just a dream after all."

Hank set off his pager, and La Fratellanza gathered to plan the next steps. The time had come to move to the next crucial phase.

—

As was the norm, Simon opened the meeting, but at this meeting, the primary topic of discussion seemed rather odd to the brothers. "It is necessary for Abner to marry. It isn't essential in the pursuit of a senatorial seat, but most definitely will be for the presidency."

The other four, perhaps carelessly, had never considered that Abner would marry, and they certainly had not considered involving anyone else in their plot. They were quite shocked and voiced their concerns.

As usual, Simon sat back to let them state their opinions.

"You're correct. That is why everything that happens going forward has to give the appearance of reality," Simon asserted.

"Okay, where are we going to find a wife?" Hank quickly injected. As soon as the words passed his lips, he knew it was a mistake.

Of course, Simon had planned that as well.

"I have crafted the perfect profile for a first lady."

The others rightly suspected it had been in place for years.

"She has to be intelligent," he explained, "but not as intelligent as Abner, and she has to be tall, but not as tall as Abner." He also felt that being a lawyer would be a tremendous plus, but not a graduate of the University of Chicago Law School, so there'd be no risk of them sharing experiences from the same campus.

Again, the four brothers voiced their concerns, this time about Abner and his proposed wife being in the same profession.

"You're forgetting Abner graduated first in his class, aced his bar exam, and along with his license to practice law in the state of Illinois, he can play with the best of them."

Simon continued his monologue and said she had to be from the Chicago area because a long-distance relationship was hard enough to manage; to manipulate one would have been impossible. He proudly laid out the details of how he searched the databases for the graduating class of 2002 at the other top four law schools in the Chicago area. He pared the list down to three candidates and was able to obtain information about each of them from their college records. "In addition, I was able to get a more recent photo, along with height, weight, and current address from the Division of Motor Vehicles. Extremely vital statistics," he noted with a wink.

After taking a bow for his technological wizardry, Simon, with a half-smile, half-smirk, declared, "I have found the perfect First Lady. She is attractive, slightly shorter than Abner, slightly less intelligent, having finished third in her class, but equally passionate for social justice. After graduating from the DePaul University College of Law, she joined the law firm of Spence, Darrow, and King, where she is a practicing civil rights attorney. Her name is Marianne Townsend," Simon announced proudly.

"I know a little about dating, but how are you going to make this happen?" Paolo asked.

Simon, ignoring his question, turned to Hank and asked him to hire her as co-counsel to work with Abner, to help lighten his workload before he left to hit the campaign trail.

With a genuine smile this time, Simon said, "We'll let Abner take it from there."

—

La Fratellanza swung into high gear.

Its members had perfected their craft beyond reach. Now, working as a team, they truly believed Abner had an excellent chance of eventually becoming unbeatable.

Hank would manage the campaign with the help of the others. Seymour would devise a campaign message and a slogan. He would then design the ad campaign with sound bites using his inventive 527 organizations and create a 501(c)(4) to start bringing in the donations. Of course, there were additional donations that would pour in from Uncle Rob, under a torrent of different names, which Simon would manage. Chase would manage the campaign finances, including the implementation of the fund-raising techniques designed to raise "legitimate" donations. Paolo, who had already written several campaign speeches, would revise them to deal with current issues.

"It would be helpful if we could slam the 'Chicago Political Machine' and talk about changing the way of doing business," Paolo offered. The Chicago—or rather, "Daley Machine"—was often challenged for questionable politics, even though they concluded those tactics might prove useful in the days to come.

"I agree," Seymour added. "It would help my negative campaigns ads and increase their effectiveness."

Paolo and Seymour would work together on managing the media and the message.

It would be Hank's job to convince both the Illinois governor and the mayor of Chicago to take the heat temporarily for political advantage. Both understood they would be rewarded in the future. These two cronies were certainly not merely cogs in the wheel. They were more the crank that kept the wheels moving. Fortunately, they wholeheartedly supported Hank and his foundation, which forged a symbiotic relationship that lasted for years. His get-out-the-vote effort for them was a positive and prominent election factor.

"We all have our work cut out for us, and while a lot of our efforts will take place behind the scene, everything out front must give the appearance of reality," Simon declared.

—

Up to that point, everything felt more surreal than real and they began to feel more like a gang of four. But then the full impact of their endeavor was about to hit home.

Hank's Chestnut Foundation had been running effectively in the capable hands of his second in command. Hank simply continued to devote 100 percent to Abner's U.S. Senate campaign, putting his personal life on hold.

Naturally, Abner accepted Hank as his campaign manager.

Abner knew nothing about Paolo and Seymour. Therefore, Hank arranged for them to meet and discuss their potential roles in the campaign. After their meeting, Abner felt comfortable hiring them as speechwriter and communications director, respectively.

Paolo, in the midst of wrapping up a project for a local official in Washington, had already made provisions to enlist Abner as his next candidate.

Seymour, similar to Paolo and Hank, had delegated his responsibilities to an associate to manage his company. However, Seymour had the luxury of traveling to his studio in L.A. to utilize his production equipment for producing the print ads and film clips they would use during the campaign.

Chase became finance director, understandably, based on Hank's recommendation. He was in charge of fund-raising and completing the mountains of paperwork. Chase was less than thrilled at the prospect of taking a leave of absence, but he had committed for the long haul and didn't have much choice. There was no way he could manage both as treasurer for a political campaign and CFO for a major bank. Managing his family would be another issue with which he had to come to grips.

Everyone knew that Simon was able to pursue the plan vigorously since he was the instigator and leader. Chances were that this was all part of his master strategy. Simon's formal role was to serve as the focal point, to collect voter registration lists, set up Web sites and blogs, and take full advantage of the modern technologies the Internet had to offer. And Simon was the logical choice to be the one to find or create the chinks in the armor of the opponent. He would also pay the group's expenses.

In the meantime, they were to return to their respective homes, arrange their schedules and personal lives, and prepare to spend several months working on the campaign.

They agreed to reconvene one month from the day.

14

THE CAMPAIGN TRAIL

During the last four weeks, Hank had been involved in a flurry of activity.

First on the agenda was to explain to Abner, in considerable detail, that the time had come to enter the 2004 race for the U.S. Senate. Over the past three years, Abner had studied hard, worked earnestly, and crammed multiple years of knowledge and experience into this short period.

As anticipated, Abner was more than ready to leave the starting gate and accept the challenge.

Hank then proceeded with the plan, to hire Marianne Townsend as co-counsel, which Abner accepted with delight, given his heavy workload.

—

Abner and Marianne worked tirelessly for several weeks reviewing his caseload, specifically focusing on one crucial case that was plaguing the organization. The federal government had charged the Chestnut Foundation with violating IRS tax laws as they pertained to electoral advocacy.

Marianne, paraphrasing the Internal Revenue Code under Section 501(c)(3), stated, "The law specifically prohibits organizations from directly or indirectly participating in any political campaign on behalf of a candidate."

Admittedly, Abner explained how members of Hank's foundation trained—or more specifically, indoctrinated—thousands of volunteers, which Hank referred to as his "foot soldiers." They worked vigorously in various aspects of lobbying specific legislation, or in electoral activities. Get-out-the-Vote drives were one of their principal assignments.

Abner clarified. "The training staff at the Chestnut Foundation provides specific training sessions to prepare the volunteers to convey a consistent effective message during their door-to-door campaigns."

He continued to explain that the foot soldiers learned to encourage the first-time voters to register by citing their civic duty as citizens. They explained the emotional term *underrepresentation* and the effect it had on them as individuals, and the importance of getting involved in the election process. Then the volunteers would explain the voting process. If necessary, the volunteers frequently took it upon themselves to ad-lib.

"The goal was to take the necessary steps to convince potential voters to participate," he stressed. "The volunteers would continue to steer the dialogue until the voter-to-be would finally ask the volunteers for whom they should vote at the polls. It was all part of a structured script to achieve an outcome. With the proper training they received, they would say in a rote fashion, 'We are not allowed to endorse any specific candidate.'"

"Thus far, I believe we are in good standing and can defend our position," Marianne offered confidently.

"Let me finish, there are some gray areas that may surface in the trial that we'll need to address." Abner continued, "For instance the volunteer, in a guarded and somewhat hushed voice, would confide, 'It is possible the Chestnut Foundation will be endorsing a candidate…' We use this standard technique in training sessions. You can guess the rest."

Marianne listened to Abner astutely while formulating a case strategy in her mind.

Abner reminded her, "The neighborhoods they canvas are minority and relatively undereducated." He agreed with Hank's premise that the voters would not likely admit their lack of knowledge, but would vote for the same candidate endorsed by a powerful foundation known for fighting for social justice. "Hank felt safe in crossing the line, and as a result, increased voter turnout in record numbers for his candidate," he assured her.

"I agree at times that the ends justified the means and acknowledge it is unlikely these new voters will admit their ignorance," Marianne noted. "Given that, I believe the best strategy is to subpoena twenty or so select witnesses, to testify as to how they came to register to vote."

"As you are aware, the Chestnut Foundation is continuously under attack, and has already been on the government's radar for challenging the tax code," Abner reminded.

"The prosecution's case is weak at best, based on flimsy evidence with a lot of innuendos and assumptions," she countered in her usual self-assured manner.

—

Abner, extremely pleased, reported to Hank. "Marianne is more than capable to handle this case on her own."

Hank agreed.

They had appropriately placed their confidence in Marianne. All the witnesses she called testified that they had registered, believing it was their civic duty. All confirmed the volunteer never mentioned a specific candidate's name. The witnesses admitted they felt compelled to speak with others in their neighborhoods to learn more about which candidate would best represent them. The prosecution did not succeed in its efforts to get the witnesses to declare that they voted for the Chestnut Foundation's recommendation.

When Marianne cross-examined each of the witnesses, she asked directly, "Did you ask the Chestnut Foundation volunteer for which candidate you should vote?"

Each responded in a similar fashion. "Yes, but the volunteers said they were not allowed to express their views on any one candidate."

Clearly, Marianne had coached them well, for they did not perjure themselves. They simply left out the whispered name at the end of the volunteer's answer. The strategy was brilliant despite the questionable tactics, and Marianne won a crucial case. The victory was vital. It was the same technique Hank had planned to use for both the senatorial and the presidential races.

As soon as the government dropped the charges against the Chestnut Foundation, Marianne and Abner began to collaborate on a different, more personal case—each other.

—

Evidently, Simon has a feel for human nature, thought Hank. His psychology studies paid off, because in a few short weeks Marianne and Abner were a hot item.

Hank relieved Abner of his duties at the foundation so he could concentrate on his campaign by day, and leave time for wooing at night. He then promoted Marianne to fill the vacancy created by Abner's departure.

Of course, Abner was never far away, as the courting intensified. Within weeks, Marianne had invited him to escort her to her brother's wedding, a full-fledged family affair, and the first real test for Abner at a formal social gathering. Marianne found Abner's charm, intelligence, and passion for community causes captivating. Hank, being rather cynical and overprotective, felt she found the idea of his run for the U.S. Senate equally enchanting.

—

Hank leased another office space, this time on Michigan Avenue in downtown Chicago, and set up campaign headquarters. Forgoing the "testing the waters" activities usually conducted by an individual considering running for office, Hank assisted Abner in filing the necessary FEC Form 2, "Statement of Candidacy," with the Federal Election Commission. Hank asked him to list "Baari for Congress" as his designated principal campaign committee, opting not to designate other authorized committees.

"The less complicated, the better," Hank explained.

Hank then asked Chase, as the appointed treasurer, to file the FEC Form 1, "Statement of Organization," within the next ten days.

There was one more obstacle to overcome. Hank had to convince both the Illinois governor and Chicago's mayor to deflect any attacks on their administrations during the campaign free-for-all. He would remind them of the voter's short-term memories.

—

The past month had gone by quickly, and when La Fratellanza reconvened, its members were in the final stages and almost ready to launch the senatorial campaign.

Predictably, Simon, never at a loss for words or ideas, was the first to speak.

"We just got our first real break," he gleefully announced. "I just learned that a state senator from the first congressional district of Illinois is stepping down due to a personal illness. This district just happens to contain most of the South Side of Chicago, where sixty-five-point-five percent are African American and four-point-eight percent are Hispanic." Feeling a need to point out the obvious, he said, "Baari's platform will surely appeal to this segment of the population."

All suspicious eyes were on Simon, he innocently denied being involved in any way. "It was simply a lucky break," he stated. Ignoring their doubting thoughts he asked, "Hank, can you possibly con the governor to appoint Baari as interim state senator?"

"Sure. There are only eleven months until the end of the term. I assume the state would willingly want to forgo an expensive and possibly contentious runoff election."

The others jumped in to express their opinions, cutting Hank off before he had an opportunity to continue. All except Simon and Hank believed it would be too much, too soon, and Abner needed to focus on the U.S.

Senate election, as well as continue to sharpen his skills.

"If he slips up in any way it will be devastating for the campaign," Seymour argued, which didn't evoke any retort.

Hank, however, supremely persuaded that his protégé was ready for the national stage, believed he could also handle a short stint in the state senate as a precursor. "With the exposure at the state level, Illinois constituents will be so enamored with Abner that, based on the campaign for United States Senate, no one will even focus on his brief time in the state senate," Hank assured. "All he has to do is show up, cast a few votes—or, as Illinois protocol permits, simply vote present—and avoid any major controversy."

Simon concurred, pointing out, "When it comes time to run for president, another leg of experience will be crucial."

"I'll support it, but it will be up to Hank to control Abner," Paolo noted, less effusive than usual.

Seymour and Chase concurred despite their misgivings.

Hank injected a positive note. "I have been able to get the governor and the mayor to agree to take the heat from the political, carefully calculated campaign assaults on the Chicago Machine. I'm sure appointing Abner as interim state senator will be a piece of cake. Both elected officials will take any strategic measures to increase their influence in Washington, and especially in the White House," he added with a touch of cockiness.

Within the week, Abner Baari was sworn in as a member of the Illinois State Senate.

It was a substantial leap toward their ultimate plan.

—

That same week Seymour unveiled his campaign slogan.

"Action, not Promises," he trumpeted. "The mantra is 'Fighting for the will of the people and not the politicians' will.' If we attack the inaction of any incumbent and of Washington at the same time, setting the stage for the 2008 presidential campaign, Abner's lack of any meaningful experience will fade into the background."

"Especially lacking business or legislative experience in Washington," Paolo reminded Seymour, as he looked Hank's way.

Seymour, ignoring the interruption, continued. "I also set up a studio at campaign headquarters where I plan to film Abner giving various speeches—sometimes seated, sometimes standing—always with the American flag to his right and the Illinois state flag to his left."

It was Simon's turn to interrupt. "Just make sure he always looks very presidential."

Seymour, not relinquishing the floor, briefly described his design for several ad campaigns citing the campaign slogan and attacking the incumbent for inaction.

Support for the campaign and the approach was unanimous.

As they congratulated Seymour on his campaign strategy and the tools he had created, Simon once again intruded, "Also attack the senator for misuse of campaign funds."

"I was not aware of any malfeasance on the part of the incumbent," Seymour responded.

"I'll find a way. Just create the ads," Simon said, with his famous Cheshire cat smile.

Chase recoiled, but the others were blasé.

Within the week, Paolo had produced five speeches, each containing a central theme, and replicating the rest of the core content. "I've been coordinating my effort with Seymour, having checked in with him several weeks ago, and have incorporated the campaign slogan into the speeches. I have to admit, when I heard it was 'Action, not Promises,' I knew it would fly with the rest of you. The speeches are ready to go," Paolo proudly stated, gesticulating in Italian fashion, a mannerism he never lost.

"While you've all been having fun, I was busy working with Simon to set up the Web site for our 501(c)(4) group, which we named ActionForward.org," Chase groaned. "Admittedly, I am happy to report the donations are starting to come in. Now I'm inundated with forms and reports that must be filed with the FEC," he added with even less enthusiasm.

"That's the spirit, Chase," Hank teased. "It's the American way." Not missing a beat, Hank announced, "I've been busy scheduling a multitude of speaking engagements for Abner, and you may have noticed that when he is not standing at a podium or shaking hands and kissing babies, he is with Marianne."

—

In fact, Abner and Marianne were dating so seriously that Abner sat down with Hank one evening and rather sheepishly asked, "Will you be my best man?"

Hank was thrilled, but not surprised, since Abner had left obvious clues.

They had been dating for only six months, which would seem unusually quick, but out of necessity everything was operating at warp speed. Hank's foremost thought was, *I couldn't have planned it better myself.*

"I proposed to Marianne last evening, and without hesitation, she accepted," Abner reported with a grin, reminiscent of the one he had displayed when he first arrived in Chicago. He elaborated that they had planned a small, unassuming ceremony and set the date for the following Saturday. Then he asked for a few days off for a quick honeymoon in Mexico. Both he and Marianne felt that time was of the essence, especially since the campaign was accelerating. "Besides, we are committed to each other and there is no point in delaying the inevitable."

"I will relieve Marianne of her duties at the foundation, but when you return from Mexico I'd like her to join the campaign," Hank requested.

"I don't see that as a problem. I'm sure she will be thrilled."

Hank rearranged Abner's speaking engagements, and two weeks later, Mr. and Mrs. Abner Baari hit the campaign trail.

—

Abner's constituents were electrified by his oratory, and the media was in awe of his liberal idealism. His opponent was enraged, complaining to everyone and anyone who would lend an ear. The governor and mayor of Chicago survived the masterly cloaked attacks from Seymour's fierce negative ads. The turnout of voters on Election Day was phenomenal, a result of the enthusiasm generated.

"It shouldn't have been so easy," the La Fratellanza members concluded.

However, six months after returning home from his honeymoon, State Senator Abner Baari was sworn in, this time as one of the United States senators from Illinois.

That evening, the junior senator and his wife celebrated their win with his campaign staff.

—

On the South Side of Chicago, Simon was planning his own celebration. The champagne was on ice and the foie gras and cigars were in abundance as he waited for the other members of La Fratellanza to arrive. Simon sensed his brothers' restlessness to return to a normal life, but he desperately needed them for the final phase. The celebration was more about appealing to their egos than Senator Baari's accomplishment.

Close to midnight, each arrived, still on a high from their sensational victory.

Simon seized the moment to compliment them for their hard work and reminded them of the incredible feat they had pulled off so smoothly.

"Congratulations! As a team, we plucked a young man from the streets of Florence and catapulted him to the U.S. Senate." Half believing it himself, Simon insisted, "The difficult part is over. The next and final phase will just be a repeat of 2004," he added rather casually. "The constituents of Illinois know their young senator. Our mission now is to plant the same message in the other forty-nine states."

Detecting it was time to change the subject, for the moment at least, Simon directed them toward the elaborate setup on the conference table. Once they were well into the champagne and relaxing with their cigars, Simon took the opportunity to inform them that he had wired a bonus into each of their bank accounts—not to their personal accounts, but to the accounts he had initially set up to transfer money that would pay their expenses. "Tomorrow, you will find an increase in your balance of fifty thousand dollars, compliments of Uncle Rob."

They smiled and thanked Simon once again for his generosity. However, this time it was with less than the usual enthusiasm. All the members of the group were suspicious of Uncle Rob, and had been for some time. Perhaps it was denial, and the largesse it brought them, that caused them to look the other way. They no longer questioned the source of the funding. Simon's talent for tapping into databases and creating identities continued to amaze them. It was a much-discussed subject when out of Simon's earshot.

Their inquiring minds also had some difficulty rationalizing certain fortuitous events that defied coincidence.

Hank did not share these concerns.

In fact, the "gang of four" seemed more like the "gang of three" as time went on. The others suspected that Hank was clued in on what was happening behind the scenes and would doggedly do what was needed to see the "game" to fruition. They knew Hank loved being the senator's personal advisor.

What was in it for Simon, they didn't know.

15

A NOBLE DOCTRINE

It was a glorious day for the newly minted senator, as Abner Baari settled into his new office in the Dirksen Senate Building on Capitol Hill, preparing for the first of many committee meetings.

A short distance down Pennsylvania Avenue, Director Hamilton Scott sat in his office at the White House, fretting over looming threats. The director's chief objective had always been to keep American citizens safe, but now, in 2005, his primary role was to focus on those threats specifically at home by supervising all intelligence within the borders. Among his many other duties, he provided daily briefings to the president.

Looking back to 1996, Hamilton Scott had then been the director for an elite group of research analysts at the CIA. Their primary function was to investigate all known members of terror cells, those currently operating within the U.S. borders and those that operated from abroad. The director knew the American public was not fully aware of the dangers they posed.

Director Scott, a tall, brawny man in his mid-fifties, possessed a full head of white hair and piercing blue eyes. He had a booming voice: husky, stern, and commanding. He was highly respected inside and outside of Washington, having served his country well for many years. Not surprisingly, in 2003, when the CIA established the States Intelligence Agency in response to September 11, Hamilton Scott was considered the ideal person to head up the new organization, given his record of success.

"I was reluctant to take on the added responsibility," he would later admit, "but I understood it would give me enormous power and put at my disposal all the government tools essential to solving some of the most serious offenses against our country."

However, at the time, he did not fully grasp the extent of those powers. He certainly did not entirely understand how those powers would become vital to his uncovering one of the most diabolical plots ever put in play. Unsuspectingly, he first became involved in the case almost twelve years earlier.

—

When the director transferred from Italy back to Washington, his first assignment was to track down, what the CIA thought to be, an amateur computer hacker—a new breed of enemy created by the latest innovative Internet technology. The FBI had been trying to track this particular hacker, whom they assumed to be a man. With no success in finding him, they requested the assistance of the CIA.

After the director was assigned the case, he and his team of analysts were able to learn that the elusive hacker was siphoning off exactly eleven dollars of the monthly interest applied to randomly selected consumer bank accounts, with balances over one hundred thousand dollars. On the eighth day of every month, the hacker would arbitrarily choose twenty banking institutions, large and small. The institutions he selected all appeared to be located in one-third of the country. As one analyst explained, the first group of banks selected was on the East Coast, the second in the Midwest, and the third on the West Coast. The hacker would then work his way backward; in the fourth month, he would choose the banks from the Midwest, followed by the East Coast. The hacker had worked in this pattern for several years.

"All I could visualize was following the light on a copy machine or scanner as it passes back and forth," an image the director would share.

Eventually, the director's analysts were able to ascertain that each month the hacker, at random, had selected one thousand individual accounts from each of the chosen banks. When the hacker returned to a particular region of the country, he would select twenty different banks. The hacker never hit the same bank twice. The director estimated that the hacker's total take was roughly two hundred twenty thousand dollars per month, or eleven thousand dollars per bank. Based on the amount, the individual banks considered it chump change and not worth pursuing, especially since insurance covered most of their losses.

On the surface, this case seems rather amateurish and lame, the director thought. "There are hundreds of junior hackers out there, and it appears that many of them are more intent on wreaking havoc, than profiting directly from their hacking and committing a serious offense," he told one analyst.

However, within a year, this particular hacker's method quickly escalated into a major crime. During a five-year period, the hacker's estimated take was close to thirteen million dollars, but they suspected some instances had gone unreported. And while the director and his team were able to track him, they were unsuccessful in apprehending him.

Relaying the details of the case to his superior, the director explained, "I was never able to trace where the money went, and he literally left no trail, with one exception. When the hacker removed the funds from each of the accounts, he'd leave his calling card, the insignia ☪, next to the remaining account balance. It appears to be the crescent moon and star, which represent either the Carthaginian goddess Tanit or the Greek goddess Diana, depending on whose history you believe, according to one of the analysts."

In the end, the team agreed the hacker was trying to be a bit too witty, imagining himself an enemy in a *Batman* episode. Ultimately, they concluded it carried no real significance. With no additional leads to pursue, the hacker's activities quieted down and eventually he vanished.

It was the weirdest case, the director reflected, but in the end, there were more notorious criminals looming about to merit his attention. So he wrote the case off as an unsolved theft, and Director Scott's team moved on to more imminent threats.

While all the director's assignments had led to successful conclusions, his first case at the CIA haunted him. For a time, after he officially closed the case, he continued to investigate but always on his own time. For the director, it became a personal challenge. "I wasn't about to let some clever thief tarnish my perfect record, even if it was only a concern to me," he often brooded.

He continued to review his copious notes over the years, and finally his patience reaped its overdue reward. After examining one of the case files, he noticed that out of thousands of account numbers the hacker had invaded, one account traced to a regional bank in Boston. The hacker had stolen the eleven dollars of monthly interest from the same bank. However, next to the ending balance in that account, there was no ☪ symbol next to the dollar amount. In fact, the bank had credited the money, not debited it from the account.

Following up on this lead, Director Scott was able to establish an address for the account, which was the same address to which the bank had mailed statements. The address was an apartment in Cambridge, Massachusetts, a short distance from the Harvard campus. However, when he sent agents to check out the apartment, it was unoccupied and had been for some time. The only furniture remaining was a round table, six chairs, and two telephones sitting on the floor. Nevertheless, he ordered a forensic team to scour the place. Aside from a few partial prints, the evidence led nowhere.

The only other information Director Scott was able to obtain was the name of the renter. Fortunately, the landlord had remembered. That name, still written on the manila file folder containing the only evidence that a crime had even been committed, was Hal Simmons.

But that was then.

—

I have cases that are more pressing, and certainly, after 9/11, my task first and foremost is the concern that terror cells are infiltrating the U.S., he would remind himself.

The world had just witnessed nineteen men of foreign descent who had entered the U.S. illegally, infiltrated cities, befriended neighbors, and carried out a plot to kill thousands of U.S. citizens. Therefore, with the director's newly appointed power, he decided to establish a secret vetting department and needed an extraordinary analyst to be its "director of one."

He had the ideal candidate.

Noble Bishop was a recognized research analyst at the CIA who had an excellent reputation and was considered extremely intelligent by his superiors. *He is inordinately talented, with a charming, quiet demeanor. He is unquestionably a top-notch analyst,* the director recollected.

Noble was tall and lean, with dark brown hair and hazel eyes. Without question, women found him handsome. His affability, along with many other qualities, would have made him the perfect mate, but evidently, it was not in the cards. Research was the only companion he needed or wanted for the time being.

Noble and the director worked in different divisions at the CIA, so other than having met him briefly on a few occasions and knowing his reputation, the director had no inside information. He obtained his profile on record and discovered that he graduated from Harvard with a master's degree in computer science. After Harvard, Noble earned a PhD in technology from MIT. Since then, many of his assignments at the CIA were spent developing computer tracking systems to facilitate the various intelligence requests from the agency.

One system allowed cooperating agencies, such as the CIA and Interpol, to download all information they had on various terror cells, as well as data on suspected leaders of those cells. This included surveillance tapes: both audio and visual, fingerprints, and other pertinent information on file.

Noble's system processed, crosschecked, and verified the information to produce a profile that was more accurate than any single agency could supply. A precise profile gave the agents an enormous advantage in selecting their targets. This system was not only a tremendous tool for agents in the field; more important, it also helped to keep them safe and out of the crossfire. Noble's ability to develop these systems helped him gather the intelligence, and use his talents to uncover the "undiscoverable," rivaling other analysts.

The Department of Defense also utilized the models he created to enhance identity recognition and computer network intelligence. These improved techniques for collecting data would address the cross-community challenges facing the country in the future.

Noble is truly a genius, and I need him for this special assignment, thought the director.

Oddly enough, as the director perused Noble's bio, he noticed that he had attended Harvard during the same time as Hal Simmons, the renter of the Cambridge apartment.

The director placed a call to the young analyst and asked if he would meet with him, to discuss an unusual project he might find of particular interest.

Noble agreed.

—

The following day, at CIA headquarters in Langley, Noble Bishop left his cubicle on the third level below ground and met with the director at the White House to discuss a possible transfer to SIA.

After the usual opening cordiality, the director asked Noble to be seated.

"For some time now, I have been observing the vetting process conducted for elected officials, and I believe it is superficial at best, leaving the country possibly vulnerable," the director alleged.

"It is true the responsibility of vetting newly elected officials to the Congress seems to be limited to the constituents, the candidates, and sadly, the biased media," Noble mentioned. "I understand the only careful vetting process performed is for diplomats and cabinet appointees.

"I know from my personal experience at the DSS," the director explained, "that diplomats go through an FBI check, interviews with the White House counsel, and finally through a confirmation hearing with the Senate Foreign Relations committee. In contrast, cabinet appointees go through a slightly more rigorous process, beginning with completing a grueling sixty-three-item questionnaire."

"I've seen the questions, most of which should be limited to confessionals," Noble quipped.

Smiling in agreement, the director continued, "Following the questionnaire, the FBI conducts a full background check and the U.S.

Office of Government Ethics looks for financial conflicts." He explained how several committees then put the appointee through probing interviews relating to the appointment, and finally the appointee goes through the Senate confirmation process, where the legislators from both sides of the aisle interview the appointee.

"While the process would appear to be comprehensive, I always believed the White House did a miserable job, primarily because it was in the president's best interest, as well as his party's, to push these appointments through," opined the director, "at times conveniently overlooking vital information."

"I recall," Nobel interjected, "mostly the media, repeatedly followed the trail to uncover essential items such as unpaid income taxes and unpaid withholding taxes for nannies and house cleaners."

"Clearly, the tax avoidance issues are not as trivial as they may seem on the surface," the director volunteered. "In the past, the media have revealed several appointees to cabinet posts owing back taxes in sizable amounts. This oversight, intentional or not, caused many of them to step down, which became a major embarrassment to the president. Back on point, my main concern is the fact that more and more elected officials entering the U.S. Congress may not be native-born U.S. citizens. As I am sure you are aware, the president and the vice president must be natural-born U.S. citizens. However, members of the Congress must be or become U.S. citizens."

"What you'd like to know is how many are not native-born?"

"Precisely."

"If my memory serves me correctly," Noble said, "in the U.S. Constitution, Article One, Section Two, Clause Two, it states that a representative in the House must be twenty-five years or older and must have been a U.S. citizen for seven years. Similarly, in Article One, Section Three, Clause Three, it states that a senator must be thirty years or older and have been a U.S. citizen for nine years before qualifying to run for office."

"Now you understand my concern," the director injected, pleased at Noble's grasp of the facts.

"Congress is truly becoming a house of cultural diversity, and I can understand why the vetting process is becoming more and more difficult to manage," Noble acknowledged.

"I firmly believe that if the country is concerned with the possible infiltration of terror cells," the director stressed, "then we need to take extra steps to ensure these terrorists are not working in our government, and first and foremost, that they are not elected officials. That is why I've asked you to consider transferring to the SIA. I need you to design and program a computer system to aid in the vetting process."

"I've always been impressed by the tasks assigned to the SIA, and I do believe it could be another intriguing project," Noble offered.

"Please take some time to think about the position, but in the meantime, I ask that you discuss it with no one."

During the interview—or rather, recruiting session—the director asked one last question.

"I noted that you attended Harvard from 1995 to 1997. Perhaps you knew a man by the name of Hal Simmons?"

After careful thought, Noble replied, "No, I'm sorry, the name doesn't sound familiar."

—

Noble took a week to mull over the job offer, and although he was professionally satisfied and very much at home at headquarters, he concluded it was time for a career change. Fortunately, for the director, Noble accepted his new assignment, one that would be more deeply undercover than any he'd held before.

In December 2004, Noble moved from his "home away from home" at Langley to his new office just a few blocks from the White House. The office was located in the same "undisclosed" building as the other SIA research analysts, where covert starts at the front door.

Noble had enjoyed many years at Langley, and even though it was the headquarters of the CIA, he was not part of the political sphere he was now entering. Although he was reticent about moving into the lion's den, so close to the seat of power, intellectually he looked forward to a new and exciting venture.

Noble's new position was not publicized, and only those in the know would regard him as merely a research analyst, working on special projects for the director. In fact, there would be only two people who would be aware of this ultra-top-secret assignment.

—

It wasn't until his first official meeting with the director, that Noble fully recognized the scope of his role and the vast power it encompassed.

"First, it is imperative that only you and I know about the existence of SAVIOR," began the director. During the interview, the director held off giving the specifics of SAVIOR, but now he explained, "SAVIOR is the SIA Appointee Vetting Internal Official Records system I want you to design and program. You must program the system to link the CIA, FBI, and IRS databases, among others."

"Regrettably," the director explained, "it will need to be done without the knowledge of these agencies, whose political ties impede them from operating efficiently. Forgive the cliché, but it was one of those 'easier to get forgiveness than permission' situations and most certainly we don't have permission."

Noble quickly absorbed the gravity of the situation. "I assume there would be no forgiveness, but certainly the administration would tolerate our activities if we ever uncovered a terror cell infiltrating our government?"

"Should that happen, I will take full responsibility," the director stated, "although I understand should you have second thoughts."

"I've always shared many of the same concerns, and from my time at the CIA, I've been privy to the facts of the extent to which these terrorists are penetrating our country." Noble assured the director he was onboard and the director was more than pleased.

Noble said confidently, "It will require six months to develop SAVIOR, at which time I will be ready to start vetting all new junior senators and representatives joining the Congress, during the 2006 off-year elections."

"There are two rules I insist on," the director demanded. "One, no vetting the president. Two, only information that threatens our national security will be divulged—surreptitiously, of course—and upon my approval. The first rule is mostly out of respect for the office of the presidency and not the man himself, for whom I personally hold no sway either way," the director admitted. "One of my major concerns is the threat of terrorists making their way into the U.S. Congress. SAVIOR will investigate all members running for office, both in the House and the Senate. The non-U.S. citizens who became U.S. citizens and then ran for Congress merit scrutiny. I specifically want to add them to our Watch List."

"I understand. You can count on me to follow your directives, Director Scott."

"One more rule, call me Hamilton."

16

OH, LORDY

The April showers disappeared and the May flowers, along with the June brides, had come and gone. Six months had passed and Noble was in the final stage of beta testing SAVIOR. Pleasantly satisfied with the overall outcome, he scheduled an appointment to meet with Hamilton to review the results.

On that day, as he strolled down Pennsylvania Avenue enjoying the warmth of the sun on his back and the moderately cooler breeze on his face, he suddenly heard someone shout, "Ciao, Lordy!"

Noble had not heard that name since his college days.

As he turned toward the voice, he saw his classmate from Harvard, Paolo Salvatore. He crossed the avenue and quickly received Paolo's Italian embrace and a kiss on each cheek. The affectionate greeting instantly reminded Noble of the generosity of his college mates, all those years ago.

"My friend, it is so good to see you, what a pleasant surprise!" Paolo beamed. "We must go someplace now where we can catch up. It has been much too long."

"Paolo, it is wonderful to see you as well, and while I'd love to, right now I am late for an appointment. Can we get together later this evening?"

"*Perfetto*! Where shall we meet?"

Noble arranged to meet Paolo at the Blackfinn American Saloon, a popular hangout among politicos, both those who worked on the Hill and the political analysts who critiqued them. It was a strange mixture of patrons, but after hours, ideological views were secondary to friends sharing a few drinks.

—

During happy hour at the Blackfinn, Noble and Paolo, sitting on the two end stools at the bar, reacquainted themselves. Over several hours, a few beers, and some appetizers, they reminisced about their time at Jake's, followed by the usual twenty questions posed by Paolo, the extrovert.

"What have you been doing since you left Harvard?" he quizzed, adding a wink. "Is there a special woman in your life?"

"Starting with your last question first, I am still single, by choice," Noble answered with a remarkably convincing smile. "After leaving Harvard, I attended MIT and earned a PhD in technology, and then I was hired as a research analyst at the CIA." Noticing Paolo's raised eyebrows, Noble quickly added, "Nothing covert, just basic routine intelligence gathering."

Anxious to hear more, Paolo simply returned a smile and urged him to continue.

"Then last December I transferred to the SIA. It's a fairly similar job, just the focus is more directed toward illegal immigration. I imagine it is pretty boring stuff to most people, but I like the fact that I can work alone."

"You are still such a loner, Noble," teased Paolo.

"It suits me. Now it's my turn to interrogate you," he offered, returning the raised eyebrow. "I recently became aware that you were working for Senator Baari." Embarrassed at his admission, Noble assured him, "I had every intention of getting in touch with you, but I've been involved with a project that has monopolized my time."

"Apology accepted."

"I'd be fascinated to hear about the inner workings of a senatorial race. It must have been very exciting."

Paolo took the opportunity to touch on what it was like to work for the senator, and at the same time filled him in on Hank, Seymour, and Chase, and the contributions they had made to the campaign.

"What about Simon?"

"I have no idea where Simon is or how to locate him," Paolo alleged, diverting his eyes in an attempt to hide his deception.

"Ever since leaving Harvard I've been trying to locate Simon to repay him the tuition money he loaned me," Noble explained. "He seems to have vanished."

Paolo, quickly changing the subject, began to talk of the various speeches he had authored. "My words have catapulted many into elected office," he boasted.

Noble listened to the long list of names attached to those speeches and was reasonably impressed.

Then Paolo turned to the personal aspects of his life, explaining that he lived in Washington, actually just a few blocks from the Capitol, on Tenth Street near the H Street Corridor.

"A few years ago I bought a two-bedroom row house that functioned as my office before I started to work for the senator. And, yes, I too am still single. Although I have a long string of choices to occupy the dating scene, of course," he bragged. Paolo admitted, however, none thus far had captivated him.

The two of them appeared to be enjoying themselves as they continued for another hour of kibitzing about the usual topics discussed inside the Beltway. They became so absorbed that time got away from them, so they agreed to call it a night and reconnect another time.

Noble and Paolo gave each other a solid hug and made plans to meet again, and soon.

—

Aside from his sister, Natalie, and his dinners with Hamilton, Noble didn't normally delight in, or miss, other companionship. However, he found his time with Paolo unusually pleasurable. It obviously was mutual because Noble and Paolo, after their first reunion, met on many occasions, as a rule, at their favorite saloon for a beer and a lot of chatter.

As might be expected, many of their conversations focused on their Harvard experience, especially their classmates. Previously, Paolo had described the positions their fellow classmates held working for Senator Baari. But Noble, struck by the fact that they converged to work together, thought it seemed like an odd coincidence.

On one occasion, he asked Paolo, "How did it happen that four of you ended up working for the senator?"

"We've all remained in touch throughout the years," he replied. "One day I received a call from Hank while I was working on a reelection campaign for the governor of Arkansas. He asked me if I'd join him on the campaign trail for a friend who was running for the U.S. Senate. It sounded challenging so I agreed."

"So Hank and the senator were friends?" Noble asked.

"Yes. Abner Baari worked for Hank at the Chestnut Foundation for years, and after law school, he was hired as its legal counsel."

"So they've known each other for a long time?"

"I believe he started working with Hank from the beginning, back in 1998, when Hank established the foundation. Anyway, shortly thereafter, Hank asked me if I knew how to contact Seymour, which I did, so I passed the information on to him." Paolo continued to explain that Hank enlisted both Chase, with whom he had kept in contact, and Seymour, based on the information he had given him. "That's how we found ourselves working on the campaign together," he explained. "It was a fortunate combination of circumstances."

Naturally, Paolo made no mention of the fact that they planned to continue working for Senator Baari—on his presidential campaign.

Nonetheless, Noble was extremely interested in what Paolo knew about the senator, because through happenstance, Senator Baari was one of the first people he had planned to vet.

—

Several months passed, and both Noble and Paolo were enjoying their time together immensely.

At Harvard, Noble had admired Paolo more than the others members of the group. It seemed he in particular was always on top of the world, and he was genuinely kind. Noble believed that Paolo, being oblivious to his own handsomeness, helped to contribute to his aura, causing him to be more congenial than daunting. But something was different.

While reconnecting with Paolo after several years, Noble sensed a touch of loneliness amid his braggadocio statements. Over the months they spent together, he came across as being even more charming than Noble remembered, and he was less inclined to dominate the conversation. He was more relaxed and even a bit more self-effacing. On the occasions at Harvard when Noble had joined the group at Jake's, he had not seen this side of Paolo, a side that Noble came to admire.

—

A few weeks before Christmas, Noble finally invited Paolo to his home for dinner. He lured him with the promise that there was someone he wanted Paolo to meet. It was a rare occurrence for Noble to entertain a guest, and unthinkable that he would have ulterior motives.

Paolo, being the proper gentleman, arrived at the appointed hour.

When the door opened, a tall, slender, attractive redhead greeted him.

"Welcome, I'm Natalie, Noble's sister."

From the look on Paolo's face, he was visibly stunned.

"I see I've taken you by surprise. Excuse me, but the temperamental chef is in the kitchen. He promised to join us shortly."

Regaining his composure, he managed to utter, "Obviously you know I am Paolo, a former classmate of your brother's?"

Natalie smiled.

As Paolo's heart was melting, she offered him a glass of wine. After the customary toast, the conversation flowed without letup, and with warmth usually reserved for a longtime friend.

From the kitchen, Noble was eavesdropping on their conversation, and as he had hoped, they seemed to have an affinity for each other. His plan seemed to be working, so he decided to busy himself a while longer.

Paolo, encouraged by Natalie, spoke about how he began his career as a political speechwriter, naming many of the candidates he'd helped win elections. "Now I am currently working for Senator Baari."

She was fascinated by his career, and mesmerized by the unmistakable trace of an Italian accent.

Paolo was entranced long before she began to speak about herself.

"I'm afraid my career is a lot less glamorous. After graduating from Georgetown University, I was hired by the law firm of Bracewell and Giuliani."

Paolo was familiar with the firm, known for defending the rights of lobbyists that permeate the Washington scene.

Natalie explained that after making partner, she developed a true distaste for that branch of the law and decided she was better suited for teaching, rather than practicing law. "So I returned to Georgetown University to teach trial law," she expressed, without a trace of regret.

The entire evening went perfectly. The wine, food, and conversation flowed between Natalie and Paolo. Actually, the wine and food were almost inconsequential.

After Paolo bid Natalie a good night, with an extra-long cheek-to-cheek kiss, Noble escorted him to the door.

"I remembered you had a sister, but why didn't you ever tell me she was a knockout?" Paolo whispered. "As well as being extremely intelligent to boot. Obviously a family trait," he said, all the while grinning.

"You weren't ready for her at the time!" Then returning the grin, Noble whispered back, "Good night my friend."

From the kitchen, Noble could hear pots clanging and the water running as Natalie prepared to clean up after their dinner. It was obvious to Noble that Paolo was smitten big time, and when he returned to the kitchen, he found out quickly that his sister was too. Paolo and Natalie already had a date scheduled for the next night, to meet at the Kennedy Center for a concert.

—

Over the next ten months, there would be countless dates and numerous dinners, many in Noble's home. On several of those occasions, Noble would invite Hamilton to join them, which he wholeheartedly accepted, avoiding his solitary dinners at home.

The director, divorced and estranged from his children, built his life around his work. Interestingly, his work life mirrored Noble's. In fact, Noble and Natalie provided the only real companionship he enjoyed. In many ways, he treated Noble like a son and they were becoming his family. Any invitation he received from them, he accepted with pleasure.

Hamilton met Paolo at one of those dinners.

At first, he sensed Paolo was uncomfortable in his presence, and it was obvious that Paolo made every attempt not to show it. Over time, however, Paolo appeared to relax and enjoy the conversations that ensued between them. Eventually they developed a friendly relationship, but always within the context of dinners with Noble.

Ultimately, Noble, Natalie, Paolo, and Hamilton became quite accustomed to spending time together.

—

Paolo managed to save most of the money he had earned during his participation in a couple of brutal gubernatorial campaigns and for his efforts to get Abner elected senator. As it was, he had little time left in which to spend his earnings. At the same time, a major change was taking over his life outside the demands of the campaign.

He was now devoted to Natalie.

Paolo lavished her with gifts, and wined and dined her at some of the most chic restaurants. Attending the opera became part of their dating routine. Naturally, he favored Italian opera, and before long, Natalie became a devotee.

Paolo was so in love with Natalie and deeply engrossed in their relationship that he cleared his mind of thoughts—of La Fratellanza—and Noble's potentially menacing career progression.

Finally, he couldn't resist any longer. He faced reality and proposed.

When he told his La Fratellanza brothers, they were happy that he had finally found the woman of his dreams and wanted to settle down. They were ecstatic that he scheduled a date for a wedding, and while they were disappointed not to be invited, they understood that the couple had decided on a small private ceremony.

Paolo, in a bittersweet moment, smiled as he remembered Seymour's offer, "That doesn't preclude us from throwing you a bachelor party." At the same time, he was saddened because he knew it would be impossible to invite his brothers to the wedding, especially because of the guest list.

Many months would pass before Paolo would finally tell La Fratellanza about his encounter with Noble Bishop. He knew his brothers would never understand how he allowed his relationship to flourish with Lordy, especially considering his chosen profession. Even for Paolo, the relationship went beyond his expectations from the first encounter.

He obviously chose to withhold information about his personal relationship with Hamilton Scott, director of the SIA. Paolo reasoned that if "nervous Nellie" Chase was aware of how close he had become to Noble, Chase would opt to walk away from the whole plan, at a time when they were so close to accomplishing their goal.

They still had to complete the final phase, the phase that would place Abner Baari in the Oval Office. Once achieved, they would be free of all commitments to La Fratellanza and free to go their separate ways. Alternatively, they could choose to continue in their current roles and enjoy the notoriety they attained.

Paolo was holding on for that moment.

—

After a hasty courtship, Natalie and Paolo were married. Noble was proud to walk his sister down the aisle on that beautiful June day in 2006. It was a simple but lovely ceremony. There were no bridesmaids or groomsmen.

"Actually, it was a strange conglomerate of bedfellows. The director of the SIA, a national security analyst, a law professor, and a member of La Fratellanza all in attendance," Hamilton would later recall.

17

MANIPULATORS IN CHIEF

Throughout the senatorial race, both Paolo and Seymour worked assiduously to obtain a United States Senate seat for an obscure candidate, which they did successfully. Their contributions became well known, and they enjoyed the political limelight. They were now prepared to apply their skills to the presidential campaign.

Chase's feelings toward his role never changed. He had little interest in politics, although he reluctantly felt obliged to continue as financial director. Unlike the others, his dream position was CFO of a major bank in New York, and not in the political swamp of Washington. Much to his dismay, he wasn't willing to back out, as he had become too entrenched in the "game." He unenthusiastically took another temporary leave of absence to work on Senator Baari's campaign for the presidency. Given the prominence he had achieved, his superiors offered no resistance.

On the other hand, Hank happily continued as the senator's aide-de-camp. He was perpetually at the senator's side. First, to help Abner recruit his staff, and to ensure the applicants would not be a threat to La Fratellanza's ultimate goal. Second, to organize various speaking engagements at several nationally recognized organizations, such as the National Labor Union and the AFL-CIO, both of which proved to be huge supporters; they energized their membership to campaign vigorously—not to overlook the gigantic campaign contributions their dues machine generated.

Senator Baari happily retained the four staffers to manage the campaign, and while their roles were well known, their clandestine relationship to each other was not.

—

During one of his first meetings with the new U.S. senator, Hank highlighted two major concerns in the state of Illinois, which Abner could seemingly support.

"The governor's initiative 'Keep Warm, Illinois' campaign is designed to prepare the state residents for record-cold temperatures and high-heating costs. It is a cause you need to rally around, and it will give you more exposure," Hank advised.

"I'm sure its support the governor will welcome openly"—Abner smiled—"especially since he turned the other cheek during the campaign when we criticized him."

"That brings me to the second concern, which will appease your constituents greatly—political reform," Hank said, waiting for the backlash.

"So you want me to ingratiate the Illinois governor, and then you want me to tick off him and the Chicago mayor at the same time," Abner complained.

"They won't like it, but they will tolerate it. Trust me, it will make you look strong, and you'll be standing up for the people."

Senator Baari followed his recommendations and continued to heed Hank's advice when given. All the while, Hank was sure Abner had no idea that he was still grooming him, and this time for the ultimate political leap.

—

After the senator's swearing in, there was a period of relative calm.

Then, in the second year in office, the gang of four started to become antsy about their futures, including Hank. Ignoring Simon's overzealous statement that the presidential campaign was just a repeat of the successful campaign they just ran, they were beginning to consider the consequences—and of greater importance—the risks.

Fortunately, for Seymour, he was free to travel between Los Angeles, Chicago, and Washington during Baari's first two years in the U.S. Senate. While on the campaign trail and in Washington, he captured many photos and film clips. He was able to use them to produce a mini-documentary titled *Rising Star, Abner Baari*. It portrayed—or more accurately, inflated—Baari's accomplishments in the Illinois State Senate and then in the U.S. Senate. Seymour took generous liberties with the material but was confident that the vignettes of the powerful speeches given by the gifted senator would overshadow any inaccuracies, which would fade away in the minds of the electorate, known for their short-term memories.

He was most happy to be able to work from his studio in L.A., although oftentimes he would need more material, requiring additional visits. He was always fully aware he would still have to produce some of the future political ads, as needed, for the inevitable run for the presidency. Fortunately, La Fratellanza was not as demanding during the interlude between elections, which pleased Seymour immensely. More time allowed him to manage some of the smaller projects of his company, MediaLynx.

Paolo naturally continued to write the speeches for the senator for all occasions, while simultaneously constructing new material in preparation for the upcoming presidential election. Despite the demands of his job, he was always able to be with Natalie. After a year and a half of marriage, they still behaved like newlyweds, never seeming to tire of each other.

It was also a dark time for Paolo as he began to question his career choices, wondering whether he made the right decision. He knew that even more of his time would be in demand once Senator Baari reached the White House. His interest in politics began to wane as he became increasingly critical of the senator. Often Paolo would be upset when the senator strayed from the prepared remarks, and even more so when the senator would spontaneously change the thrust of the message completely.

Natalie never complained, but Paolo knew she was starting to detect a change in his behavior.

During this same period, Chase was wrapping up the accounting from the senatorial campaign and filing the myriad of forms required by the FEC and the IRS. Luckily, he could complete most of those tasks in New York. Although he was temporarily on a leave of absence, he still maintained his bank office, a place where he felt the most at ease.

In the course of those first two years, Hank spent most of his time observing his protégé, the junior senator. Totally out of character, he, of all people, began to feel queasy about some of the events that had occurred—it was a drama, in which he played a leading character.

All the members of La Fratellanza struggled with their multiple roles. One face was for their brothers, another for the public, and yet one more for their families. Coping with the façade maintained for their families was particularly wrenching.

On an entirely different plateau, Abner was quite at ease with his identity, as if he had abandoned his prior self. He intellectually and emotionally had transformed into Abner Baari, a United States senator from the state of Illinois.

At times, Hank would attempt to trick him, as he had in the past. On one occasion, he fired off facts from Abner's previous life, only to have him pass the test with flying colors and return an all-knowing look that conveyed, "Keep trying."

Shortly after the senator was sworn in, Hank with some trepidation, sat down to inform him that his political and financial backers expected him to gear up for a try at the 2008 presidential race. Hank was speechless when

Abner replied, "Of course, that's what this has all been about, me becoming president. I've been picking up the signals from my team for a long time."

Equally alarming was Abner's apparent lack of curiosity as to the identity of his "backers." In the beginning, he would continuously prod Hank, always receiving the same response, "They wish to remain anonymous." As time passed, he no longer asked, projecting the notion that it didn't actually matter. Worse yet was a certain arrogance, suggesting that not only did he not care, he didn't really need them.

Does this include me as well? Hank began to wonder.

Hank's apprehension amplified considerably when he noticed Abner breaking the first three cardinal rules he had initiated. When he first approached him to run for the Senate, Abner agreed to do whatever his "backers," by way of Hank, instructed him to do. He wanted the prize and was happy to follow orders.

Shortly after, he broke the first rule. "Never veer from the words on the teleprompter. Always stay on message," Hank stressed repeatedly, thumping the desk occasionally.

The second rule was never to vote for a bill other than those specifically identified and approved by him. Otherwise, Abner would be reported as "Not Voting." This was a departure from the Illinois State Senate, where he was able to vote "Present," one of the preferred ways to duck an issue.

And the third rule was never to take on a cause without Hank's explicit written approval.

There were other sacrosanct rules that La Fratellanza had adopted to reach its lofty goal, but Abner had broken the fundamental three rules, which they considered crucial.

While the senator quickly glossed over each infraction with an air of indifference, Hank began to notice Abner's arrogance was expanding rapidly. Senator Baari's behavior emitted a feeling of superiority. Almost to the point where he thought he was solely responsible for his own success.

Hank chose not to share his concerns with La Fratellanza. He surmised they would simply push the problem back to him to resolve, but a certain uneasiness settled in, and Hank started to think about playing the defense.

—

On a Friday night, Simon activated the pagers. The gang of four knew that this time, the final phase had arrived.

During the planning stages, they always met one week from the day of the page, and the display on the pager was always ***LF***. Since the senatorial campaign began, the time and day of the week would appear. This time the pager read "9:00 a.m. Monday."

As La Fratellanza convened at the office on the South Side, a certain annoyance prevailed. Having received the summons at the beginning of a weekend demanded that they travel on Sunday to arrive in Chicago on time for their meeting.

Simon was the first to arrive. Shortly thereafter, the others strolled in—one by one.

"Simon, why couldn't this meeting have taken place on Tuesday?" Paolo complained. "You knew I was already scheduled to be in Chicago to review a speech with the senator. Oh, you should know he is speaking at Marianne's alma mater, DePaul University, on Wednesday."

"Next," Simon stated, waiting for the next grievance.

"I was flying to Washington on Wednesday and could have easily arranged a stopover," Seymour barked.

"Chase, is there something you would like to say?" Simon asked.

"I'm here, am I not?" Chase, of course, would have been happy not to be disturbed at all. He was enjoying the time he was able to spend at his home in Connecticut with his boys and in his office in New York.

"May we now get started?" Not expecting a response, Simon turned his back on them.

They were stunned to see him facing the whiteboard already packed with bullet points, and the TV set up with a DVD ready and waiting for him to push the play button. The atmosphere in the room changed the feeling to "let's rock and roll," so as they began to "rock," the apprehension they felt in their stomachs began to "roll."

"The time has come for the final phase, the appointed hour, to plan the presidential campaign," Simon announced, something the others already had discerned.

It was now May 2007.

The general feeling pervading the air was that they were still licking their wounds from their previous political battle, and yet they were forced to step into the ring once again.

"Hank, why don't you start by reviewing Abner's performance in the U.S. Senate? And we are well aware of the senator's defiance, so you can skip that part," Simon chided.

"I will manage that part. Abner understands how important it is to stay on script. I am happy to report he is scoring higher on the recognition factor according to several independent surveys, which he gained from his appearance at a number of major events."

"The polls show that Abner is dazzling the electorate with his oratory. Moreover, his campaigns across the states are also well received," Seymour contributed.

"Thanks for the plug," grinned Hank. As for supporting legislation,

Abner has voted appropriately on all but one bill."

"We are acutely aware," Paolo interjected. "Tell me more."

"I understand it is easier to defend a non-vote than an explicit vote that could come back to haunt you," Hank said, "which I continually remind the senator. In the same vein, I believe keeping Abner somewhat of an enigma is more effective that offering him up as a target. We just need to find the right balance. The campaign will be won by dint of idealistic speeches and a populous platform."

The others concurred.

"Staying under the radar," Hank added, "should be the modus operandi for the time being."

Hank also reported that Marianne had become a terrific asset on the campaign trail, and now, with their two-year-old baby girl in tow, they truly painted a perfect picture of the First Family, a scene appealing to the masses.

"There is no doubt she is ready and willing to campaign wholeheartedly for her husband to be the next president," he promised. "In fact, I've picked up vibes that she wants it as much as Abner, if not more. The Baaris are prepared."

"I'm ready to go as well," Seymour reported. "I'm making the final edits to the documentary, and I plan to run excerpts on YouTube. I think it is tantalizing enough to induce a major network to run it in its entirety. Of course, it will have to meet with everyone's approval first. I'll have it completed for your review by the end of the week. I am assuming we are all still comfortable with the Action, not Promises campaign?"

The others nodded in agreement.

Seymour went on to explain how he planned to use the TV and Internet ads used previously, altering them only to change the challengers and focus on their vulnerabilities. He would also gin up his 527 organizations to attack and counterattack by activating his Web site, ActionForward.org. The site had already received national recognition and had accumulated significant financial support during the senatorial campaign.

"Everything is already set in place," Seymour stated self-assuredly. "Chase, would you prepare to begin managing the donations that are sure to flow in, and add them to our coffers?" he asked, adding with a hint of disgust, "Of course, there will be millions of donors offering small donations, compliments of Uncle Rob."

Paolo, wanting to steer the conversation away from Uncle Rob, chimed in. "I've revamped all the speeches to give them national appeal, and I will fine-tune them as we go along. In fact, the senator already committed to memory the key speeches, and he adjusts to the new wording the moment I make the changes," he reported, shaking his head in an expression of amazement. Paolo was still astounded at Abner's ability to retain so much information, although this time around, something seemed different.

"I'm concerned with the senator's delivery." He paused. "During the senatorial campaign, when the vernacular pertained to issues of social justice, Abner read from the heart, but now they appear to be just rote phrases from the senator," Paolo lamented.

"Are you concerned about the senator, or the possibility he doesn't like your words?" Hank prodded.

"Both! I poured my heart into those words, but the fact that the senator seems too detached is the point. More important, will it be apparent to the voters?"

"Point taken; I will speak with Abner to see if there is a problem."

Then, in a rare moment of dejection, Paolo said, "Perhaps I misnamed our fraternity all those years ago at Harvard. Instead of La Fratellanza, perhaps I should have recommended the name *Padroni del Burattino,* which means Puppet Masters, even if the puppet is not responding."

None of the others found the humor in his remarks.

Ignoring his brothers' stares, Paolo, with a bit of uncharacteristic sarcasm, asked, "I assume you haven't overlooked two major obstacles? Abner first has to win his party's nomination and, second, has to defeat the challenger for the White House! In the first instance, I've had experience working on a campaign against the current front-runner. Haley Collier's political machine looks unbeatable. In the second instance, there are so many players in the race, it is too early to predict who will lead the pack, but we need to be prepared." Paolo continued, reminding them, "Illinois was a cakewalk compared to the national scene, which we are about to enter." He believed it was time for a reality check—a turning point—"Do we walk away now or run the risk of a rout?"

The others were stunned to hear Paolo so dispirited.

Seymour tried to intervene but only worsened matters when he invoked Natalie's name. "Paolo, you may be feeling overwhelmed knowing the pressures you will face in the campaign. By definition, it will occupy much of your time, time you'd prefer not to spend away from your new wife. What is important is that Natalie supports you, and she will be waiting for you when this is finished." The moment the words left his mouth, he knew he had stepped out of bounds. "I'm sorry, Paolo, that was uncalled for," Seymour offered apologetically.

Looking more melancholy than ever, Paolo said, "You really don't understand." His defining moment continued when he proceeded to tell his brothers of his encounter with Lordy.

They were naturally happy to hear that he had reconnected with him after so many years.

Then Paolo dropped the bomb. "Lordy works for the SIA as a research analyst, reporting to the director." As if that wasn't bad enough, he dropped the megaton bomb, all the while looking at Simon. "Noble Lord Bishop is Natalie's brother."

They were shocked into disbelief, and while the group had never seen Paolo so disheartened, they had never seen Simon so incensed. Up to that point, Simon had remained silent. Now he lit into Paolo using several expletives, following each one with the word *stupid,* an odd choice of a word, coming from Simon.

"Of all the women you could have laid, why did it have to be her, the sister of a federal agent?" he shouted.

After the personal assault, and once the crimson began to drain from Simon's face, everyone breathed deeply and tried to remain calm.

Simon continued, this time in his typical measured speech, laying out their options.

"All of our lives are at stake, and should there be any leaks at this point, we all go down, including our families. We have just spent the past several years of our lives together and through our sacrifices have delivered the impossible. We are in the home stretch of our ultimate goal and it is no time to abandon all we have accomplished. Does anyone else have secrets to share?"

Dead silence followed.

"Senator Baari has survived three years in the public limelight with no debilitating gaffes," he reminded them. "We can do this! It is not insurmountable for La Fratellanza." In an odd moment of humbleness, Simon offered, "As agreed when we started the 'game,' if anyone wants out, we'll recast our votes, and should three brothers favor ending it, we'll all walk away this time."

He looked around the room, his eyes landing on Chase, assuming he would probably want the chance to return to the cushy job he loved.

"Let's vote."

Simon handed each of them a piece of paper and saved one for himself.

"Write either IN or OUT, fold it, and return it to Paolo. We'll let him have the honor of reading the votes."

A few moments later, Paolo called out each vote aloud. The others were apprehensive as they heard him read, "IN, IN, IN, IN, IN."

Ultimately, even with all his own doubts, Paolo could not bring himself to part with his brothers. In fact, he read his vote first, not knowing how the others would cast their ballots.

After several awkward moments of silence, Simon asked Hank to reopen the campaign headquarters, and urged them all to be prepared to swing into action in two weeks.

18

ON THE ROAD AGAIN

La Fratellanza had maintained the lease on the storefront on Michigan Avenue, so all that was necessary was to open the doors, dust off the desks, and round up the volunteers.

Hank and Chase agreed to work together to file all the necessary forms, including the "Statement of Candidacy." Once completed, Hank would start marshaling his foot soldiers and prepare them for the get-out-the-vote drives, this time on a national scale.

"It is time to use our full arsenal of weapons," asserted Simon.

Seymour agreed. "I will have the 527 organizations going at each other in no time, utilizing the 'Willie Horton' technique to the fullest."

Paolo and Seymour arranged to work together, to polish the speeches and the ad campaigns, bashing the current administration that would create questionable links between the challenger, once identified, and Washington.

"I will line up the speaking engagements and limit the number of venues where Abner will have to field questions," affirmed Hank.

"All of us working together must create a media blitz, one that will make the senator seem larger than life, a sort of messiah," Simon insisted.

The others thought Simon sounded a bit like one himself as he continued. "The country is at a pivotal point in its history, and its citizens are primed for someone just like the Chosen One. All the elements are in place. We can really make this happen!" Toning down the rhetoric slightly, he said, "Remember the American people will be less probing about Senator Abner Baari. They will be influenced to focus more on his opponent's incompetence and his ties to the current administration. The electorate's wrath will lead them to vote for Abner. He will constantly be on the offensive, holding out an image that will take them in a totally new direction that will be life changing."

After a minor pause, giving the other's time to absorb his words, Simon boasted, "I'll focus on what I do best, finding the ammunition to attack the opponent—and if necessary, creating some."

Ignoring Simon's pontification, Hank assured them. "We're good to go. I'll tell the senator tonight."

—

The beginning of the campaign was unlike the well-oiled machine they were accustomed to running. As they proceeded, it was fraught with on-the-trail glitches and personal dilemmas. Then, in the midst of a string of successes, and with eight months to go before Election Day, there was total agreement among La Fratellanza, and the Baaris followed the script.

Not only were many of the potential voters in the United States leaning toward Senator Baari, enchanted by his silver tongue, but also avid supporters in large numbers surfaced overseas. This fresh, new face of America became an instant hit akin to a rock star. The positive press from his international debut was enough to grab the attention of the people at home.

It was Paolo's idea to give Abner international exposure and it worked like a charm.

While the others complimented Paolo enthusiastically on his brilliant strategy, there were still some nagging doubts about his lasting commitment.

—

At the end of that first year, the campaign encountered the one serious obstacle Paolo had predicted accurately. The party's front-runner, Haley Collier, appeared to be unbeatable with his well-established organization.

"The situation could work to our advantage, especially against a relative unknown. The Collier campaign's overconfidence will lead them to make mistakes," Simon pointed out. "We just have to wait for it to happen and then be prepared to go in for the kill."

Frequently, Simon liked to recite his knowledge of psychology. The others assumed it was a diversion from his overly technical mind.

Amazingly, as if Simon were clairvoyant, four months later the unraveling began.

First, they hurled accusations at the opposition for planting softball questions at town halls. Then, a revolving door of hiring and firing took place during crucial periods of the campaign, and finally, the most dreaded campaign fear happened—the campaign coffers began to dry up and donations slowed down to a trickle—Collier's campaign was in crisis.

Those donations began to flow toward Senator Baari, as his campaign gained momentum.

Again, that daunting question passed through the minds of the brothers, as to whether Simon was clairvoyant or only manipulative. Nonetheless, what was more important was the major political upset that defied the pundits' earlier predictions.

Senator Baari won the nomination—history was in the making.

Then the final challenge began, or so they thought.

—

The opposing party had finally elected a candidate from the array of presidential wannabes. Interestingly the nominee, Josh MacDonald, a decorated war hero and two-term senator, was gaining in the polls.

The country was at a pivotal point in the war against terror, and the American people placed a higher priority on national security than on the economy. A potential setback for Senator Baari was the one vote he cast without Hank's approval that was in favor of the Troop Reduction Amendment. Voter support was turning away from him.

Senator MacDonald was solidly behind keeping U.S. troops in the war theaters, in both Iraq and Afghanistan, which he felt was vital to national security interests. He was outspoken in his conviction, removing all doubts about his position on the issue. This conflict flew in the face of the position Senator Baari—or rather, La Fratellanza—supported on the campaign trail.

Baari's potentially fatal weakness was the lack of tangible foreign relations experience, an insurmountable obstacle that even the infallible Simon couldn't resolve. The international excursion to woo overseas supporters helped, but was not enough to trump a war hero with substantial foreign policy bona fides.

Senator Baari was gaining in the home stretch, but voters still focused primarily on the war and on Senator MacDonald's background. It appeared that Baari could not overcome his opponent's clear advantage.

He was about to lose the election.

Then, shockingly, and providentially for La Fratellanza, the unthinkable happened.

A scandal in the subprime mortgage market surfaced, similar to the one Chase predicted in his thesis. Chase understood that the foundation for the major debacle in the economy that followed started back in 2007. Moreover, during the heat of the campaign, the housing market collapsed totally, resulting in the sharpest drop in home sales in two decades, which ultimately triggered an unprecedented number of evictions and foreclosures.

The banks that created the toxic instruments known as subprime mortgages, which fueled the financial disaster, were on the verge of insolvency. The entire financial system spiraled downward: first with the banks and their cohorts, then with the other mortgage lending institutions, and then it spilled into the stock market. It traveled from Wall Street to Main Street.

It was January 2008, when the stock market suffered its first significant downturn, and in March, the Dow Jones Industrial Average was at its lowest level since October 2006.

By June, the Senate Banking Committee desperately proposed housing bailouts, followed quickly in July by the sitting president signing into law the Housing and Economic Recovery Act, guaranteeing up to $300 billion in new thirty-year fixed rate mortgages for borrowers.

In September, the federal government took control of Fannie Mae and Freddie Mac, two of the largest mortgage holders. In combination, they either owned or guaranteed $12 trillion of the mortgage market. It was a once valid concept gone wrong—investors worldwide backed $5.2 trillion of these debt securities, which they purchased from various U.S. sources.

During the same month, Lehman Brothers, a premier global financial services firm, collapsed, as the Federal Reserve loaned $85 billion to American International Group, known as AIG, an equally premier financial services organization, to avoid total insolvency.

As problematic as these events were, it was easy to understand why consumer lending dried up, and consumer spending came to a screeching halt.

Not only was the American public in a panic, so were Senator Baari and La Fratellanza, all except Simon.

"I have a plan to stop the spiraling economy, but I don't think we should put it in place until after Abner is sworn in as president," Simon explained, in an effort to console his brothers.

"I agree. That way, he will get full credit for saving the country from a financial collapse, and it will give him an abundance of political capital, which he will need," Hank said in approval.

"We have only two months to go, and I'm convinced we can hold on until then. Remember, I have the ability to suspend trading on Wall Street if necessary, along with other controls if it truly starts to fall apart," boasted Simon. "The current administration is still responsible, and they appear to be doing all they can, but we must monitor the situation closely."

For the moment, they forgot about Abner, and focused more on their own financial futures and those of their families. The gang of four, ignoring Simon's boasts that he could fix the situation, pleaded with him to stop the problem immediately.

"For the sake of the election!" they shouted.

"It will work itself out," he calmly assured them.

—

A week later, in mid-September, to their surprise, amidst all the lunacy, a young, highly intelligent economist who worked with the current secretary of the Treasury developed something called TAP, the Toxic Asset Plan. *Toxic* was a term created to describe nonperforming assets.

The economist had designed TAP to transfer trillions of dollars to various banks to buy their failed assets. The objective was to help free up the frozen credit market to stimulate the economy. The most threatening risk was that the federal government would then own an enormous portfolio of exotic mortgage instruments created out of thin air. A few weeks later, in October, the sitting president, still under tremendous pressure, signed TAP into law, providing $700 billion of government funds to purchase assets. Their true value was indeterminable.

However, before this new infusion of capital took hold, the stock market suffered its worst week in seventy-five years, down 40.3 percent from its record high in October 2007. As an emergency measure, the Federal Reserve provided $900 billion in short-term loans to banks and another $1.3 trillion directly to companies outside the financial sector.

They pulled out all the stops to end the bloodletting, but in the new global economy, shock waves still hit the stock markets around the world. In spite of all the massive federal spending that created an unprecedented number of bailouts, it appeared to reduce the panic in the streets, and there was a massive sigh of relief. It became apparent that the federal government's intervention had a salutary effect and began to stimulate the economy to a small degree—long enough to take the focus off the war and redirect it to the economy.

With less than a month before the election, the financial crisis caused Baari's challenger to lose significant ground.

On November 4, he was defeated.

Senator Abner Baari won the election.

The unimaginable had happened, and no one celebrated more jubilantly then La Fratellanza—first, in earnest for all it had achieved—second, for finally coming to the end of a long, hard-fought "game."

—

After the swearing-in ceremony, Hank was still attached to Abner's hip, but this time as chief of staff. He worked diligently with the new president and aided him in selecting his cabinet appointees. One of the first appointees Hank recommended was the young economist that developed TAP. The economist became the new secretary of the Treasury.

The president, with Hank's glowing endorsement, made two other appointments.

He appointed Seymour the president's documentarian. Seymour was delighted, as it suited him well.

"I recognize you were the point person that made me look good," Baari said, "and in addition to the documentary, I want you to produce short clips to promote key agendas—to be aired on television, on the Internet, and all other forms of communication, as necessary."

"Thank you, Mr. President."

Initially, the president offered him the position of communications director, continuing in the role he performed during the campaign. However, Seymour believed that position was more demanding and restrictive, and not wanting to be so entrenched in the administration, he convinced him that Paolo would be a better choice.

Seymour was happy to be able to pop in and out of the White House at will, as he documented the president's life for the film, *First 100 Days in Office*. He was also eager to return to his neglected company, MediaLynx, and to resume his career as filmmaker. He had no qualms about managing both.

The president then appointed Paolo to the unusual role of communications director, along with maintaining his role as speechwriter.

"I'm well aware it was your words that propelled me through two successful elections, and I finally accepted that by and large I was only the reader," he graciously admitted.

"I appreciate your words, Mr. President."

"I also recognize your uncanny ability to predict public sentiment and to be fully prepared with statements to minimize any concerns. I want you to be the man at the podium, as my press secretary."

"Thank you again, Mr. President, but with all due respect, I don't believe my Italian accent, however slight, will be well received in that role. I can, however, recommend an excellent candidate who worked with me on the campaign."

"Let's look him over, but since he reports to you, make sure he shields me and suppresses the frequency of question-and-answer sessions. I don't want to provide the press corps and others with ammunition to be used against me later."

"Yes, Mr. President. I understand."

The president had little direct contact with Chase, but Hank already had a candidate for budget director. So Chase blissfully returned to his CFO position at the National Depositors Trust Bank in New York, putting his involvement in the "game" behind him.

No one knew exactly what Simon's plans were, nor did he shed any light on them. At that point, his brothers were less apprehensive after their fantastic coup.

It was over—or was it?

19

THE POLITICAL UNSPIN

It was a bitterly cold morning in February 2009, but inside the George Washington University Hospital, there was nothing bitter about the gurgling seven-and-a-half-pound baby boy named Mario Salvatore.

As the proud father, and equally proud uncle, stood counting fingers and toes, Natalie laid back looking stunning.

Hamilton watched from outside the hospital room door, not wanting to intrude. He was honored to have been included, and it warmed his heart as he gazed at his extended family.

Shortly after that blissful occasion, the Salvatore family returned home and acclimated to a new routine. Paolo's consisted of Mario's midnight feedings and performing his duties at the White House by day. Spending those intimate moments watching his son's face as he drank from his bottle—contrasted with facing the president each day—intensified Paolo's inner doubts about his role in the plot. He became noticeably concerned for his wife and his new son.

Natalie observed the increasingly negative changes in Paolo's demeanor, but continued to ignore it for the moment. She was dealing with her own adjustments, having taken a sabbatical from Georgetown University to stay at home with Mario.

During the little time alone with Paolo, she would often ask, "Is there anything I can get for you?"

"No," he'd snap.

"Would you help me with Mario?"

"I'm busy right now," he'd grumble.

"Is everything okay?"

"Yes," he would respond, and then leave the room.

This atypical behavior continued for weeks.

At the time, Natalie thought he was overwhelmed with the pressures of fatherhood and exhausted from having just come off the campaign trail. She had no way of knowing that Paolo's increased tension, verging on paranoia, was brought on by his close relationship with Noble and Hamilton, which conflicted with his commitment to La Fratellanza.

As President Baari settled into the Oval Office, Paolo was struggling to balance his life between family and the White House.

—

Concurrently, Noble had just finished vetting a string of senators and congresspersons that were on the 2008 election circuit. It was also during this time that Noble's curious streak overcame him. His inquisitive nature was most often his greatest asset, but there were other times it became a bit of a hindrance.

He knew the severe consequences of delving too incisively into the president's personal life. He would not only put himself at risk, but also the credibility of the agency. Considered part of a "super snooping" agency by some, any intrusions they uncovered would reflect on the entire organization. Naturally, it would raise questions about how far and deep they had strayed.

However, some questions were gnawing at Noble, driving him to the limit.

I'm not sure what it is, but something doesn't compute. It has something to do with how the president ascended to the lofty office, and I won't find peace until my doubts are satisfied.

He began to have flashbacks of the theses he had read while at Harvard, and something kept drawing him back to their pages.

This convergence of events gave rise to what became the beginning of the "political unspin."

—

One of the odd jobs Noble had at Harvard was to catalog all the theses submitted and subsequently published by the graduates.

A few years prior to his attending Harvard, a highly controversial thesis, reported stolen, was held for ransom. For this reason, the university kept all theses in a special room, under strict security, only accessible to the author and a few others, including Noble.

When Simon Hall asked him to join the inner sanctum of the study group, he declined, but that didn't stop him from being inquisitive about its members. Especially after he began to spend more time with them.

Noble enjoyed the occasional beer at Jake's, or a spontaneous dinner with the group, but that was the extent of his socializing. Clearly, he was an introvert at heart.

I'm just curious as to what these guys are like on a deeper level, something I'm not privy to, since I'm not officially part of their group, he would often ponder.

He concluded that reading from their theses would gain him more insight about his comrades. He surmised that the theories they had constructed and their conclusions would expand his understanding.

Noble never intended to be malicious, but again, his intellectual curiosity compelled him to uncover some answers. One evening, he decided to take the five hardbound books from the Pusey Library, with the intent to read and return them quickly to their rightful place. Then there was that horrible fire, and it became impossible to return the books. Noble, ashamed and dissatisfied with his waywardness, placed the books in a box with other memorabilia and stored them in a safe place.

But not before reading the theses.

He remembered he found the theories original and quite ingenious, although he never fully understood their applicability. He certainly didn't comprehend how their conclusions would apply in today's world. Noble never made the connection, until recent events caused him to recall the theories embraced between the pages in those etched leather bindings.

The banking crises, followed by the swearing in of the first minority president in the White House, are two events that seem frighteningly familiar.

Noble desperately needed to get his hands on the books, but could not remember where he had stored them. He thought of them possibly being in his home, in the boxes that he had piled in the second bedroom, or in the storage locker he rented for his other possessions. Then, of course, there was his family's home in Kansas, which he and Natalie had never allowed themselves to sell.

—

When Noble vetted Abner Baari earlier in 2006, along with the other senators, he detected nothing suspicious. The president's grandparents reared him in Kansas when orphaned at birth. He graduated from Northwestern, and after working several years with the Chestnut Foundation, he attended the University of Chicago Law School. Everything that followed was public record and exploited ad nauseam during the campaigns.

After the swearing in of the forty-fourth president, Noble could no longer control his curiosity— he broke the director's cardinal rule.

He began checking and rechecking, in infinite detail, the various databases. Based on his exhaustive analysis, he was aghast to discover that the information on the president's file entered into several different computer systems—only a few years before—was fictitious. Furthermore, Noble, who happened to have grown up in the same hometown as the Baaris, didn't know the family. He was also able to uncover that John and Sara Baari died as reported in an automobile accident, but they had no children. Then he checked the elementary and high school records, only to find that those records had been fabricated as well.

He was overwhelmed to learn that it would have been impossible for Kathleen Baari to have worked for the Peace Corps and been assigned to Libya in 1970, at the time of Abner's birth. During the 1970s, the Peace Corps did not assign women to Libya, especially since the tensions were high between the United States and the rogue nation. Muammar al-Qaddafi had forced all U.S. personnel off the military bases and required the renegotiation of oil production contracts. It was during this time Qaddafi began using oil embargoes as a political weapon to drive up the cost of oil. It was also an attempt to force the United States to end its support of Israel.

Noble recalled that the tensions had heightened again in 1986, when the U.S. bombed Libya in retaliation for the death of two American soldiers in the bombing of the Berlin discotheque. Noble also recollected that during the retaliatory strike, Muammar al-Qaddafi's two-year-old adopted daughter was killed. He reviewed the reports carefully and, to his amazement, he discovered a family in Qaddafi's complex, including a sixteen-year-old boy, had also died in the bombing. On the surface, the information didn't appear to hold any grave significance.

Then what Noble did uncover was explosive.

However, before he took the information to the director, he needed more proof. He also feared Paolo might be involved and wanted absolute certainty before he risked destroying his sister's life.

He needed the theses to fill in the blanks.

20

THE FINAL OBSTACLE

After the election, the financial crisis simmered down a few degrees. Then during the Christmas season, consumer spending was abysmal, and after the inauguration, the crisis started to bubble up again. The financial crisis continued, but this time it spiraled downward relentlessly.

On March 6, 2009, the Dow Jones closed at 6,627 points. Other markets around the world were experiencing similar volatility, adding to an already unstable situation. Investors, dazed by the turmoil, began to recalculate the value of their portfolios, only to find their personal wealth had taken a lethal blow. The stock market dropped 50 percent from the prior year.

No answers seemed in sight.

And La Fratellanza, along with some of the greatest economic minds throughout the world, didn't know when, or if, the downward trend would stop.

The gang of four in particular was in a panic, primarily because they felt responsible for placing their man in the Oval Office—a man they knew had never faced a crisis of this magnitude.

They needed Simon. He claimed he could fix it.

Surprisingly, Chase was the first to activate his pager, which didn't post a time or day, only the word NOW.

It was a Friday and the market was about to close. It was also a difficult travel day at best, and with pandemonium in the business world, it was sure to be a nightmare.

Hank happened to be in Washington, along with Paolo and Seymour. They didn't know where Simon was at the time, but they all would need to make travel arrangements to leave on the next flight.

Hank activated his pager with the word SAT.

—

The members of La Fratellanza arrived Saturday morning and convened in their office on the South Side, all accounted for except Simon. Sitting around the round conference table, they strategized for hours. By six o'clock that evening, they had a sinking feeling that Simon wouldn't be arriving. The fact that they'd had no correspondence from him during the past terrifying week was atypical, suggesting that something was dreadfully awry.

"Is it possible something has happened to Simon?" Hank conjectured.

Initially, their immediate thoughts were about his well-being, especially Hank, having the closest relationship with him.

"It is not like Simon to ignore his pager or not try to contact us in some way!" Chase snapped.

"Something must have happened to him." Seymour reasoned.

They gave Simon the benefit of the doubt as they recalled his acts of kindness, each recapping a particular incident. However, that mood changed quickly and dramatically with the tenor of the conversation. The gang of four began to express doubts as to whether they were simply pawns in something they didn't fully comprehend.

"The game may be over, but one wonders if Simon is involved in the crisis," Paolo speculated. "The real question is why would he want it to continue?"

"Simon has no reason for wanting the crisis to persist," Chase defended.

"Paolo, do you really think he is setting us up?" Seymour quizzed. "We work for the president. Simon understands what a disaster this would be for all of us."

The devastated looks on the other's faces gave him his answer.

"Remember at Harvard, when Simon boasted about how he had set up Noble," Paolo recalled.

"Yes, but it was Simon who was also there for Noble at a crucial time of his life," Hank cautioned, still grasping at the hope that it was all a misunderstanding.

Whether it was doubts he had concealed or a result of his state of panic, Paolo blurted out the unthinkable, "Was it possible that Simon caused the death of Noble's parents?"

Paolo, sensing the others had tentatively considered the prospect, quickly added, "If Simon is capable of such a monstrous crime, is it possible we have been used as pawns to accomplish a goal that goes beyond winning the presidency?"

"Is it possible Simon has a plan of some sort that we were not privy to?" Hank asked with dread.

They conceded that Simon was a master at manipulating people beyond anything they had ever experienced. Hank alluded to the possibility that the fine hand of Simon was behind many of the events that occurred. Paolo harked back to the time when he suggested they change their name to Padroni del Burattino.

"Actually, I should have said *Padrone*, not *Padroni*. There is only one master." He sighed. "There's no denying it, Simon is the one pulling the strings, and we are his puppets."

"Back on point—the economy continues to be in shambles, and the Treasury has yet to release the much-sought-after TAP Funds!" Seymour shouted. He reminded them, with panic clearly in his voice, "Initially, the Treasury made the announcement informing the public about the TAP Funds, but it was only a promise to release the money at some future date. But as the banks wait, more and more are defaulting."

Hank informed the group, "I heard rumors the Treasury has instituted a waiting period until the banks pass a so-called stress test to determine which banks are worthy of being saved and which should be allowed to fail."

Chase, noticeably silent throughout the exchange, chimed in. "The president should force some of the major 'solvent' banks to take the TAP funds, even though they don't need them or want them. Then the Treasury must allow the banks to repay the funds after all the 'stress tests' are completed." Chase believed it would give the appearance TAP was working and instill confidence that the Treasury funds would eventually be repaid. "It will also encourage the banks to unfreeze the credit market and start lending to consumers and small businesses."

"It might work," Hank mumbled.

They all agreed the president lacked the experience to cope with the crisis on his own, as they agonized over the fact they were in many ways responsible for putting the country at risk. Shortsighted as it may have been, La Fratellanza's focus had been on their ultimate goal, not on the ultimate consequences.

Now harsh reality befell them.

"Hank, you are best equipped to guide the president through the labyrinth before it gets out of control, along with our careers and our futures," Seymour insisted.

"Chase, I'll need your help to lay out a plan, one I can get the president to accept!" Hank demanded.

As more calm set in, this select group of intellectuals, began to work together to find solutions.

"While Hank and Chase work together to bring the financial crisis under control," Paolo concluded, "we need to find Simon. He may be the only one who can help us climb out of this mess." Paolo waited a moment, then looked at each of them intently and said, "The only sure way to find Simon is to enlist the support of Noble."

They acknowledged they didn't know what was on Simon's agenda, but concluded it had to be more than just their "game." There had to be something even bigger in it for him. They agreed and felt Paolo should be the one to approach Noble.

"You'll have to admit to Noble that you knew of Simon's whereabouts all along," Seymour reminded.

"I'll make my mea culpa, but then I'll have to bend the truth a bit and tell him there are rumors Simon was involved in some unknown way in the financial crisis."

"Don't tell him they were rumors," Chase suggested. "Convince him that Simon was the one who instigated the crisis. I can give you enough information to make your case believable."

"You should also tell Noble that Simon was working hard to gain access to the TAP funds at the Treasury," Hank added.

"All we really know at this point is that he just simply walked away," Paolo argued.

"I agree, but if we need to intensify our efforts to find Simon," Hank implored, "we can escalate the search with the help of a number of competent sources. We didn't elect a president without acquiring some power!"

"We also agreed that we don't understand what is happening, and if we involve anyone else, we run the risk of exposing La Fratellanza—and, worse, the president," Paolo appealed. "Noble is our only hope."

Hank backed down. "Point taken." Then he strongly cautioned Paolo. "Do not mention anything about La Fratellanza or any of our activities."

Paolo agreed and left for Washington to meet with Noble.

21

THE CONFESSIONAL

Noble was surprised to receive a call from Paolo so soon after spending time together, especially sounding so agitated. Only a few days earlier in the week, Noble enjoyed a delightful dinner with Natalie and Paolo at their home in Reston. They engaged in their usual intellectual repartee and laughed at most of what was flowing from the political rumor mill. The camaraderie was what they enjoyed most.

It was Sunday morning when Noble received the call.

"I need to meet with you as soon as possible, somewhere completely private," Paolo stammered.

Noble's first reaction was fear that something was wrong with either Natalie or the baby, but there was no evidence of it at their dinner.

He remembered the time when Natalie had confessed, "It was his irresistible charm that led me to fall in love with him and marry him so quickly." During their whirlwind courtship, Paolo oftentimes referred playfully to their relationship as *kissmet*.

"I was never sure whether it was his clever play on words or his Italian accent that made it sound so endearing," Noble once admitted to his sister.

Feeling partially relieved as he reflected on his memories, Noble suggested Paolo meet him at the Blackfinn, but he resisted. He said he needed a place more private, so Noble agreed to meet him near their favorite watering hole in Franklin Park, near the corner of K and Thirteenth Streets.

However, Paolo had one more person with whom he needed to speak.

—

Since the birth of baby Mario, Natalie became increasingly suspicious that something was horribly wrong—Paolo was not his former self.

Sometimes, Paolo was distracted, as if his mind was completely absorbed. Other times he would be irritable, a trait Natalie had not seen before in her husband. When he seemed withdrawn, she tried to reach out to him by engaging in conversation, which often led to arguments when she attempted to gauge his thoughts.

"*Lascia mi stare,*" was his usual retort. She had learned painfully that it meant, "Leave me alone."

The Paolo of old always displayed a keen sense of humor and an upbeat attitude, but his disposition had changed dramatically. While Noble didn't pick up on the signs, Natalie couldn't miss them, and she feared her life with Paolo was at risk. She pleaded with him several times to confide in her, without success, and it only heightened the tension. Finally, Natalie found the situation unbearable and decided to confront Paolo. She wanted him to explain his strange behavior.

However, Paolo reached the breaking point first. It happened the day before, after his meeting with La Fratellanza, a meeting he believed would probably be his last.

Before Paolo met with Noble, he knew he first had to explain his abnormal behavior to his wife.

As he sat across from Natalie, her hand in his, he told her everything: about La Fratellanza, about the president, and about his plan to meet with Noble.

He began with his time at Harvard and worked up to his most recent meeting with his fraternity brothers. Going against La Fratellanza's wishes, he left out nothing. After he divulged everything he knew, and had exhausted all his explanations, he pleaded with her, "Please, my love, I ask you to be patient, and I promise I will set things straight, for you and for Mario."

Initially glaring with the impassioned look of a prosecutor, Natalie sat painfully silent. However, when Paolo had finished, and she attempted her cross-exam, she broke down in tears. Not all her legal training had equipped her to cope with the situation, and she melted in her husband's arms. Her love had not faded, and she wanted the man she married to return.

As much as Paolo hated to leave, he relaxed his arms from their passionate embrace and softly whispered, "*Ti amo più della vita,*" telling her he loved her more than life.

Then he rushed off to meet Noble.

—

For a Sunday afternoon, the park was unusually empty. Washington had either more churchgoers or more sinners—Noble suspected the latter—and that they were sleeping off their indulgences. While the sun was warm, the air was chilly, and Noble had hoped he could convince Paolo to move their meeting to the Blackfinn once he arrived. Edging up to twenty minutes after the appointed hour, Paolo finally entered the park where Noble was patiently waiting, and trying not to shiver.

After a quick apology for being late, he began rapidly sputtering words that sounded more like Italian, but in fact, they were English. What Noble was able to glean from Paolo's rants was that he had confessed to Natalie, telling her everything, about something, about which she promised to say nothing. And he trusted her.

So far, he wasn't making any sense.

Now Noble was seriously concerned that his family was in trouble. The cold he felt before was now a chill of a different sort. He could have never imagined what he was about to hear. With heart-wrenching sincerity, Paolo expressed regret to Noble for all the distress he had caused his sister. At that point, he demanded, "Paolo, sit down and explain to me what's going on!"

Thanks to Paolo's behavior, Noble was approaching his own state of panic.

Paolo proceeded to share the intensely personal conversation he'd had with Natalie. Then he pleaded, "I need you to understand what I've done, and then I need your help to undo the harm."

As they sat on a bench, away from the few pedestrians, Paolo took a long, deep breath and then started from the beginning. First, he went over Simon's role, then told him about La Fratellanza, and then about the president. He expressed regret repeatedly for not having divulged any of this to Noble before and for lying about Simon's whereabouts.

As Noble listened and took in the seriousness of the matter, he was also thinking about the many opportunities Paolo had before to tell him the truth. Their weekly get-togethers at the Blackfinn would have been an ideal, opportune time—and certainly, he had opportunities before he married Natalie.

Noble caught himself fighting the temperature, shivering as his thoughts drifted back to the Blackfinn, where it would be warm and cozy. Now, despite the cold, he desperately wanted Paolo to continue, uninterrupted.

Paolo carried on for another hour. Sometimes in a highly emotional state, other times composed. "The financial crisis was not engineered by us, it was just a lucky break, which we used to our political advantage," he stated emotionally. "All it took was some effective spin from La Fratellanza to catapult Baari into the Oval Office."

He calmed down slightly, and spoke about Uncle Rob, about the microchip, and the "shadow" thesis hidden in their theses. After a slight pause, in an awkwardly measured voice for Paolo, he said, "We now fear that Simon has disappeared."

Slowly, he removed his Rolex watch from his wrist and gave it to Noble, turning it over and displaying the initials ***LF*** on the back, and indicating the location of the microchip. A microchip that contained each thesis detailing what was supposed to be their imaginary plot to defraud the American people.

"It started as a game, and now the game is over." Paolo sighed, feeling totally spent.

Noble could feel his face flush, and not from the cold, but as he remembered the leather-bound copies somewhere still in his possession. *Where are they?* , he asked himself.

In an attempt to persuade Noble further, Paolo avowed, "Over the years, we had convinced ourselves that while we were aware we were straddling the line of justice, we had never crossed it." He paused. "It was always Simon who managed to lure us in, just to do one more thing to ensure success. However, 'one more thing' never stopped. Now the president is in office, the economy is in a free fall, and Simon left all of us to take the rap," he whispered in dismay.

He admitted La Fratellanza was afraid they would be held accountable for manipulating the system and placing a totally untested person to lead the country at such a fragile time. "While each of us feels we are not directly responsible for the crisis, we are beginning to feel responsible for the outcome," he confessed.

During that cathartic moment, Paolo explained that his fraternity brothers, out of fear, instructed him to tell Noble that they thought it was Simon, who had converted the college game into reality—and more important, that he had devised it on his own.

"That was all I was supposed to divulge." Bowing his head, Paolo said, "But out of love for my family, my country, and my loyalty to you, I've left nothing out, and truly want to set things straight. We know you have the resources to ferret out Simon, and we need your help. I promise if you find him, La Fratellanza will devote all its efforts to solve the financial crisis." Paolo, sounding more like Natalie than he did the president's communications director, had presented his case.

Throughout his summation Noble remained silent, allowing Paolo's words to flow. All the while, he felt distraught over his brother-in-law's participation and over the pain he and Natalie must be sharing.

Noble let the silence fall between them for a while longer. Then he proceeded to tell Paolo what he had already uncovered. "I suspected that the president is a fraud, but I was never able to discern the ultimate purpose."

Paolo appeared shocked, but Noble didn't react.

Now, with the disappearance of Simon, Noble was able to confirm his suspicions—at least that the plot was more involved than he had originally believed. Noble did not share his feelings directly with Paolo, but assumed he had reached the same conclusion.

Noble needed time to study the theses on the microchip, especially the "shadow" thesis. He needed to find clues within its pages, leading him to the ultimate end of the game. As soon as he gathered sufficient evidence to support his findings, his next step would be to review all he had discovered with Hamilton.

He needed to return to his office immediately.

"At this point, I don't know what, or if any, crimes have been committed, but I am giving you advance warning that we may have to interrogate all of you." He promised Paolo that the information he had supplied, other than what La Fratellanza had instructed him to convey, would stay confidential, at least as to its source.

Paolo appreciated his brother-in-law trying to protect him, but knew he wasn't out of the woods yet.

"Go home and say nothing to the members of La Fratellanza, other than the fact that you reported their suspicions about Simon, and I will start the investigation."

They left the park in opposite directions.

—

Noble hurried through Franklin Park and down Thirteenth Street. While on the way to his office, he called Hamilton on his cell phone. "I just had an epiphany!" he cried out. He explained to the director that he had just met with Paolo, who dropped a mega bomb of information on him and some startling revelations came to light, but first he needed to check out one more piece of the puzzle.

"I need to see you first thing in the morning, eight o'clock, in your office. It is of vital importance."

Noble's revelation came when Paolo made the statement that they did not engineer the financial crisis, that *it was just a lucky break*. He knew the truth lay somewhere in the theses.

Ironically, Noble had just rushed past the Church of the Epiphany on the northwest corner of G Street.

—

Noble returned to his office and locked the door behind him. He then reached into his desk and retrieved his microchip reader. It was the latest in technology, a Datamars ISO MAX V Microchip Scanner. The 2009 technology made the reading and downloading of information relatively easy. Fortunately, this particular Datamars model was capable of reading nine-, ten-, and fifteen-digit microchips operating up to 134.2 kHz.

"Thank you, Simon, for creating the microchip with nine digits at one hundred twenty-five kilohertz," he said aloud.

Noble quickly attached the USB connection cable and downloaded all five theses into an Adobe format on his secure computer. He inhaled deeply, let out a long breath, then sat back and began to read the text.

Even though Paolo had filled him in on the outlines of each thesis, and about how Simon's suggestions became the basis for the "shadow" thesis, Noble decided first to skip to each title page to get the gist of their topics. His head was spinning and he needed to refresh his memory.

The first one read, "Effects of Political Campaigning on the Web" by Seymour Lynx. Then "Political Speech: Creator or Interpreter of Ideology" by Paolo Salvatore. Next to follow was "Internet Activism: Campaigning for Social Justice" by Hank Kramer. After Hank's was "U.S. Banking Deregulation: The Catalyst for a Housing Crisis" by Chase Worthington. Lastly was "Internet Security: Pandora's Box of the New Millennium" by Noble Bishop.

Noble did a double take, and in sheer disbelief, he reread the title and name of the author of the last thesis. There was no time to understand Simon's sick joke. He knew that once he found his own thesis, with his name inscribed, the idea that he was a suspect—or even more remotely, that he was Simon Hall—would be laughable on its own merits. Now, there was something even more disturbing: the insignia ☪ placed under each of the author's names.

Noble spent the next several hours combing intently through the information that was on the microchip looking for the "shadow" thesis, trying to find a common thread, anything that would connect the dots of a plot that potentially could do more harm. There had to be a purpose, an even more diabolical reason for spending years, money, and the devotion of a few, just to have Baari elected.

It didn't make sense, not to Noble's logical mind.

He trusted Paolo had told him all he knew, but something was definitely missing.

The puzzle was incomplete.

—

The next morning, Noble arrived at the director's office in the West

Wing. Seated in his office on the ground floor, only a stairway from the president, Noble briefed Hamilton on his conversation with Paolo and on the contents of the theses. Then he mentioned the insignia next to each author's name and said he found that fact most troubling of all.

The director had never mentioned the calling card from the hacker case he investigated in the early nineties, because he felt it had no significance. He only briefed him on the general details of the case that eventually led him to Hal Simmons.

"Odd, this is the same insignia my hacker left after each crime!"

Noble, as always, still looking for more clues, asked, "Would you review the details of that case with me again? Please don't leave anything out."

At the time, Hamilton didn't fully comprehend the importance of a case fifteen years old, or how it could possibly involve Simon Hall, but he felt Noble was onto something. He repeated the story about the computer hacker who had transferred eleven dollars from twenty banks on the eighth day of every month, and each month he would attack a different set of banks. He never understood why eleven dollars, an odd amount, or why on the eighth day. "I admit, at the time, my focus was more on tracing the movements of the elusive hacker than his motive."

As Hamilton continued to elaborate on the other details of the case, he noticed Noble, while appearing to listen, kept staring at the floor as he repeated, "eleven-twenty-eight," several times under his breath. When he finally looked up, his expression conveying a eureka! moment.

"I previously checked, and according to the calendar cycles in the years the transfers occurred, there were over one hundred days where the eighth day was on a Sunday, the day banks are closed."

Hamilton could see a shift in Noble's mind-set as he went into overdrive.

Noble's brilliance came to the fore as he multi-processed at an astounding rate. He was still tossing it around in his mind. "Why did the transfer always have to be on the eighth day? The hacker had either predated or postdated the transfers to make them look like they happened on the eighth day," he rightly concluded. Then downshifting, with a slower-paced voice, Noble simply stated, "There were always twenty banks at a time: twenty represents the twentieth century. And when you enter the number eight for the day on a computer, it is entered as zero-eight, and the eleven dollars represent the eleventh month. November 2008, the presidential election!" he erupted with gusto.

The director was stunned.

Then the ultimate jolt hit.

"As you rightly recalled the hacker's calling card, at the end of each bank balance, was the same symbol Simon Hall placed at the end of each thesis."

"You mean Simon Hall is Hal Simmons!" Hamilton roared in disbelief.

"The location of the apartment, the study group, the bank where Chase Worthington was a bank manager, it all seems to fit together. Now, are you ready for an aftershock?"

Hamilton, still in a state of wonderment, urged Noble to continue.

"The symbol ☪ did not represent the Goddess Diana, as relayed by one of your analysts during the Hal Simmons investigation, but is the symbol for the Islamic faith."

The common symbol, the plot to elect the president, and the missing Simon paralyzed them momentarily, as the severity of the situation sank in.

"I feel as though I just received a right jab to the solar plexus, compliments of Mohammed Ali in his heyday," Hamilton said. "Are you implying that the money *my hacker* had stolen, so many years ago, contributed to the growing slush fund affectionately named Uncle Rob, and was used in preparation for the 2008 presidential election?"

"In a word, *yes*!"

Simon Hall had been plotting his master plan long before he arrived at Harvard. He had planned everything that occurred at Harvard, including his selection of students to become part of his choice study group, far in advance, through an ingenious computer selection process.

Noble remembered with relief, "I was supposed to be part of La Fratellanza."

"There is still something amiss," heeded Hamilton. "The puzzle is not complete."

Noble agreed.

"We must interview all members of the La Fratellanza," Hamilton insisted. "And we need to find Simon Hall."

They both agreed it was imperative to conduct the investigation covertly, including the interrogations.

"We must keep the information top secret, especially from the president, until we have all the pieces of the puzzle," Hamilton cautioned. With the thought of the president eerily in proximity, Hamilton shared a revelation of his own, one he had almost forgotten.

"When I started working for the Foreign Service, I was posted to the U.S. Diplomatic Security Service in Rome." He explained that his duties were to manage the security detail for the U.S. embassy, particularly for the ambassador, but while he was in Rome, he received an assignment to go to Florence to oversee the investigation of the murder of an American tourist. It was in 1995.

"As I recall the victim was a fifty-eight-year-old man, from Asheville, North Carolina, who had been stabbed to death with a knife. It took place on Via Terme near the Mercato Nuovo, the new market. There was never any real evidence, other than the ten stab wounds and the missing wallet—no murder weapon—no witnesses to the attack."

Hamilton explained it was also a time the Carabinieri were at odds with the African street vendors, blaming them for an increase in crime. This happened to be one such crime, and in the end, it led to the arrest of a nineteen-year-old Senegalese.

"What does that have to do with this case?"

"I'm getting to that, and you'll be quite surprised at the conclusion. What made this crime so interesting was the trial itself." He continued to explain that there were no witnesses for the prosecution and virtually no forensic evidence, but there was one witness for the defense. "At this time, I don't recall the name of the defendant, but the witness's name was Hussein. He was a young Libyan, similar in age to the defendant. It was his testimony I found most fascinating, as did the jury."

Hamilton explained that Hussein described his role as the organizer of a group of African street vendors, teaching them Italian and English, how to hawk the tourist, and how to work as a harmonious unit. He boasted their take was quite lucrative and, as a group, did not tolerate any crime. He vouched for the defendant and said he was with him at the time, so it was impossible for him to have killed the tourist.

"The jury bought his persuasive argument, and they released the defendant. The prosecutor seemed quite relieved as well, having no countervailing evidence and additionally averting any further friction between the street vendors and the local government. I know I am rambling, but the point I want to make is that I believe I know the young Libyan. Even more disturbing, I was in Florence at the same time as Simon and Hussein." Shaking his head he continued, "I've always harbored this feeling that I had met Baari in the past, but was never able to make the connection until now—now I believe Hussein is our President Baari."

While it was a shocking conclusion to the director's story, there was no reaction from Noble. He had been listening, but multiprocessing as usual. He was also shuffling through the papers in his briefcase, until suddenly he pulled out a photo of a young man sitting on the low branch of a tree, and handed the photo to Hamilton. In the background was a small wooden frame ranch-style house with a front porch, surrounded by wheat fields.

The lad on the tree limb was the president.

"I do remember the photo was used in some of the political ads promoting his presumed small-town, Midwestern values," Hamilton said, shaking his head in utter amazement.

Then Noble explained that on closer inspection, he discovered someone had superimposed another photo of Baari sitting in the tree onto the backdrop. He patiently explained, "The tree was a baobab tree, which contains a highly nutritious fruit. It is a tree that is indigenous to Africa."

"Clearly, Baari must have supplied some old photos of himself as a child, which Seymour then was able to crop, cut, and paste," concluded Hamilton.

Noble then showed him a photo of the same house, but without the tree.

"I combed through hundreds of film clips of houses, clips Seymour would also be able to access with his connections at MGM, until I came across the one I've just shown you. It is the photo of a house in Liberal, Kansas, which was the house used in the making of the 1939 MGM film *The Wizard of Oz*."

Noble smiled. "I guess we now know who is behind the curtain."

"We have to move fast!" shouted Hamilton, still shaking his head in disbelief.

—

Within hours, the director sent four agents to deliver a summons to each member of La Fratellanza, requesting he report to the director of the SIA for confidential questioning, along with a word of caution that it might require more than one day, so he should plan accordingly. Actually, it wasn't an ordinary request, but a summons compelling their attendance.

It was Monday, so Hamilton scheduled the appearance for Friday at 9:00 a.m., providing enough travel time. He gave orders to the agents not to leave their sides as they personally escorted them to Washington on Thursday. He then arranged to have three of them sequestered in different hotels overnight and transported to CIA's headquarters the next morning.

Paolo received his summons within the hour, followed by a call from Noble, ensuring him that his role would remain as a "confidential informant"; the others would not know the source of the additional information. He told him an agent would accompany him as well.

22

THE INTERROGATION

Over the past several days, Hamilton and Noble reviewed all the evidence they had collected thus far. They needed to be fully prepared to conduct one of the most vital interrogations the agency had ever performed—it had to be perfect.

It was Friday, a day they hoped all the pieces would fall into place.

Hamilton's office was in the West Wing of the White House, but he housed most of his departments in secure locations around Washington, for national security reasons. Often, when it was necessary to interrogate a suspect or an informant, he would use the facilities at the CIA in Langley, a fifteen-minute drive across the Potomac.

This is where he decided to conduct the interrogations.

Following September 11, the CIA fingerprinted all persons, after passing through the metal detector—La Fratellanza was no exception.

Shortly after following the entry procedures, the agents escorted the members of this band of intellectuals to the reception area outside the interrogation room. The receptionist on duty observed that none of the members of this illustrious group seemed surprised to see each other, and they limited their conversations to small talk about their kids, family, and sports. They were correct in assuming she was a trained listener who would report what they had said, and she did.

Three quarters of an hour later, the gang of four was ushered into the interrogation room.

Director Hamilton Scott stood up from behind the desk in the corner and greeted the group of men, who were visibly tense. "Thank you for your patience. I'm sorry you had to wait," he said apologetically. "We'll get started momentarily."

He first introduced himself to Chase Worthington, with the traditional handshake, as he reached across the desk. He sent a nod of acknowledgment, with the hint of a smile, to the other three, with whom he was acquainted. Obviously, both Paolo and Hank were on familiar terms with the director, from having attended many briefings with him and the president. Naturally, he knew Paolo from the many dinners they shared at Noble's home, unbeknownst to the others. He recognized Seymour because his office was located near the White House Photo Office, on the ground floor, across from the Secret Service, the legendary protectors of the president. Seymour was in and out of this office many times, as he worked on various assignments for President Baari.

The director invited them to sit at the conference table in the center of the room, placing each of them in a particular seating order. Still standing at the desk in the corner, the director began to shuffle papers, appearing to look busy, but all the while watching them from the top rim of his glasses. He did glance directly at them, long enough to offer the coffee and pastries on the credenza at the back of the room.

They declined—hunger was not on their minds.

As the director continued to observe their expressions, they attempted to feign indifference. All the while, their eyes were fixated on the crude etching, in the center of the table, the carved initials ***LF***.

They were dumbfounded to see it was their special table from their Harvard days.

Director Scott always believed that table held some significance; he referred to it as a "gut instinct." Therefore, after the police had removed the yellow tape from the apartment in Cambridge, an apartment thought to be a crime scene, the director returned and bought the table from the landlord. It had remained in his conference room ever since that time, and for the past twelve years, the director considered that table a reminder of the missing Hal Simmons.

The forensic team, in 1998, was able to uncover several partial fingerprints from the table. They ran them through IAFIS, the Integrated Automated Fingerprint Identification System. The system, maintained by the FBI, contains fingerprint identification and criminal history for more than sixty million subjects. But there was never a match.

That was then.

Now, Noble was able to match those earlier prints against the fingerprints obtained from La Fratellanza that morning when they entered the complex. While they detained the group in the reception area, the director awaited the call from Noble. When the call came, he used the information to place each of them at the precise location around the table where they had sat before.

It was a surreal moment, as the members of La Fratellanza were able to examine the initials signifying their brotherhood from the same vantage point they had so many times in the past.

I admit, it serves no real purpose other than personal satisfaction, but for that moment, the look on their faces made it well worth it, the director mused.

Six chairs fit comfortably around the table, and now he was able to conclude exactly where Simon sat. The director walked over to the table and took Simon's seat.

On cue, Noble entered the room and walked to the empty chair. "I assume this one was meant for me?" he inquired with a touch of despair. Before he sat down, he reached behind and turned on the video camera aimed directly at this close-knit group sitting around the round table that held so many memories.

The director chose to let their stunned silence take hold while gazing at them, with what Noble called his "death stare." Then he proceeded to tell La Fratellanza the evidence he had already uncovered. He enlightened the group, informing them that Noble had discovered the real identity of the president, along with the details of the plot. He also uncovered their involvement in the hoax.

"I don't need you to tell me about Simon's specific role. Nor do I need you to tell me about the plot itself, outlined in your theses—I obtained that information from the microchip," the director divulged.

The gang of four spontaneously checked their wrists; then the others glanced over to Paolo's left wrist, and noticed that his Rolex was missing. Paolo also reacted, forgetting for a split second that he had given it to Noble.

Noble was expressionless.

A slight blunder on the director's part, but now La Fratellanza understood the SIA had the table and the microchip, and the director had skillfully led them to assume that he had much more.

Now he had their full attention.

He went on to expound that he had been able to trace back to the inception of Simon's plot, long before he arrived at Harvard, and he made it painfully clear that Simon deviously selected them and used them for his own personal gain. It was an official confirmation of what the group had long suspected to varying degrees.

"We know Simon is missing, and believe the game has not ended as far as he is concerned," Noble declared. "What is vital for us to understand is the exact role each of you played, as the game was converted to reality."

Director Scott and Noble conveyed guarded assurances that the members of La Fratellanza might not be at great risk if they cooperated fully with the investigation.

Previously, the director had decided that Noble would conduct the first two interviews. He felt the group might feel less intimidated, having had a relationship with Noble in the past. Noble also had firsthand information based on Paolo's confession.

Naturally, the director would continue to assert his authority as necessary.

Noble started with Seymour, only to discover most of what they had already surmised was true. They did, however, learn the names of the two 527 organizations, ChangeNotHope.org and ActionForward.org, and how he manipulated their messages. He reluctantly explained that each Web site presented sound bites and dozens of photos of the family, Baari at law school, and traveling abroad. He admitted he cropped many of the photos, but the sound bites were real, or at least as real as he needed to make them.

"ActionForward.org was designed to support Baari, and all the political ads highlighted his indisputable accomplishments, thanks to Simon's handiwork," he confessed.

Alternatively, Seymour said he designed ChangeNotHope.org to be extremely over-the-top negative. He explained how he produced small, embarrassing film clips that aired on the Web site, presumably exposing the senator as having questionable ties to terrorist organizations, along with holding other radical beliefs.

"The clips I produced were confected to be so outrageous they swayed the fence-sitters, the Independents, and moderate Democrats to vote for Senator Baari," bragged Seymour. He noted that he timed the ads to flood the airwaves in October, a month before the election, both as televised ads and on the Internet. Seymour's experience taught him time was of the essence. "With Hank's special talents, we were able to prove his theory of locating the tipping point of negative campaigning he had conjured up at Harvard."

Hank, incredulous at Seymour for including him in the plot so casually, sniped, "It was actually another one of Simon's theories."

"I have not yet called on you, so please remain silent," the director cautioned.

Letting Hank stew for a while, Noble turned to Paolo.

Paolo clarified how he had been able to predict public sentiment with unusual accuracy, permitting him to write many of the president's speeches far in advance of their actual delivery. He then used many of those speeches as teaching aids for Baari while he was grooming him for the race for the senate and then for the presidency. He added that, in many cases, Baari's speeches were so well memorized they became rote.

"Of course, that wasn't necessary because Simon required Hank to force Baari to use a teleprompter for fear he would go off message. The other members of the group also contributed their expertise to lessons for

Baari, which Hank taught and supervised."

The director and Noble stared Hank's way, but he did not respond.

"In the latter half of the campaign, we all started to notice Baari becoming more and more arrogant and harder to control." Paolo volunteered, which seemed odd to the others that he would find it worth mentioning. "Funny," he said, "it seemed to get worse as the president settled into his role, and at times he acted as though he didn't need me anymore, and in a way I'm thankful."

Paolo acknowledged he didn't have much more to add, except that he was trying to withdraw as the president's communications director and speechwriter, but it would take some time. "I have my family to consider," he added.

Noble thought his statement was inconsistent, since Paolo had told him earlier that the reason he became involved was that he dreamed one day of becoming the speechwriter for the president of the United States. Noble let Paolo's more personal statements go unchallenged.

The director and Noble suspected that the roles Seymour and Paolo played were innocuous relative to the others. They believed Chase was instrumental in aiding and abetting Simon with his banking transactions, to what degree, they still didn't know. They assumed Hank was not only the direct link to the president—but also more likely— a direct link to Simon.

The interrogation had been going on for over five hours, and everyone needed a break. Each had eventually made his way through the breakfast goodies, but by then the remaining pastries were stale and the coffee was cold. The director offered them an opportunity to stretch and take individual breaks to the men's room, escorted by an agent.

Meanwhile, Director Scott and Noble recapped the morning's events.

"Are you planning on giving these guys immunity for their testimony?" Noble inquired.

"I don't know yet, it depends on what more they have to say. What I do know is I want the bigger fish—I want Simon—and I want this game to end!"

—

As they reconvened for round two, several large boxes of pizza arrived from Papa John's, along with two six-packs of Pepsi. After granting them a few minutes to fill their plastic plates, pop the tabs on their soda cans, and settle back into their assigned seats, they continued.

The director opted to move to Chase next, and this time he chose to conduct the interview. Twisting in his chair to face Chase squarely, the director started the dialogue by asking him to explain, in full, his relationship with Simon.

To everyone's surprise, he unhesitatingly described the time when Simon established a bank account, at his branch bank in Boston, and deposited a sizable amount of money. "As a high-net-worth client, it was my responsibility to court him, during which time we became friends." He explained how Simon convinced him to attend Harvard, even to the point of helping him through the admissions process and lending him the tuition money.

The other three envisioned what the admissions process entailed as they smirked.

Chase paused, having noticed their expressions, looked away, and focused on the carved initials in the center of the table. Regaining his composure he continued, "Years after Harvard, when I was promoted to CFO at the National Depositors Trust Bank in New York, Simon requested I give him access to the bank's online banking system." This time looking straight at the director, Chase averred, "I knew no reason to distrust Simon, and I was indebted to him for the help he had given me!"

Still trying to divert his eyes from the others, he couldn't help but notice the disappointment on their faces.

"Shortly after I granted access to the bank's database, Simon assured me he only planned to set up several untraceable accounts to transfer the funds out of the community bank in Boston, which still retained the 'trust fund' money from Uncle Rob." With genuine sincerity, he admitted, "To this day, I don't know why I agreed to let him use my computer and password to access the system."

The director appreciated Chase's candor and suggested they move on to talk about his subprime theory described in his thesis. "I found it surprisingly prophetic, considering what is currently happening in the financial markets," the director observed in a complimentary tone.

Evidently, the director hit a raw nerve, because instantly, Chase became noticeably withdrawn. He slouched in his chair, clutching his Rolex so tightly that his knuckles appeared as though they were attempting to puncture the skin. Then suddenly, he sat upright and announced with complete composure, "I engineered the financial system meltdown—but I believed it would be short-term."

All eyes darted to Chase, wide-eyed in disbelief.

As everyone regained his composure and settled back, Chase submitted. "Simon pointed out that we were in the eleventh hour of the campaign, and we needed something to take the electorate's focus off the war on terrorism and refocus it on the economy at home." He reminded the others that the challenger was stronger in foreign affairs, one of Baari's weaknesses, and was a threatening miscalculation on the part of La Fratellanza.

"Simon said we needed to foment an economic crisis, a crisis he assured me could be reversed after the election through some of his machinations. He insisted he had a plan in place, and was confident the current administration could manage the crisis for at least the next three months, past the upcoming election. Simon promised that once Baari was in the Oval Office, he would administer his 'antidote,' as he called it. I foolishly believed him because he had always delivered in the past," he ended in a whisper.

Chase understood that Simon considered it vital to the outcome that he hype the causes of the subprime fallout and leak it to the media. "I crafted a self-serving white paper and sent it anonymously, to Bill O'Reilly at Fox News, and to the editors at *Mother Jones*, *Politico*, and *The Weekly Standard*, along with a few other investigative journalists. It appeared to be enough to spur the media to go full speed ahead," he offered apologetically.

Then his remorsefulness quickly turned to defensiveness, and he began spewing some of the rationale Simon had used to prep him. He attempted to make the case that when a company goes bankrupt, and the government bails it out with the taxpayers' dollars, it is not necessarily a financially unsound strategy. He pointed out, that in many cases, the government forces the company to restructure, and when it returns to financial stability, the company repays the government at a profit to the public.

Chase cited the situation in 1970, when Penn Central Railroad almost went bankrupt, before the government granted it $676 million of loan guarantees. It used the money to consolidate other struggling railroads, thus becoming Consolidated Railroads, or Conrail. Then in 1987, the government sold Conrail to private capital for $3.1 billion.

"Do the math," he crowed, feeling he had regained his stride.

Citing another example he pointed out that, in 1971, the government bailed out Lockheed with $1.4 billion in loans. Then in 1977, the company was able to repay all loans, plus an additional $112 million in associated fees.

Chase finally ran out of steam and, feeling defeated, admitted, "I understand it is risky business when the government gambles with the taxpayers' dollars, and it doesn't always pay off."

The director and Noble could detect from the faces of the others that they honestly thought the subprime crisis was their lucky break—the event they needed to turn the tide of the election toward their candidate.

In opposition, and in chorus, they avowed they would have never supported such a dicey proposition, even if Simon had requested it of them.

Chase once again focused on his Rolex.

Paolo was furious. "If I had known what you had done, I could have crafted responses for the president to address the issue. More important, we might have been able handle the crisis in the early stages, instead of allowing it to get out of control!" Paolo stormed.

From the look on Seymour's face, he was even more outraged than Paolo, but chose to keep silent for the moment.

Hank, of course, had no problem speaking out. His outrage was even more vigorous, but his rage was born out of ego rather than a duty to country. He believed that Simon should have kept him more intimately involved, especially regarding his conspiracy with Chase. He considered himself not only the president's alter ego, but Simon's as well.

Director Scott and Noble sat back, deciding to let the verbal punches fly until nothing further was uncovered. They wanted to avoid the possibility of La Fratellanza recognizing the speed with which the entire plot was unraveling.

During the earlier testimonies, members of the group had confirmed that Hank was the person most directly connected to the president. Now waiting impatiently for his turn, and in an irate state, the director thought it an opportune time to have him speak. He interrupted their subdued free-for-all and launched into his interview with Hank.

Hank wasted no time spewing an abundance of information, mostly claiming that he was the sole creator of the president. "I picked a young radical off the streets of Florence and turned him into the most powerful man in the world." He did give a nod to Simon, who had first encountered Hussein Tarishi in Florence, in the early nineties. "But it was I who gave the president his voice, a voice promoting a progressive socialist agenda as the new form of government."

Finally, he stepped down from his soapbox, relaxed, and then calmly outlined the most astounding details about the actual grooming of the president.

Hours had passed, Noble had replaced the memory stick in the recorder several times, and everyone was exhausted, but something was still missing.

There was a vital piece of the puzzle they lacked.

Hank was the only link between Simon and the president, and the director believed there was something Hank wasn't telling them.

It was time to turn up the heat.

He abruptly interrupted Hank. "Our country is in the midst of an economic crisis. Unless we find Simon, I will ensure that each of you is convicted of defrauding the United States government," he warned. "The crime is a class E felony under the section of the penal law 195.20, and it carries with it a sentence of five to ten years in a federal prison."

Hank, resisting the director's threat, continued to yack as if the director were not present. Unrelenting, he returned to his soapbox and continued with his previous rant. "I created the president; I personally schooled him and prepared him to run for the Senate, and then the presidency. And you are threatening me?"

The director, unmoved, let him continue, even though he was already aware of most of what he divulged; Paolo had covered those details in his informal statement to Noble. Hank did give, however, specific information about his time with Hussein in Florence, facts which the director and Noble were not aware.

I still have a hard time grasping the fact that Simon, Baari, and I were all in Florence at the same time. The director reflected, shaking his head.

Hank persisted, but this time uncharacteristically in a measured, soft tone. He spoke as though he was slowly composing his message as the words were leaving his mouth. "Simon asked me for a seemingly innocuous favor, but now that I know Chase's part in precipitating the financial crisis, I have additional information that might be useful."

The others in the room could see Hank was visibly tormented by the fact he was not a complete insider with this president. Now with great curiosity they all listened, as his brothers jointly thought—*What else don't we know?*

"Long before the subprime scandal was disclosed, Simon asked me to introduce a friend of his to Senator Baari," Hank disclosed. "He was an economist Simon met at Harvard who was currently working in a low-level position in the Treasury Department. Simon said he was brilliant but wasn't much of a self-promoter, and thought meeting the senator would give him a boost, encouraging him to aspire to a higher level."

Now everyone was waiting for the proverbial shoe to drop.

Hank admitted he arranged the meeting, and Senator Baari believed he was a likeable, competent chap. Then the senator asked him to follow his career closely.

"I honestly thought it was quite innocent, that it would lead nowhere, until the crisis began. Then a month later Simon informed me that he had sketched out a recovery plan and had given it to his friend, the economist." Hank then looked directly at Chase, who was now making eye contact, and said, "He called it his 'antidote.'"

With this news, everyone became extremely uneasy, the director and Noble included.

"Please continue," urged the director.

Hank, his speech even slower and more measured than before, continued. "Simon insisted that after the inauguration, when President Baari started to assemble his cabinet appointees, he wanted me to ensure that Baari appoint his friend secretary of the Treasury. He punctuated his support by emphasizing his candidate was best equipped to see the country through these difficult economic times."

"And was he appointed?" the director asked.

"Yes."

The director and Noble bolted out of their chairs and left the room, with the video still rolling.

The gang of four sat frozen in their seats, not moving or speaking, only eyeing each other furtively.

—

Hamilton and Noble agreed they had a lot of explosive information, but still needed time to sort through it all. They were stunned to think the secretary of the Treasury might be involved in some way, so they needed to proceed with extreme care. In the meantime, they couldn't afford to let any of their deliberations leak to the president, the secretary, or to Simon.

They both believed La Fratellanza had been less than altruistic, but truthful, telling all they knew. But La Fratellanza's loyalties still ran deep, and they weren't prepared to trust them entirely.

"Go back to my office and start sorting through what information we have collected thus far. Look for any clues that will lead us to Simon," Hamilton ordered.

—

Director Scott returned to the interrogation room, this time without Noble. He informed La Fratellanza that he was sequestering them for the night at a safe house nearby, with a promise of comfortable quarters and proper meals. They were required to surrender their cell phones, and any outside communication was prohibited. He assured them it was for their own safety, and that he and Noble needed time to fathom Simon's next move.

"The game is not over," he said, reiterating Noble's earlier remark. "Only you, along with Noble and me, know what has transpired in this room today. The agents standing by are not aware of any facet of this case, and it would be in your best interest to limit your conversations for the evening," he cautioned. "Noble will contact you in the morning with information regarding the next steps."

The director bade them a good night and left the room with the last of the memory sticks.

After arranging to have the table moved back to his conference room the next day, he headed to the White House.

23

THE DISCOVERY PHASE

On returning from Langley, the director arrived in his office to find papers strewn across the desk and Noble tapping furiously away at the keyboards of the two secure computers sitting in front of him.

Noble turned around abruptly as Hamilton entered the room. Obviously, he was startled, and Hamilton could see that Noble was utterly exhausted.

Time was not on their side—and they both knew it.

"We have to keep the president at bay and definitely find Simon," Noble underscored.

"First, we have to make sure all of our facts are straight. We are dealing with the presidency of the United States, and there is no room for error," Hamilton reminded him. "There is one more piece of the puzzle I must clarify. I need to speak with the Treasury secretary." Hamilton told Noble he had called the secretary's office before leaving Langley. "Fortunately, he was meeting with the president at that moment, so I requested that the secretary stop by my office before he walks across the street to the Department of the Treasury."

It was early evening, but within the hour, he was in the director's conference room.

Noticing the red light blinking on his phone, Hamilton announced, "The Treasury secretary just arrived. I'll return shortly."

—

After a few pleasantries, Hamilton asked the secretary, "Do you know a man named Simon Hall?"

"Yes."

"How did you come to know Simon?"

The secretary mentioned he had taken a few classes with him at Harvard. He didn't know him well until a few years ago, when he ran into him at a local restaurant near the Capitol. "We met occasionally over a period of a few months and chatted about the topic of the day. Usually it involved the financial crisis, a subject about which he was well informed."

"Mr. Secretary. With all due respect, who conceived the idea for TAP, the plan to buy the toxic assets from the banks?"

"I believe it just gelled from the many conversations I'd had with Simon and a number of my peers, but it was Simon who suggested the broad outlines of TAP," he replied quite openly.

The secretary conceded that he was quite surprised to learn how knowledgeable Simon was about the Savings and Loan crisis of the late eighties and the current crisis. "His expertise goes far beyond technology. He often spoke of how profitable it proved to be for the government when it bailed out the S-and-Ls. The TAP concept emerged out of those conversations," the secretary admitted.

The director then asked what he suspected to be true, yet no less frightening. "Did you hire Simon to design and program TSAR?"

"Yes," he replied, with a bit of hesitation. The secretary, feeling the need to defend his decision, explained he knew Simon's reputation for being a phenomenal computer systems designer and programmer, and he screened him, along with many other highly qualified applicants. "Simon, however, was head and shoulders above the rest in his dossier and performance. Ultimately, I hired him to design the Treasury Sorting Accounting and Reporting system you referred to earlier as TSAR. TSAR was a directive from the president," he stated, this time with more self-assurance.

"It's my understanding, correct me if I wrong, that the purpose of TSAR is to track the outgoing and incoming TAP funds?" questioned the director, looking for confirmation.

"Yes, that was the original plan, but the president also requested it track many of the other appropriations, and direct certain portions of those funds to be set aside and used for certain designated projects of the president. Some observers referred to them as his 'pet projects' to fulfill his campaign promises."

"So TSAR became a sort of 'self-appropriated' account separate from the TAP funds?" probed the director.

"Yes, one might call it that."

"Excuse me, Mr. Secretary, but didn't you think it was outside the realm of acceptable government appropriation standards?"

"It falls within the broad outlines used in the past. Furthermore, I serve at the pleasure of the president," he stated with unusual sternness.

When the director asked him if anyone other than he and the president knew about TSAR and the president's special account, he responded, "No one else, except Simon, the programmer, of course. Director Scott, may I ask you what this is about? I'm not comfortable in the way this is all unfolding."

"To answer your question, at the moment I'm not sure."

The director extended his arm, signaling the meeting had ended. He shook the secretary's hand and thanked him for his time.

They both left the conference room and the director returned to his office.

—

When Hamilton walked into his office, he noticed the large bag sitting on his desk. He had forgotten that he had made a stop on his way back from Langley; it was dinner. After some urging, Noble agreed to take a break and chow down on some beef with broccoli and the house fried rice Hamilton had picked up from the Hunan Palace on Vermont Avenue, one of Noble's favorites. Although the food had lost its original appeal, both of them were too hungry to care.

As they sat in the two overstuffed chairs on opposite sides, deftly wielding chopsticks, Noble informed Hamilton he had made a phone call to Natalie earlier. "I knew she'd be worried, and I needed to explain why Paolo wouldn't be returning home tonight. More important, I reiterated that she must not discuss any of the information Paolo had shared with her." Noble sensed from the tone in her voice that she was fearful. Natalie said Paolo's last words to her were not in his normal passionate voice; it was a voice filled with uncertainty. "I assured her everything would be clearer in a few days and asked her to be patient."

Earlier, while Hamilton was meeting with the Treasury secretary, Noble was in the midst of constructing a timeline of events known to them thus far. Before Noble began to review those events, Hamilton first apprised Noble of his conversation with the Treasury secretary, which uncovered a vital piece of the puzzle.

"Are you ready?"—Hamilton cautioned—"Simon designed TSAR!"

Noble was dumbfounded, even though he had considered it a possibility; hearing confirmation of what he had suspected left him speechless. In part, it was a reaction to having to add another factor to an already long list of issues, creating an even more massive problem to solve.

"My friend, we've shared many dinners together dominated by a lot of lively conversation, but did you ever think we would be discussing a breach of such magnitude?" Hamilton bemoaned as he shook his head.

"I'm pleased my inquisitive nature produced results, but the results are frightening—I'm afraid I am the one who got us into this mess." Noble sighed.

"Thank God you did!"

As Noble was poking at the remains of the fried rice, he reviewed with Hamilton the events, starting with those that followed the subprime scandal, many of which were revealed by Chase during his interview. "For the moment, we can set everything aside, all that preceded the financial crisis, and the time spent on grooming the senator and then the president."

Hamilton agreed. "We have the evidence on Baari's culpability, which we can deal with later, but evidently the game did not end with the inauguration."

"All the facts thus far point to Simon, and in turn—as you've discovered—are linked to TSAR," Noble said dejectedly.

—

A few days before they held the interrogations, Noble explained to Hamilton that on a whim, he decided to locate his personal copy of his thesis. "Seeing my name in print on the cover page of Simon's thesis was troubling and persistently intruded on my thoughts at a time when I needed to focus. I wanted to find my copy, once and for all," he fumed.

Fortunately, he discovered it in one of the first boxes he unpacked. He was relieved to learn his thesis had been in the spare bedroom closet all that time. When Noble dumped the contents of the box on the rarely used bedspread, he had found it also included several other mementos from his days at Harvard. Among them, he found the tuition slip receipts and stub of an airline ticket to Kansas, all paid for by none other than Simon, on his personal credit card.

"I immediately deduced that if he had the balance due on his credit card automatically debited from a checking account, I might be able to trace those charges to a specific bank account, and hopefully an address," Noble exulted.

"And were you able to locate the bank where the account is held?"

"Yes. I traced the credit card to an account at the National Depositors Trust Bank branch in Menlo Park, California, which included an address for the account, Simon's address!"

Noble admitted he was able to access, or rather hack, Simon's bank account, and found the usual monthly utility charges and debits for a few grocery stores and gas stations, but nothing that indicated a slush fund. It appeared Simon had paid Noble's expenses out of his own account; it was not compliments of Uncle Rob, based on the available information. "Why

Simon would do that is another question."

"Perhaps, he had true affection for you, born out of admiration," Hamilton counseled.

"I don't find that very comforting."

"Take comfort in that fact that we might be getting closer to finding Simon."

Hamilton immediately requested that the Menlo Park Police send two officers to the address, with instructions only to report their findings, along with strict orders not to apprehend the occupants.

As it developed, the police officers reported the house was stripped clean, and it appeared no one was living there. Menlo Park was not equipped with an evidence team, so Hamilton immediately contacted the chief of police, an old friend, at the San Francisco Police Department, and asked for a personal favor. He requested that the chief send a crime investigation unit to look for prints, hair, anything that could link it to the occupant. He explained it was a rather delicate situation and requested that the chief instruct his crime lab not to pursue the investigation further, only to turn the evidence over to him. Hamilton didn't care to mislead a friend, but in this instance, he thought it was vital; the fewer people involved the better.

Much to their disappointment, all they were able to retrieve was one lonely fingerprint on a light switch near the front door. Hamilton and Noble hoped that, somehow the print would lead them to Simon—and if not to Simon directly—then to his next move.

—

While Noble continued to review the events with Hamilton, the computer beeped.

An e-mail had just arrived from the police chief in San Francisco, with the scanned fingerprint from the Menlo Park house. If Simon had been fingerprinted in the United States, there would be a record of him in the system. That print was now in the process of running through IAFIS.

Still sitting in the overstuffed chair, Noble kept glancing across the room at the computer on the right side of the credenza and noticed the data on the screen was still spinning. With great anticipation, they hoped the print might be their first significant break in the case, a print that came to them under an unconventional set of circumstances.

Minutes later, in the midst of their discussion, they heard the computer beep again, this time— *No Match*—appeared on the screen. "There is one more thing I can try. It may not be over," Noble opined. As he dashed across the room, he announced, "I'm scanning the print to Interpol. Perhaps they will find a match. All we can do at this point is wait for a response."

Noble returned to his comfortable chair and continued to summarize the events on his timeline since the financial meltdown began. "We learned Chase was the catalyst behind the subprime scandal, which caused a panic in the housing and financial sectors, resulting in the rapid decline in the markets around the world. We know it occurred during a heated campaign, while the focus was on the war on terror."

"And we personally witnessed the crisis shift almost overnight to the economy, and Senator Baari became President Baari on January 20, 2009," Hamilton added.

"And we surmise La Fratellanza, specifically with Simon at the helm, was behind the manipulation." Noble questioned, "What was the motivation?"

"That is the trillion-dollar question." Hamilton winced.

Adding to the "what we know" scenario, Hamilton reminded Noble that he was able to confirm from his conversation with the Treasury secretary that the purpose of TAP was to transfer over $700 billion to various banks to buy their "toxic assets," which in turn would help free up credit to stimulate the economy. He also discovered the secretary knew at the time, of the announcement about TAP, that there would be a time lag in the distribution of stimulus funds.

"Therefore, the secretary was urged to make a 'promise' of funds to be forthcoming, which would be paid out in the near future," Hamilton assumed.

"Very interesting; in Chase's testimony, he claimed the strategy was his idea. In a separate white paper, he suggested a 'promise' of stimulus funds geared to placate the public would be enough to calm the financial markets," Noble recalled.

Initially, the strategy produced some positive effects, visible in the world markets, a fact on which Senator Baari capitalized and reaped the political advantage from the intervention.

"Whether it was manipulated or not, he won the election," Hamilton carped.

Based on the further testimony of Chase, they discovered that President Baari ordered the Treasury to force the major banks to draw on the TAP funds. Then the Treasury was to refuse to allow the banks to repay the money until after some proposed stress test, scheduled for April. They touted the stress test as a means to determine the financial health of the banks.

"Am I to assume the communications chain of our government starts with Simon, formulated by Chase, passed on to Hank and then to the president?" Noble asked caustically.

"Obviously, the government intends to create the appearance of cracking down on the financial industry, and to simultaneously create the appearance that TAP is successful, based on the illusion of positive effects," Hamilton implied.

"Let's not forget the other extraordinary piece of information I discovered when questioning the Treasury secretary. The president has earmarked not only the returning TAP funds, but also other appropriations. He plans to use his 'private stash' for social programs he intends to push through."

Noble chimed in, "In fact, Hank confirmed in his testimony that the president's agenda had always been to push through as many of his social programs as possible, before the end of the president's first term, presuming it would ensure his reelection."

"It was the 'strike while the iron is hot' political theory, known to generations of politicians," Hamilton reminded him.

Their thoughts returned to the young economist, the same Harvard graduate Simon had befriended, the same person confirmed as secretary of the Treasury. Finally, with utter wonderment, the enormity of what they had uncovered struck them like a bolt of lightning.

It was a moment in history that would leave an indelible mark.

They sat staring at one another, feeling a mutual chill, quickly followed by a sense of dread. They also recalled that it was the president, who wanted yet another type of tsar—and it was Simon who had programmed the Treasury Sorting Accounting and Reporting system—as a holding tank for an astronomical amount of funds.

"TSAR was structured to house the $700 billion in TAP funds, but also many of the other appropriations, such as the $300 billion in Housing and Economic Recovery funds, and the $700 billion for an Economic Stimulus Package. The list keeps growing," Noble recapped, with dismay in his voice.

Hamilton grimaced. "I also asked the secretary how they tracked the funds going in and out of TSAR. He said he received a daily report indicating the balance from the previous night. He appeared unconcerned, stating that everything looked copacetic."

"There are many ways around that!" Noble said, his words bursting out. "Simon could have corrupted the reporting system, but then it could be easily discoverable if another programmer were asked to create a different report. If he were truly transferring the funds out of TSAR, he could have programmed a parallel system to run in tandem. One reporting the actual transfers, Simon's transfers, deducting the funds from TSAR, and then crediting the funds to the parallel system, one virtual dollar for each dollar removed."

"Then both systems would appear to seem accurate and in balance?"

"Exactly!"

"Could all this have been orchestrated by Simon?"

Ignoring his query, Noble asked, "More important, was Simon siphoning off those funds, and if so, for what use?"

Hamilton, unnerved as all this was shaping up, avowed, "If this is truly the case, and if Simon is siphoning cash, we not only have to find him, we have to find some way to retrieve the misappropriated funds before it becomes known to the world at large. I officially authorize you to play 'unofficial' hacker one more time. You must locate and tap into all of Simon's bank accounts, and into TSAR. We need to follow the money," Hamilton insisted.

It was 1:30 a.m., and Noble especially needed a clear head before infiltrating the various banking systems. They needed to go home and get some rest.

Noble wrapped up his work and they left 1600 Pennsylvania Avenue. Hamilton headed for Dupont Circle, and Noble headed for Georgetown.

24

THE DOUBLE STING

The director arrived at his office the next morning at seven, only to find Noble already working at his desk.

As he offered Noble coffee that he had picked up en route to the office, the computer signaled an incoming message. Noble spun his chair around to face the computer and opened the e-mail immediately.

It was from Interpol.

He turned back around slowly to face Hamilton. While the color drained from his face, he stumbled over the words, "They found a perfect match."

At that moment, things went from awful to devastating.

Hamilton bolted over to the computer screen to find it was not Simon Hall. The lonely fingerprint belongs to Mohammed al-Fadl. He was the head of a notorious sleeper cell, a cell the agency had been tracking for years.

"Incredible." Noble gasped. "The photo in the upper-right-hand corner staring back at me—is the face of Simon Hall."

"If Simon is Mohammed al-Fadl—who is Hal Simmons?" Hamilton shouted.

Noble had the same thought as he turned and asked Hamilton to retrieve the file with the evidence he had collected from the apartment on Cambridge Street. Without questioning, he scoured through his files and found the folder, and then handed it to Noble. Noble removed the copy of the partial print that led nowhere fifteen years earlier and compared it to the scanned fingerprint he received from San Francisco.

Thanks to improved technology, he was able to make another perfect match.

"Unbelievable. Hal Simmons, Simon Hall, and Mohammed al-Fadl are all one and the same," Noble spoke in a shocked voice.

The one indisputable fact they had was that Mohammed al-Fadl was responsible for orchestrating the bombing of several U.S. embassies around the world, killing citizens and military officials. He still had ties to al-Qaeda, but operated independently, and his lone-wolf activities in the United States had always been a mystery.

"Now we are searching for Mohammed al-Fadl, our Simon?" Hamilton queried with absolute astonishment—then he recalled something—"In the interrogations, we discovered Simon had set up an account at Chase's bank in New York. It was the same bank where Chase allowed Simon access to the banking system."

Noble started tapping the keyboard furiously once again. He began with the account number from the Menlo Park branch of the National Depositors Trust Bank and found it linked to the account in New York. Earlier, when he accessed Simon's bank account at the Menlo Park branch, he guessed at possible password choices, until he typed in 1-1-2-0-0-8, the date of the presidential election. He got the user ID on the first try, using *Fratellanza*, exposed initially when Paolo described the computer lab in Simon's apartment.

"Simon is brilliant, but luckily for us he is prone to being a creature of habit." Noble smiled.

Noble continued to hack into the numerous accounts on Hamilton's secure computer, until he was able to access Simon's account in New York. Probing his other accounts, he discovered, involved a labyrinth of transactions. Simon would enter one transaction, but would immediately transfer the funds through a maze of ten randomly selected banks before the money rested in the designated account. Noble found it extremely challenging to trace the pattern Simon used, but eventually he was able to locate twenty new links to other accounts in banks across the United States, all with sizable account balances.

However, none was sizable enough to suggest the source was TSAR.

Hamilton had learned a lot about the Internet, thanks to Noble. They both agreed Simon must have designed his own wire transfer system, piggybacking off the system at the National Depositors Trust Bank. Without a special system, it would have been impossible to manage a task of that magnitude.

"If you can locate Simon's wire transfer system and hack into it, we can shut him down, at least for the time being."

"You know Simon well enough by now to know he always has a backup plan," Noble replied.

"I have a hunch this case might come full circle. Hear me out. Check to see if Simon transferred any money overseas, specifically to a bank in Italy."

While Noble tapped away, Hamilton called the agent standing guard at the safe house. He instructed him to inform the La Fratellanza group that they would need to remain there for the weekend. In addition, the agent was to mention that Noble expected to meet them Monday to explain the situation, and then they might be free to go. Hamilton couldn't run the risk of any of these gifted intellectuals contacting Simon, and especially the risk of Hank contacting the president, at least until he had an opportunity to speak with the president first.

It took most of the morning with Noble hammering away on the keyboard, but he was eventually able to uncover several straw parties, dummy corporations, phony foundations, hawalas, and overseas bank accounts linked to Simon's bank account in New York.

Simon had wire transferred the TSAR funds to the New York account and then from the New York account to multiple accounts in banks in Zurich, Singapore, Liechtenstein, Luxembourg, and Bermuda, and one other account located, not in an offshore protected account, but at the Banca Nazionale, an elite private bank in Florence, Italy.

Hacking into international banks, where secrecy dominates, proved to be more difficult, but within several more hours, Noble was able to calculate that the total balance in the accounts combined was slightly over $500 billion from funds originally transferred from TSAR.

Hamilton was horror-struck.

"Can you reconfigure the online banking systems for Simon's accounts, so when he accesses them he can only see the account balances, but not the transactions, and at the same time freeze his ability to transfer funds?"

"It may take some time, but I won't give up until I do."

Stepping out of character, Simon had carelessly used the same user ID and password for most accounts. Noble also deduced his carelessness was attributable to his vintage overconfidence. He told Hamilton he was now sure that Simon had also installed a "backdoor" in each of the banking systems.

"The backdoor is an undocumented method a programmer uses to access a program or a computer," Noble explained. "Initially, it provided a way for the programmer to stop a program or computer gone awry, but later its use was for more nefarious reasons. It has been reported that unscrupulous programmers, hired to design a system, would use the backdoor as their 'private entrance,' returning later to steal data or money."

"I suppose I could use Simon and TSAR as an example," Hamilton scoffed.

"Precisely!" Noble quickly changed Simon's access on the front end by resetting the passwords. Now he had to work, at breakneck speed, to change the security code needed to access through this backdoor program.

First, he faced an enormous task—he had to find the backdoor.

—

The sun had been up for hours and the clock had just peeked past nine. It was Sunday morning, and they both had worked tirelessly through the night. Noble, visibly exhausted, was still beating on the keyboard at a rapid pace, obviously driven by nervous energy. Hamilton, awakening from one of his power naps on the sofa, was designing a strategy for their next steps.

Moments later, Noble bellowed, "*I got it!*"

Startled, Hamilton walked over to his desk as Noble rambled. "I kept thinking about Mohammed al-Fadl, not Simon, and Mohammed's affiliation, al-Qaeda. I had tried everything related—*jihad, Taliban*, frontward and backward—they were fruitless attempts. Until it dawned on me Simon is Mohammed, and suddenly the copy of Simon's thesis with my name as the author flashed before my eyes."

"I'm not following."

"Simon would tell me periodically that I was a much better programmer. Knowing Simon's ego, I assumed it was an insincere compliment to co-op me to join his group." Noble exclaimed, "I am better!" Then he muttered, "But I have his number. He's still trying to set me up."

He admitted that when he first read Simon's thesis, he was still stung at the thought of his name on the cover and was so distraught by the events that he merely skimmed his dissertation. Therefore, he went back and analyzed it more scrupulously, and that is when he discovered how Simon proved his theory on the penetrability of computer security systems.

"I had focused on a password, not on a programming code. Simon developed a programming code that would unlock the security code for almost any system. He called it NOBLE"—he smirked—"which stands for **N**o **O**perands **B**etween **L**ogical **E**xpressions."

"You've really lost me now," Hamilton admitted, totally puzzled.

Noble attempted, in laymen's terms, to explain that an operand is a computer instruction that describes an object or objects capable of manipulation. "For example, two plus four equals six; the two and the four are operands, and the plus is the operation; six is the result of the operation; if there is no operand, the result of the operation is *nullary*. Everything becomes null, or zero, and then the user receives a 'runtime' error message."

As Hamilton's eyes started to glaze over, Noble conceded, "I know its complex, but that's how I am going to shut down the backdoor. Simon will be totally locked out from all his accounts. Just stay with me, try to follow this through, okay? Simon wrote a program to allow the code to execute repeatedly, finding itself in a loop, until after what seems like an infinite number of tries, will eventually give up and permit access to the system."

"Like knocking down a locked door," Hamilton volunteered.

Noble smiled and continued to clarify how Simon must have written a basic code, probably in C, which is a general-purpose programming language used to develop portable application software. It is the best code to use because it supports the use of pointers. These pointers can address the location of an object in memory, specifically the executable security program files.

"All of this occurs at millions of bytes per second, and in a short space of time Simon would have access to the programmer's code. He may need to decompile the files using a hex editor, which is quite easy, even for an amateur hacker. I know it sounds complicated, but the fact is, it is quite simple."

"Do I really need to know all this?" Hamilton protested.

"Come on, it's exciting. Think of it as the opposite of when you enter an incorrect password a number of times and you are locked out, but instead of locking you out, it gives up and lets you into the system," Noble noted excitedly. "Now I have his programming code, so I can get in and reprogram the source code, changing the backdoor access, basically disable NOBLE—and, more important—disable Simon."

By that evening, he was able to lock Simon out of all online banking options with the exception of retrieving his actual bank balances. Of greater importance, he was also able to lock him out of TSAR, where Simon had set up a parallel system with the ability to transfer funds undetected.

Of great significance, Noble was also able to determine the money Simon had siphoned out of TSAR was not from the various appropriations accounts, including the TAP fund, but was being drawn from the president's personal "holding account"—his self-appropriated funds.

"Am I to assume Simon has a heart, or a twisted sense of humor?" Hamilton asked.

"The latter."

Noble wasn't finished; he had one more overreaching trick up his sleeve.

He described how he was unable to shut down the parallel wire transfer system because Simon had designed it to tie into the bank's own wire transfer system. If he did shut it down, he would have totally destabilized the National Depositors Trust Bank's online system.

Noble admitted that there was a high probability Simon had other accounts he might have missed, so to avoid the risk of further transfers going unnoticed he created a type of virus. "Actually, more like a Trojan horse. This doesn't infect and spread, but attaches itself," he explained. "Each time Simon tries to transfer money from any account I haven't discovered, my Trojan horse will act sort of like a GPS tracking device and will attach itself to the transaction. I can then continuously trace the transfer of funds to its final destination."

"Brilliant."

"Oh, and anytime Simon attempts to transfer money, I will receive an SMS text message on my cell phone. Then all of Simon's bank accounts can be shut down individually."

"I take it back, extremely brilliant," Hamilton cheered.

"Thank you!"

Noble cautioned that Simon could possibly decipher his moves and eventually reroute to negate the changes in the programming code. "Hopefully we'll have him in custody by then." Noble smiled.

"Hopefully, which is why we really need to move with alacrity," Hamilton emphasized. "While you were working your magic, I made a few calls. After invoking national security as a reason and citing the president's approval"—Hamilton grinned—"I was able to get the Swiss Central Bank to agree to set up several accounts in four different banks in Zurich. They understand that large sums of money will be deposited over the next several hours, and they will put a lock on the funds until further instructions are given. These are the account numbers. I want you to park all the funds from those accounts to Zurich, except for the one at Banca Nazionale."

"But Simon has over five million euros in that account."

"Hold on! Then set up fund transfers from Banca Nazionale, so that every hour, two hundred and fifty thousand euros are transferred to one of the accounts in Zurich. Continue the transfers until there are only one hundred thousand euros on balance. All these transfers must be untraceable," Hamilton insisted.

"That's not a problem, but what is the plan? Now I'm the one who is confused," Noble conceded.

"As soon as Simon discovers his account balances are zero, and his Florence account is dwindling, with no way to access it, he will be forced to go to Florence."

"So the only way he can get to the remaining money is to present his bank card in person. Nice move."

"I relish the thought; the fact he will see the money siphoned off and will not know by whom." Hamilton smiled, mirroring the huge grin on Noble's face.

—

Noble was busy performing his wizardry, and Hamilton was occupied assembling the components of a sting operation to nab Simon.

He knew he'd have to involve the Carabinieri and the Polizia di Stato, from his prior experience in Italy, and justice would be slow and deliberate. This time he needed it to be swift and sure. Hamilton knew he also had to involve Interpol, and it was certain to become a circus, one that would rival any classic Italian comedy. He believed the only way to ensure they captured Simon was for him to be there personally to manage the operation.

First, he had to persuade the president to appoint him special consultant to oversee the sting operation. While the director was about to submit his resignation, he still had three more weeks before he would become a private citizen. He knew convincing the president to send him to Florence would not be an obstacle.

This will be my last case. The case closes when I finally apprehend Simon, he thought with delight.

While Noble set up the Zurich accounts and transferred the funds on one computer, Hamilton was on the other computer adding Hal Simmons, Simon Hall, and Mohammed al-Fadl to the Terrorist Watch List. When adding the names to the watch list, he added specific instructions:

If that person attempts to leave the country, he is not to be apprehended. It is imperative he reach his final destination.

Also noted in the data was that the suspect did not pose an imminent threat.

Hamilton grabbed one of the secure cell phones from his bottom desk drawer and retrieved the phone number. The airline personnel were instructed only to send a text message to mobile number (202) 555-9876, with the flight number, destination, and time of arrival. Then he booked himself on a flight to Florence, leaving Monday night.

By eleven o'clock Sunday evening Noble had successfully locked Simon out of his bank accounts and had secured the stolen funds. There was nothing more he could do. After some prodding, Hamilton convinced Noble to go home for some real shut-eye—but before his head would hit his pillow, he had one more thing he must accomplish.

Now he had to control the president.

The ground floor of the White House was shrouded in darkness, except for the illumination from the corner office, where Hamilton gathered his notes. He spent the next few hours scribbling a summation of the events that led to the most horrific crime ever perpetrated against the people of the United States. As he sat at his large executive desk facing the two secure computers with a long and slender fluorescent light casting a glow, Director Scott began to dictate. The door was locked from the inside.

25

THE PRESIDENTIAL AWAKENING

After a few hours of sleep, a hot shower, and several cups of eye-opening black coffee, Hamilton prepared to return to his office at the White House. Before leaving home, he called the president's secretary and scheduled an appointment for later that day, stating the reason was of vital importance.

Hamilton was of the opinion the American people had the right to know what had transpired, reasoning it would be the only way to prevent it from ever reoccurring. He also firmly believed that now was not the time. In his view, it was imperative for the future of the country, first, to recover from the current crisis damaging its very foundation. He was well aware of the burden he would carry until the day came to expose the president.

He returned to his office with three more hours to refine his thoughts.

After reviewing all he had uncovered in the past seventy-two hours, he finally had his script resolutely planted in his mind. The hour had arrived.

Feeling confident, he left his office, walked up the stairway, and met with the president.

Meanwhile, Noble was on his way to the safe house.

—

Noble informed the gang of four of the director's offer of full immunity in exchange for their complete silence. He emphasized that they were never to mention the conspiracy or their connection to the president and Simon.

"Under no circumstance should any of you try to contact Simon. If Simon contacts you, you are to notify me or the director immediately, no one else," he cautioned. Noble, sensing he had La Fratellanza's full attention, warned forcefully, "If anyone ever divulges the plot, we have a well-documented case on file to convict you. You will be personally responsible for bringing down the president of the United States and your fellow brothers, not to overlook the personal humiliation to your families." Noble delivered that warning with more harshness than any of them had ever witnessed from him.

"The fallout is undeterminable," he postulated, a truism he wanted to resonate in their thoughts.

He suggested strongly to Hank, Paolo, and Seymour that they extricate themselves from any employment connected to the White House as gracefully and expeditiously as possible. "I will work with each of you to devise a strategy to disentangle yourself in a way which will not jeopardize our case against Simon." Looking directly at Hank, he said, "No one is to alert the president or interfere with this case in any way." The vigor of his voice made his message undeniably clear.

While Noble spoke harshly, he was also hiding the feelings of compassion he felt toward those in the room, the men for whom he had ample affection and respect. However, in a split second of reflection, he had a flashback of his parents, an occurrence he couldn't explain. Nevertheless, it prompted him to join in the betrayal they felt from Simon, who at one time, he had also considered a special friend.

Having no other recourse, the gang of four agreed to comply with all the conditions. Each assured Noble what he wanted most was to restore his life, and to be free of Simon at any cost.

"You are free to leave. I'll be in touch."

—

As the director sat in the Oval Office across the desk from the president, he thanked him for his time. Then he offered, "Mr. President, if there are any recording devices turned on, may I suggest you turn them off during this meeting."

The president looked at the director inquisitively and then said, "There are none."

I know it isn't true, but I gave him the opportunity, he mused.

The director informed him how he had uncovered a plot orchestrated by a well-known terrorist, Mohammed al-Fadl, who also used the assumed name Simon Hall. He purposely didn't attempt to make the connection between Simon and the Treasury secretary, who he assumed was another unsuspecting pawn.

"This terrorist infiltrated TSAR and siphoned over five hundred billion dollars, specifically from an account authorized by you to house appropriations to be allocated to special projects."

The president looked directly at the director with total indifference, or so it seemed. In the past, the president proved adept at masking his emotions.

The director assured the president he had pulled all stops to locate the TSAR funds. He cautioned this was only the first step to uncover an array of bank accounts, dummy corporations, phony foundations, and other entities, to house such incredible sums of money.

"We also uncovered several hawalas where we believe some of the money had been laundered and then transferred into several bank accounts overseas. I'm sure you are familiar with hawalas, rumored to be widely used by terrorist organizations," he said, in an attempt to get a rise out of the president. He added, "They are also referred to as hundi."

"Of course!" the president snapped.

Staying on script, the director explained he had received information that led him to a home in Menlo Park, California, where Simon Hall had resided. When the agents arrived, the home was empty, although they did find a lone overlooked credit card receipt. This document led them to a bank account, which revealed a wire transfer and deposit to a bank in Florence, Italy.

"In the meantime, I placed Mohammed al-Fadl and Simon Hall on the Terrorist Watch List." Guarding his words closely, he continued. "In the last hour, I received a text message from an airline agent reporting a man fitting the description, using the name Simon Hall. He booked a one-way ticket to Florence, Italy, leaving tomorrow."

Obviously, the director did not reveal the entire conspiracy and rearranged the sequence of events. Now there was enough plausibility for the president to send him to Florence to stop the unraveling before there was a complete exposé.

"I instructed the Italian authorities to freeze the bank account, but the bureaucracy is a nightmare, which is why I am requesting that you send me to Florence to hasten the process," he said, dodging further revelations. "I believe it is essential I oversee any attempt to capture Mohammed al-Fadl and recover the funds," he appealed. "Of course, I will have to work closely with Interpol."

The director paused for a moment to provide an opportunity for the president to respond, but none was forthcoming.

"Mr. President, how ironic, this case should take me back to Florence, a place where I believe the entire plot has its roots. I am sure you are aware that earlier in my career, I worked for the DSS," he affirmed. "What you may not know is while I was posted in Rome, I was also assigned to a case in Florence."

The director proceeded to tell the president about the stabbing and brutal murder of an American tourist. "At the end of the trial, the jury acquitted an African street vendor of the crime," he explained, "a crime that has remained unsolved."

He watched the president's face carefully as he continued.

"It took place in 1995," he enunciated clearly. "At the trial, a young Libyan, a witness for the defense, provided a cogent alibi for the defendant. It was his powerful testimony that convinced the jury to acquit."

As the president continued to maintain his renowned detached stare, the director persisted.

"The Libyan's name is Hussein Tarishi, and I have irrefutable evidence you are that person."

Even at the mention of the name, the president's expression changed ever so slightly, "Why should I believe you?"

"Mr. President, I know your family was killed in a bombing in 1986, and you survived."

Then Hamilton unfolded a litany of facts that proved he had all the damaging information in his hands.

"Where are you going with this?"

The director's muscles tensed, but his face mirrored the same lack of emotion, as he laid out his case.

"The country isn't ready for another crisis, and for the sake of its citizens, I will not disclose the deception, or the missing funds, at this time." Hamilton leaned forward, looked the president in the eye, and said coldly, "You may remain in office and govern as you see fit without my interference, under certain conditions. In the meantime, you will have the full support of my agency at your disposal, to help protect your identity. However, the time will arrive when I will inform the American people, but I don't know when that day will come."

The director's muscles began to ease as he moved into the catbird seat. He took the opportunity to suggest the president would be wise to slow down the spending and unwind some of the elements in his social agenda. "Your downfall is more likely to come from the electorate than from me," he reasoned.

The president continued to appear disinterested in his homily, but the director was positive he understood the gravity of the situation.

"I am submitting my resignation to be effective the end of this month, and I request you appoint my assistant Noble Bishop as interim director while I am in Florence. Once I capture Mohammed al-Fadl and recover the funds, I will not be returning to the U.S.," he informed the president. The director then requested he ensure Noble receive a smooth confirmation as the new director of the SIA.

Saving the best for last, he said, "There is a flash drive containing all the evidence to prove how an illegal immigrant became the president of the United States. The flash drive is in safekeeping with a third party, who is not privy to the information, but should anything suspicious happen to me or Noble, the third party has instructions to send the evidence to the media. Mr. President, out of respect for the presidency, and if it is still in my control, I will give you sufficient warning as to when the information will be released."

Still smarting at the mention of the media, the president shifted in his chair for the first time, and stated sharply, "I need to discuss this with my people. I will get back to you."

"No, Mr. President, you are not to speak to anyone about this, including the First Lady!" the director spoke firmly. Toning down his rhetoric, he calmly stated, "I am willing to shoulder this heavy burden to protect my country and its citizens and I expect you'd want to do the same. Sit back and enjoy your presidency, Mr. President—and I will get back to you."

The director had expected Baari to display his typical arrogance and narcissism. He knew he had ambitions to remain in office, and possibly for a second term. Moreover, he was confident Baari knew he had no other choice but to comply.

In his usual fashion, the president cocked his head, stared down at the director with his steely black eyes, and stated dispassionately, "I get it."

Director Scott understood this was his cue to leave.

And he did leave, for Florence, Italy.

PART TWO

26

THE DIRECTOR'S SWAN SONG

Hamilton had vivid memories of being in Florence, recalling the times when he wasn't working on the investigation, or sitting in on the trial. His thoughts often drifted to those days when he would wander the streets aimlessly, enveloped by the city's magnificence.

Every corner—every turn—offered a piece of history.

"It truly is a wonderful, beautiful, walking museum," he would gush to his friends at home.

Always a history buff, he called to mind, *Florence dates back to 59 BC, when Julius Caesar established the city as a settlement for his soldiers,* a fact he still found amazing. He recollected the city was a direct route to Rome to the south, and along with the Arno River, it quickly spread out and became a thriving commercial center. Today, it's best known for the flourishing art and cultural achievements spawned by the Renaissance, starting in the thirteenth century, and continuing until around 1600.

April is the time of year when the city air smells fresh and the Tuscan countryside radiates green, so when Hamilton disembarked from the plane in Florence and took his first breath of fresh air, the floodgate of memories opened. But he understood this trip was for a more crucial investigation than the one that brought him to Florence in the first instance.

—

An agent from Interpol, assigned to lead the investigation, met Hamilton at the airport.

"*Benvenuto*, welcome Director Scott, my name is Enzo Borgini."

Egad! Another Italian investigator, thought Hamilton, and then shook his hand and responded, "*Mio piacere*. It's a pleasure to meet you. Forgive me. My Italian is a little rusty."

"So is my English." Enzo smiled.

Enzo was of average height with a friendly face and a pleasing personality. Although he was young and new on the job, Hamilton sensed they would be compatible. Moreover, he was hopeful this lad would defer to his age, knowledge, and seniority. The fact that the Carabinieri and the Polizia di Stato had to report to Enzo made the relationship even more workable. Now feeling confident that he'd actually be running the show, he felt this time around justice would be swift and sure.

As Enzo drove Hamilton to his hotel, they discussed his plan for the stakeout at the Banca Nazionale. Enzo confirmed that everything was good to go, starting later that day. Florence continues the age-old version of the *siesta*, so the bank was closed for lunch and would not reopen until three; it was currently 11:45 a.m. Therefore, Enzo agreed to return to pick up Hamilton from his hotel in two hours, giving him time to shower and grab a bite to eat.

—

As they sat across the street from the bank, Hamilton asked Enzo to review the instructions he had given the bank manager.

"I told him that when a person approaches him with a bank card for account #Z829164, he is to release all the money in the account, placing it in the black satchel."

"The satchel I gave you at the airport."

"Yes, the same one. I then instructed the manager to call my cell phone and give me a description of the person making the withdrawal."

"And now we wait." Hamilton smiled.

The plan was not to apprehend, but to follow the money. While Hamilton hoped Simon would withdraw the cash, his intuition told him Simon probably would not enter the bank himself, but would send someone in his place. They needed the description, so they could follow their suspect when he left the bank.

They waited for days with no sign of Simon or his mule.

—

Stakeouts are tedious at best. However, Enzo devised a rather pleasant routine to break up the boredom. For the next few days, between the hours of one and three o'clock, they would wander a few blocks to the Mercato Centrale, the central market in the Piazza San Lorenzo. This was where Enzo introduced Hamilton to a gourmet's delight, Perini's Gastronomia, or delicatessen, inside the market.

"You like?" Enzo grinned.

"I've never seen a more wonderful display of prosciutto; there must be hundreds hanging from the ceilings and off the walls. And look at that marvelous display of cheeses, olives, and sauces. It's a foodies' paradise."

"They spread their treats on rounds of bread known as crostini," Enzo explained.

"Yes, I remember them well."

"I'm sorry. I had forgotten you had lived in Florence before."

"I don't know how I missed this place; I had no idea it even existed. It's amazing."

"Wait until you taste their panini," Enzo said, tempting Hamilton.

Standing behind the glass cases that displayed a sumptuous feast of goodies were four busy but good-natured souls, ready to sate their customers' hunger in a very pleasurable way.

Hamilton ordered a panino with prosciutto, provolone, and sun-dried tomatoes. On his first bite, he agreed it was incredible. On the second day, he learned not to request the panini ingredients but to leave it up to the maestros behind the counter. By the third day, they were all old friends and on a first-name basis.

Two of the talented foursome were the owners, Andrea and Moreno, along with their adept associates, Simone and Flavio. Like so many Italians, the "Perini Foursome" treasured loyalty, and if a customer returned often, it would establish a warm relationship in no time.

It was also during these lunch breaks that Hamilton's Italian started to regenerate, as he became more proficient while conversing with his new friends. They also turned the tedious stakeout into tutoring sessions, much to the delight of Enzo, who was proud of his language.

—

On the fourth day, they finally received the long-awaited call from the bank manager.

He described the carrier as a tall, slender woman in her late forties, attractive, with black hair pulled back in a bun. She was wearing a pair of tight jeans and a white shirt, with a red scarf loosely tied around her neck.

"She presented the bank card and explained that she couldn't access her account online," the bank manager reported to Enzo.

"Tell her you will allow her to withdraw the money in the account. Then place the cash in the black satchel as we agreed," he directed the manager.

Hamilton and Enzo sat on the park bench across the street and waited for her to leave the bank.

"How much money has she withdrawn?" asked Enzo.

"One hundred thousand euros, all that remained in the account. I wanted her to walk away with something, hoping she would lead us to Simon."

"You suspected all along he wouldn't show?"

"He is too smart to take that kind of risk."

Enzo provided the Carabinieri with her description and instructed them to follow on motorcycles at a safe distance. He stressed again that they were not to apprehend her. Hamilton and Enzo would follow on foot.

"I forgot to tell you; I placed a tracking device inside the zippered pocket of the satchel she is carrying. This GPS device will ensure we won't lose her and—more important—Simon."

"Do you know the streets of Florence well enough to operate that thing?" Enzo asked. Knowing the answer, Enzo graciously offered to manage the GPS device as they trailed behind her. Moments later, he pointed. "There she is, walking out of the bank now."

The woman crossed the street and weaved in and out of buildings, through the Mercato Centrale, past the Duomo, and then entered the Piazza della Signoria, where she disappeared in the crowd.

Almost instantly, Enzo spotted the woman again standing among the crowd at the entrance to the Uffizi Gallery. She appeared to be holding something in her hand, which they assumed was an admissions ticket because the attendant allowed her to enter.

Minutes later, Enzo flashed something in his hand, but it wasn't a ticket; it was a badge.

The attendant permitted access to both Enzo and Hamilton.

"There she is, up ahead," whispered Hamilton.

"She is heading to the south end of the west hallway, which is usually where groups normally gather to gain access to the Vasari Corridor."

"Wouldn't that be an odd choice for her to meet Simon?"

"Yes, considering the Vasari Corridor is not that easily accessible. It is open to the public, only by appointment on specific days, within posted hours. You need to book in advance, and if the attendants manning the ticket desk at the gallery don't have a sufficient number of people, they cancel," explained Enzo.

"I read the only way out was at the other end, in the Boboli Gardens behind the gates of the Pitti Palace," assumed Hamilton, looking for confirmation.

Enzo, on the same wavelength, immediately called the Carabinieri who had followed them on motorcycles. He instructed them to stand guard outside the Corridor exit in the Gardens, with orders to apprehend the woman if she left the Corridor without the satchel. Otherwise, they should permit her to leave and then the Carabinieri should continue to follow her.

They refocused on the woman standing in the hallway, apparently waiting for someone. At that time, there were only a few other people roaming about in that section of the gallery. Hamilton and Enzo maintained a safe distance, attempting to look like tourists.

"Do you know about the Vasari Corridor?" Enzo whispered. Then, answering his own question in an attempt to show off his knowledge, continued in a hushed voice. "It is a historic landmark. You know it is considered one of the most astounding architectural masterpieces of the Renaissance. Incredibly, it was built in 1565. Only the Grand Duke Cosimo Medici and his family, the de facto rulers of Florence, accessed the corridor."

"Yes, I recall," Hamilton interrupted in a quiet tone. "Cosimo Medici commissioned Giorgio Vasari, the brilliant architect of the time, to construct a covered passageway. It leads from the Uffizi, which was his place of work, across the Lungarno dei Archbusieri, continuing along the north bank of the Arno River. Then it crosses over the top of the Ponte Vecchio, and meanders across the peaks of houses. Finally, it ends at the Palazzo Pitti, the final home of the Medici family."

"Bravo." Enzo smiled.

"Is it true that the duke did not want to have to fight his way through the crowds, nor tolerate the smells emanating from the butchers establishments located on the bridge?"

"Exactly," Enzo replied. "Therefore, after the Corridor was constructed, they removed the butcher shops and replaced them with goldsmith shops, which remain there to this day."

"I know it was considered an amazing feat for its time, but aren't there many who feel it destroyed the character of the original design of the Ponte Vecchio?"

"I've heard those comments, but those who have been in the Vasari Corridor and have seen the collection of over a thousand portraits and paintings dating back to the seventeenth and eighteenth centuries, think differently," Enzo espoused. "And did you know that Vasari had to get permission from the owners of the buildings, those the Medici didn't own, so the Corridor could be built through each of their towers?"

"You have me stumped, Enzo. Please continue."

"Make note of the odd turn we make after passing over the Ponte Vecchio. It is because the Mannelli family, one of the owners of the towers, refused, and Vasari had to build the Corridor around the tower."

"Fascinating, bravo to you," Hamilton jested, returning the smile.

While taking pleasure in sharing their prowess with history, they spotted the woman entering the door to the Corridor with a group of about twenty people. As they stood chatting, they were also eyeing the others in the group assembling in the west hallway, but none so far fit the description of Simon.

"I have a strong feeling she is planning to meet Simon in the passageway." Hamilton presumed.

"It's logical, given the difficulty to access the Corridor. The timing had to be perfect. Otherwise, she could have met him at a number of other locations," Enzo offered.

The last of the group entered the Corridor.

Enzo again flashed his badge to another attendant standing guard at the entrance. This time he signaled the attendant with a finger over his lips to be silent.

Ignoring Enzo's gesture, the attendant whispered in rapid Italian, loosely translated, "You won't find any criminals in there. The guide is a well-known curator from the Uffizi Gallery."

After they had passed through the entrance to the Corridor, Hamilton noticed the guard had secured the door behind them. Now he knew the only exit was at the other end of the Corridor, in the Boboli Gardens.

They followed the group down a long stairway, and then turned left, then right and another left, to begin their tour over the shops on the Ponte Vecchio. Crossing over the Arno River they walked past stunning paintings from the Medici collection, on both sides of the Corridor. Hamilton and Enzo, forced to ignore the magnificent renaissance art for the time being, focused solely on the woman. Her height and hairdo made her easy to spot at the head of the group, which was fortunate because the GPS, which had worked perfectly out-of-doors, stopped receiving a signal.

"These thick walls are known to cause problems, especially with a cell phone. Thankfully, mine is on a police radio frequency."

"I'm not overly concerned. We know the only way out for her is at the other end, where the Carabinieri are waiting," Hamilton remarked.

Enzo and Hamilton then began to focus on the male faces, scanning them carefully, readying themselves to pounce on Simon. It was difficult to sift through the crowd, but after three or four glances, it was obvious he wasn't among them. There wasn't a man or a woman, other than the guide and the woman they were following, who appeared to be over the age of twenty.

As the group turned left to cross over the Ponte Vecchio, Hamilton and Enzo could see her more clearly. This section of the corridor, characterized by a series of panoramic windows, faces west, looking out over the Arno. At that time of the day, with the sun low in the sky, light streams in illuminating the corridor. They spotted the woman still in the lead, behind the guide, but they couldn't see if she was carrying the satchel.

"Simon is not in the crowd. It is just a group of students, led by the guide and the woman," Hamilton observed.

They continued to keep a safe distance, but were still able to hear the guide giving his spiel, in English, about the history of the Vasari Corridor and the importance of the art it houses.

"Call the Carabinieri and tell them to detain everyone when they exit the Corridor. Caution them to be circumspect. We don't want to alert Simon, should he be lurking in the crowd. And also remind them he is dangerous," Hamilton whispered. "Have the Carabinieri also locate the attendant who was manning the entrance to the Vasari Corridor and detain him as well."

After a few more twists and turns in the Corridor, they arrived at the Boboli Gardens. The woman exited along with the others. As instructed, the Carabinieri held the group off to the side.

Hamilton and Enzo, the last to exit, were alerted by the Carabinieri that she did not have the satchel, nor was anyone else in the group carrying a case that fit the description. Quickly, they looked again at all the men, hoping they had made a mistake, but there was no Simon.

Rapidly Enzo instructed the Carabinieri to take the woman, the guide, and the attendant to the *Questura*, the local police station, and hold them for questioning, but to release the students.

Then a cold reality set in as Hamilton and Enzo realized the woman must have passed the package to someone in the Corridor.

That someone must have been Simon.

Concluding their last hope of capturing him was to double back, they ran through the half-mile Corridor, maneuvering through the twists and turns. Next to the entrance door at the opposite end, laid the satchel they had pursued.

Enzo gasped. "The money is gone! The only thing remaining in the satchel is the tracking device in the zippered pocket."

"Simon must have been behind us all the time. He had perfectly timed his entrance into the Vasari Corridor and his exit out the same way, making for a clean escape," Hamilton reasoned. "After fifteen years, I was finally within several feet of Simon, and now he has vanished again," he said in anguish.

His heart sank as the severity of the situation overwhelmed him. His feelings were indescribable, but with great despair, he said, "I'm not sure it will serve any useful purpose, but let's go to the Questura and question our trio."

—

First, Hamilton interviewed the Uffizi guide, who spoke English.

"My name is Eugenio Bresciani and I am a curator at the Uffizi Gallery. I was giving a private tour to a group of students, at the request of Professoressa Ducale. Is there a problem?"

Evidently, he had received a call from her the day before, requesting the private tour and specifying a time the group would be available.

"The professoressa is a good friend and I was happy to accommodate her."

"I'm sorry for the inconvenience. You are free to leave," Hamilton said apologetically.

"*Buonasera*," the guide said as he bade them farewell.

They then spoke with the attendant.

Mocking Enzo as they entered, he asked, "Did you find any bad guys?" Enzo translated, and then conducted the attendant's interview using the questions Hamilton provided. "Did anyone else enter the corridor other than the group of students, before or after Director Scott and I arrived?"

The attendant explained that the professoressa said her colleague was going to be slightly late. "She asked me to allow him to enter and direct him toward the group. He arrived about five minutes after you did. I found it odd that this man didn't join the group, but left only a few minutes later."

With a feeling of dread, Hamilton showed the attendant the photo of Mohammed al-Fadl.

The attendant confirmed he was the colleague.

It was Simon.

"*Grazie, può andare.*" Enzo thanked the attendant and told him he was free to go.

Professoressa Simona Ducale was the next person to be questioned, and fortunately, she spoke English.

They discovered from the guide that she was a professor of art, teaching classical drawing and painting at the Florence Academy of Art. They asked her about the satchel, first telling her that they knew she had picked up the money from the bank and left it in the Corridor for Simon.

"I was only helping an old friend, someone I had known many years ago," she stated brusquely. "I ran into him at a café a few days ago." She shrugged.

Slowly her story began to change, along with the sound of her voice.

After another hour of interrogation, she finally admitted she met Simon at his hotel and then spent the day and night with him in his room.

"Simon is staying at the Hotel Galileo on Via Nazionale," she revealed hesitantly.

Hamilton suspected her relationship with Simon was more intimate, and he took the opportunity to ask her one last question, which he knew would seem odd to the others in the room, but he forged ahead anyway.

"Did you notice a tattoo on either of Simon's wrists?"

"I can testify to the fact that Simon has no tattoos anywhere on his body," she answered nonchalantly.

Hamilton knew that would have been his link to La Fratellanza, the ***LF*** tattooed on the underside of his wrist.

They had extracted all they needed from her, and released the professoressa.

—

Hamilton and Enzo rushed to the Hotel Galileo, near the Piazza San Lorenzo, only to find his hotel room unoccupied.

As the forensics team searched the room for evidence, Hamilton stood emptily glancing out the window with thoughts of the other apartments in Cambridge and Menlo Park, and feared they'd find nothing.

Astonishingly, the view from the room was the Banca Nazionale, the bank they had been staking out for the last four days. Off to the right he could see the park bench he and Enzo had occupied. "Simon had been watching us all the time and then must have followed us into the Vasari Corridor," he lamented.

As expected, there was no other evidence of Simon having been in the room, except for the concierge's positive identification of the man in the photo—the photo of Mohammed al-Fadl.

27

THE POSTSCRIPT

Oddly, the director was feeling an unusual sense of calm. All told, he was unsuccessful in apprehending his nemesis—he was a day away from ending his personally rewarding career—and he was about to telephone the president to mislead him once again.

First, there was one other call he felt compelled to make.

"Congratulations on your promotion, Director Bishop."

"Condolences would have been more appropriate," Noble replied.

"Bad news, my friend—Simon escaped."

Hamilton told him how it all came crashing down: the woman, the Corridor, and the empty satchel. He then reviewed what he planned to tell the president, primarily, that Mohammed al-Fadl had escaped and with the TSAR funds.

Of course, Noble knew that the TSAR funds were safely tucked away in several accounts in Zurich, where he personally transferred them. Hamilton had made the decision that the funds should remain in Zurich until the situation was resolved.

"I was able to confirm our suspicion that the president was planning to siphon some TSAR funds for his own special social programs, and unless you've decided differently, he will have to report those funds as actually missing, not expropriated," explained Noble.

"What irony."

Nodding in agreement to himself, Noble continued. "According to Paolo, the president already had a planned statement reporting that the General Accountability Office made an accounting error, based on inaccurate numbers given to them by the Treasury."

"I see he is already playing defense on the assumption I wouldn't be able to retrieve the funds," Hamilton concluded.

"Hank told Paolo he suspected the Treasury was slow in producing numbers because they were covering up their own slush fund, which notion he passed on to President Baari."

"He really knows how to stir the pot." Hamilton snickered.

"Hank also alluded to the premise that the Treasury's accounting system was shady at best, but allowed the confusion could be attributed, in part, to the process itself." Noble further explained that it was his understanding the bailout funds provided to the banks were in exchange for warrants, in the form of certificates. That gave the Treasury the right to purchase shares of bank stock at an established price. If the stock price exceeded the set price, the profit would be returned to the taxpayers via the Treasury.

"So the prevailing question is—whose profit is it?" Hamilton jeered.

"The problem intensifies in that any attempt to track the warrants, the stock prices, and the flow of money in all directions, was a nightmare, to say the least."

"One has to wonder if that confusion were part of the overall strategy," Hamilton posed.

Despite this, the thrust of Baari's speech to launch the blame game, in the end, the accounting error, a colossal one at that, was likely to go unchallenged. "It will be forgotten by the limited attention span of the American public, much to their detriment." Hamilton sighed. "One day we'll make it right," he promised. "If anything should happen to me, before that day arrives, you know where to find the flash drive and the memory sticks."

"You may be in Florence, but other than that you're not going anywhere, my friend."

"I tried to state the case as clearly and completely as possible, to give it authenticity, and not sound like the ramblings of an old man. Noble, there are still so many unanswered questions lingering in the back of my mind."

"They are probably the same questions rolling around in my head, left unanswered," Noble responded. "For example, how many Simons and Baaris are in our midst?"

"Was it all just about the money?" asked Hamilton.

Noble reminded him that La Fratellanza created the "game" to satisfy their intellectual appetites without recognizing Simon's motives. "But there had to be more to it," he insisted.

Both of them believed there was a huge void of unanswered questions that engendered a belief there was a grander and more sinister plot yet to unfold.

"Is Simon only the tip of the iceberg?" Hamilton questioned.

"There has been speculation that the Muslim population in the U.S. was increasing exponentially, and by the year 2048, the U.S. would be a

Muslim country. Even the Catholic Church has expressed some concern that in five to seven years, Islamism could be the dominate religion of the world." Noble reported. "Chances are there are some terrorists in the mix."

"A frightening thought," was Hamilton's reaction.

"Is it that implausible?" Noble replied.

"I think not." Hamilton quoted Muammar al-Qaddafi, who was caught saying, "We don't need terrorists, and we don't need homicide bombers. The fifty-plus million Muslims in Europe will turn it into a Muslim continent within a few decades."

Noble repeated, "I ask again, how many more Simons are embedded throughout the world?"

"All these questions are too frightening to contemplate at the moment," Hamilton cautioned. "For now, Simon has vanished, the other co-conspirators have been silenced, and the president is under control."

Noble held the phone to his ear and listened to Hamilton on the other end of the line as he continued to defend his decision, repeating the same sermon he had given many times before.

"You know as well as anyone, my career has been devoted to the protection of the American people. Despite my misgivings, I was convinced it would have been devastating to the country if I were forced to bring down the president, especially after the dire effects of the financial crisis. As hypocritical as it may seem to others, my only course of action was to maintain as much stability as possible until the country found its bearings."

"Does that include protecting the TSAR funds?" Noble asked.

Knowing Noble knew the answer to his own question, Hamilton ignored him and continued to proffer that if he did expose the president, he believed it would provide an invitation to the terrorists to step into the breach. That led him to the inevitable conclusion to remain silent, so the president could complete his term, and possibly run for reelection.

"It is not my role to interfere with history, although some would say I tinkered with it slightly, but it was for objectively just reasons."

In an effort to let Hamilton know he made his point, Noble assured him. "I have always supported your reasoning and I will stand by your decision."

Evidently, it was not assuring enough, and Hamilton continued, but this time it was as though he knew he was making his final appeal.

"Our country is incredibly resilient. It has managed to struggle through some of the most difficult economic and social times. I have the utmost confidence that the American people will be equally resilient when this information comes to light. The timing, however, is without question the most critical factor, but it will be the one I will take to its conclusion," Hamilton assured Noble. "For sure there will be new crises, some perhaps brewing beneath the surface today, but those challenges, my friend, will be yours."

"Thank you, Hamilton," Noble responded with a hint of sarcasm.

"Let's stay in touch, and perhaps you will plan to visit me one day. I must now call the president."

—

With a bit of awkwardness, the director called the president on his private line and informed him that, regrettably, Mohammed al-Fadl had escaped with the TSAR funds, an obvious fabrication.

"Mr. President, there is nothing more I can do, although Interpol will continue to hunt him down," he said honestly. Then with less sincerity, he allowed, "Perhaps they will be able to retrieve some of the funds, but it will take time." Receiving no response from the president, the director took the opportunity to pour a little salt in the wound. "You might find it advantageous to begin crafting a statement to explain the lack of accountability of the funds, before anyone else discovers they are missing."

The president's breathing sounded heavier from the other end of the line, but there was still no verbal response.

At that moment, not having to face the president's gaze, he reminded the president of the conversation they had before he left for Florence. "The basis for releasing the evidence early also applies to Director Bishop, should anything happen to him," he cautioned, with the most authoritative voice he could muster.

Then Director Scott officially tendered his resignation to be effective immediately, and the president accepted.

The director ended the call by wishing the president good luck—said *Arrivederci*—and hung up the phone.

28

THE REUNION

It was the dog days of summer in 2016. The Republicans had control of the Congress and the Democrats reigned in the White House. In essence, the American people had maintained a balance of power by reelecting Abner Baari to a second term. The line-up of wannabes for the 2012 presidential race had been dreadful, so Baari had been a shoo-in. And although his veto pen was still in overdrive, the wheels of government were stuck in neutral.

Progress inside the Beltway was minimal, but conversely, the economy was on a steady upturn, spending was on the downturn, the deficit clock was ticking in reverse, and the socialist agenda was slowly unwinding. Jobs were still in short supply, but that problem was finally starting to sort itself out. There were visible signs of hope in the minds of the American people, that democracy was not threatened and capitalism had regained its vitality.

Then, as President Baari's second term was coming into the home stretch, the wannabes resurfaced—and thus far—the former SIA director, Hamilton Scott, who had retired seven years earlier, had not divulged the conspiracy that had been unleashed on the country and its citizens.

—

The current SIA director was fully engrossed in his work when his secretary entered the office with a priority envelope. As he glanced at the label in the center and spotted his name in all caps, DIRECTOR NOBLE BISHOP, SIA, his eyes turned upward to the return address.

What a pleasant surprise to see the words Florence, Italy, he reflected, knowing exactly from whom it came. It brought to mind the frequency with which Hamilton spoke of his beloved Florence, as they chatted often following his retirement. Noble was never certain whether it was a coincidence or providence that led Hamilton back to Florence. Certainly, it seemed like a quirk of fate that he went back to wrap up the most notable case of his career, and then remained to make it his home.

Curious, Noble opened the envelope. Enclosed he found an airline ticket and a letter, requesting him to fly to Florence. Interestingly, the request was not from Hamilton, but from an Aldo Tancredi. The only other information contained in the message was an address that he recognized as Hamilton's: Piazza degli Unganelli, Viale della Torre del Gallo, 5. The airline ticket had an open date, but Noble felt a sense of urgency. Perhaps it was the lack of information which led him to that conclusion.

Conveniently, it was August, although it wouldn't have made a difference in any event. Much of Washington was in shutdown mode, most issues tabled, and there were no compelling national security issues to address, at least not that morning.

Noble cleared his calendar and arranged to leave the next day, for a place he had romanticized but had never actually visited.

—

During much of the flight, he filled his head with reminders of the infamous "sting," Simon's escape, and the Zurich accounts. In spite of the churning thoughts, and the excitement of seeing Hamilton again, Noble managed to get a few hours of sleep before the plane landed.

Much to his surprise, his flight was on time, arriving at exactly 10:55 a.m. at the Peretola Airport in Florence, Italy. "I can't believe I'm actually here," he muttered under his breath impulsively, being only twenty minutes from the historic center of the birthplace of the Renaissance, a place he always cherished. Over the years, he had read many Florence guidebooks, as he planned trips that never happened. Though he had received many invitations from Hamilton, work always seemed to trump his desire to travel.

This unplanned trip, however, would be different. Noble had discerned that it was not going to be a sightseeing tour; what he hadn't discerned was that it would be a life-changing event.

It was Sunday, hot and sticky, not much different from the city he had just left. As he exited the airport with relative ease, he became concerned that his inability to speak Italian would hamper him. *Fortunately,* taxi *is an international word,* he thought as he glanced up at the signs spelling out the word, and then followed them to the inevitable line forming to his right. Settling in to the back seat of the taxi, he presented to the driver the address that he had written on a separate piece of paper, not trusting his pronunciation. Finally, he was on his way to see his dear friend and as excited as he was to see Hamilton again, he felt a tinge of trepidation. Perhaps it was the unorthodox delivery of the invitation.

During the entire drive into central Florence, Noble's eyes darted as he tried to take in the wealth of sights. Listening to the melodic church bells in the distance added to the emotional experience. What seemed to be only minutes later, the taxi pulled up to a modest villa in a small piazza, with a spectacular view of the historic center of the city. When Noble stepped out of the taxi, he marveled as he turned and looked below at the picturesque scene. He could see the amazing red dome on the Santa Maria del Fiore, referred to as the Duomo, the Italian version of a cathedral.

"Astonishingly, the cathedral was started in 1296 and completed by the famous architect Filippo Brunelleschi, who constructed the dome over one hundred years later in 1436," he blurted out to the driver, instantly feeling embarrassed, realizing this probably was not news to him. "Excuse me, but I had read certain facts repeatedly in the various guidebooks I'd collected, and I feel as though the Duomo and I are old friends."

"She is a friend of mine as well." The driver smiled.

The amiable driver helped Noble with his luggage and directed him to the entrance of the director's home.

—

Noble rang the doorbell and anxiously waited to see Hamilton open the door. He was taken aback when a rather distinguished looking man greeted him. He was tall, with graying temples and a pleasant face.

"*Buongiorno*, I am Aldo Tancredi. You must be Director Bishop."

"Yes, and thank you for the invitation, although I am curious to know why," he replied, as he shook the extended hand. He was stunned to discover the person who mailed the package was the valet, and later learned he was also Hamilton's caregiver. Noble was pleasantly surprised and thoroughly grateful to find Aldo not only spoke flawless English, but pleasingly, with melodic undertones of his mother tongue.

Taking his luggage, Aldo ushered Noble to a large living room and announced, "Please wait here. I will let the director know you have arrived."

The director. It seems strange to hear him say that; he was my director too, Noble reflected.

Approximately a half hour later, time enough for Noble to take in the opulence of the room, Aldo returned. "The director is ready to receive you now."

As they entered the bedroom, Noble felt tears welling in his eyes, partly for the delight in seeing his mentor after so many years, and partly for the sadness in seeing the frail, elderly man before him. Hamilton was a shadow of the man he had once known. The only recognizable features were the shock of white hair, which he always had sported, even as a young agent, and the piercing dark blue eyes that seemed to peer into one's very soul. Without those characteristic features, Noble would not have recognized him. He approached the side of the bed and took the hand before him. He held it firmly, but gently, in his own.

"Welcome, my dear friend." As Hamilton spoke, Noble was startled to hear a voice from the past, a strong, husky voice, not to be mistaken for anyone else.

They both smiled at the sight of each other, embraced in the Italian fashion, and then chatted over an hour catching up, primarily on what was happening in Noble's life. Much to his surprise, Hamilton didn't ask a lot about the Washington scene, and he never mentioned the president, or Simon.

I assume that will come later, pondered Noble.

Aside from their numerous encounters over the years, Simon's escape and its ramifications sealed their destiny. Still there were questions that only Hamilton could demystify. The revelation would have to come later as he was beginning to tire, noticeably.

"Perhaps you might want to rest for a while?"

"Yes, but when I wake up, would you like to go for a walk? Although you'll have to do the pushing," he grinned, glancing at the wheelchair stationed in the corner.

"I serve at the pleasure of the director," Noble said, returning the smile.

Noble left the room and went to look for Aldo.

—

Finding Aldo was more difficult than Noble had expected. What he discovered was that what appeared to be a modest villa was actually quite sprawling. As he wandered from room to room, taking in the extensive and expensive art collection, he wondered aloud, "How could Hamilton possibly afford all this on his modest retirement salary?" He based his assumption on his own salary as the current director.

The sight of Aldo at the end of the corridor interrupted his thoughts.

Noble, starting to feel the need for a nap himself, wanted to know where his bedroom was located, but first he wanted to know about Hamilton's health, a subject that he had steered away from initially.

As Aldo walked Noble toward his room, he said with a tremble in his voice, "The director is only going to live for a short while longer." He explained that, just a month earlier, the director received a diagnosis of an inoperable brain tumor that was growing rapidly.

"Will he suffer any pain?" Noble asked hesitatingly.

"Although there is some intracranial pressure, the director is not suffering," he assured him. "Eventually he will go into an altered state of consciousness and then drift off to sleep. The doctors assured me the director would die peacefully."

When they approached Noble's room, after winding through several corridors, Noble asked, "Please wake me when the director is ready for his stroll."

Aldo retreated, leaving Noble with his luggage and his sinking feelings of the impending loss he confronted. As Noble turned to face the open door, he gulped as he viewed a large *Under the Tuscan Sun* type of room, inclusive of Florentine furniture and a fresco painted on the ceiling. For that moment, he felt he had drifted back into another century, let alone another country, and then the sorrow of Hamilton's condition returned.

Several hours later, he heard a rap on the door, and heard Aldo's melodic voice say, "*Signore, il Direttore* is ready."

As Noble dressed in preparation for his walk with Hamilton, he found he also had to prime himself mentally as well, for whatever this visit would hold.

He joined Hamilton in the lavish living room he had entered upon his arrival. He was sitting in his wheelchair, dressed in khaki slacks and a white shirt with tails out, and appeared to be more the person Noble remembered, for which he was deeply grateful. *If now is to be the last time I will see him, this is how I want to remember my mentor and the man who considered me his son,* he thought, consoling himself.

—

Leaving the villa the air seemed less heavy, and there was a slight breeze, almost cooling, compared to that morning when Noble disembarked from the plane, only a few hours earlier. Following Hamilton's instructions, Noble pushed the wheelchair along a small alley, actually a street, named Via Giramonte. "What is that marvelous smell of smoke wafting in the air?"

"It is the last of the burning from the pruning of the olive trees, a few months before. It always makes the air smell like late autumn." Hamilton smiled as he took a whiff of the scent.

Along the winding road, Hamilton chatted about his life in Florence, how fortunate he was to live in such a wondrous city, and of the exceptional care Aldo tendered. "When I was sent to Florence to oversee the murder investigation, I vowed I would one day return to this beautiful city and make it my home."

"Ironically, you couldn't have known at the time that the most important case of your career would bring you back," Noble replied, as sadness set in by the thought, *It was a case that demanded all of his energy, and consumed much of his life, and it removed him from any hope of rearing a family.*

The director, married several times, divorced, and estranged from his two children, made the agency his life, leaving no room for romance or anything resembling a traditional existence.

Thankfully, he made time for me, within and outside the agency, for which I am everlastingly indebted. Unknowingly, he gave me a family, or at least stepped in for the father I lost as a young adult. He continued to reflect as Hamilton described the view of the countryside.

As they sauntered along exchanging pleasantries, Noble was guided by Hamilton's pointing finger, instructing, "Go this way" or "No, that way." When they turned left up a long, gradual curving hill, he described the Basilica of San Miniato al Monte situated at the top. "The monastery, complete with a bishop's palace, was built in the eleventh century. The Florentines often refer to it as the 'Gate to Heaven.'" As Noble pushed the wheelchair up the hill, Hamilton continued, "The church with its bell tower, I believe, was one of the towers where Michelangelo hid from the pope's army as they invaded Florence."

"Didn't it have something to do with Michelangelo being enlisted against his will to reinforce the city walls to defend Florence against the pope's army? The fact that the Pope was a Medici and the Medici Family had befriended Michelangelo must have created quite a problem for him?" Noble queried.

"Yes, that's close." He chuckled. "Even the most competent scholar would require a Gantt chart to sort out the players involved in the multitude of invasions of Florence, not to mention their own forays."

"Certainly it was a complicated but interesting era of history," Noble acknowledged.

Finally, they reached the top of the hill. Noble was breathless, not solely from the exhausting push up, but also by the sheer beauty that lay before his eyes. As he steered the wheelchair through the piazza at San Miniato to the wall, he found a panoramic view of the entire city.

Hamilton pointed to a specific section of the wall next to a stately cypress tree on the right. "Leave me here while you walk across the piazza and look inside the Basilica," he encouraged.

Noble obliged and inside the church, he discovered a fifteenth-century tabernacle and apse, all in mosaic. His immediate reaction was to say, "Unbelievably beautiful." He took a few more moments to walk around the inside of the church and then returned to join Hamilton, and sat next to him under the cypress.

"From the vantage point where you are sitting," Hamilton said, "look to the right of the tree, and you can see the bustling historic center of Florence, with its towering Duomo dominating the palaces and piazzas surrounding it. Actually, slightly to its left is the Piazza della Repubblica, technically the geographic center of the city. Now look to the left of the tree, and you can see the rolling countryside with its gently sloping hills, cypress trees, and villas dotting the landscape. It looks like the picturesque Tuscany you'd see on the covers of coffee table books."

"Truly, it is a view of the best of two worlds. It's breathtaking." Noble granted.

While Noble sat on the wall catching his breath, Hamilton told him about his daily treks up the hill to San Miniato. "I vowed when the time was near for me to walk through the 'Gate to Heaven,' this would be the last view I'd want to see." Then softly, Noble heard him say, "It is also the view I have always wanted to share with you." With tears in his eyes, unlike the seemingly unemotional director, he spoke about how important Noble had become in his life and said he loved him like a son. Suddenly, his voice shifted as he regained his composure, sounding more like his former self.

"Have you ever received any signs of activity from Simon?"

Stunned at the abrupt transition in thought, Noble paused momentarily, then answered, "For the last six years, I have tried doggedly to trace the money, looking for clues, but the trail has gone cold and it appears Simon has vanished."

Hamilton then began to speak about the president. "I never felt there had been a right time to expose him, until now."

Noble was flabbergasted by the words "until now," and the color drained from his face.

Ignoring Noble's sudden reaction, Hamilton continued to explain that he had been following the politics—or rather, the histrionics—in the States, and felt the American people and the United States had both regained sufficient stature in the world, as the economic crisis subsided. "Now that the president is in his final year of office, it is time to ensure the American people don't repeat history. Noble, you must insure that the proper vetting takes place in the next presidential election cycle. It is vital to our national security!" he warned.

Hamilton always managed to be current on national and international affairs. He was well aware of the problems of homegrown terrorists and was alarmed at the breaches in security. Excitedly, he said, "You recall Army Major Nidal Malik 'AbduWali' Hasan who was responsible for the Fort Hood massacre in 2009, and then Colleen LaRose, nicknamed Jihad Jane, who became a radical Islamist arrested in 2010 for an assassination attempt, and Faisal Shahzad who attempted to blow up Times Square, also arrested in 2010. Just to name a few!" he enumerated forcefully. Then, looking directly at Noble and in a calmer voice, he said, "I am officially passing the mantle to you. You must determine when and how to expose the plot. You'll have to be the one to go to the president."

Heartfelt sadness reflected in Hamilton's eyes at the thought of handing off such an enormous responsibility, which he proudly considered his own. Then, with equal sadness, he apologized. "I'm sorry to have to place this heavy burden on you, but you are the only person who can protect the American people against a repetition of a fraud of such proportions. Never did I believe that such a monstrous scam was possible," he voiced with trepidation.

Noble quickly recognized the magnitude of the responsibility thrust upon him.

When he recovered from his moment of sharp reality, he asked Hamilton several questions, particularly related to his conversations with the president.

With clinical detachment, Hamilton answered all questions directly and in vivid detail.

They continued their lengthy conversation, discussing the possible approaches Noble might take to inform the president, the recapture of the TSAR Funds, and the ultimate repercussions that might ensue.

Then Hamilton began to tire.

Feeling it might be one of his last opportunities, Noble took a stab at one last question, a seemingly unrelated question.

"How have you been able to provide for yourself all these years?"

He knew at the time it was inappropriate and was unsure why it slipped out the way it did. Perhaps, his inquisitiveness once again took hold. Not fully expecting an answer, he heard Hamilton in a sleepy monotone ask him a question, one he will never forget.

"Was the Treasury ever able to determine how much Simon had stolen, before we transferred all the money out of his accounts?"

Noble knew Hamilton was not looking for an answer.

I'll never forget the look in his eyes, almost a twinkle, and the angle of his mouth, practically a smile, as he drifted into a deep sleep.

The walk, or rather push, back to the villa was quiet. This time Noble took in the views as Hamilton slumbered. It seemed like a long, slow push down the circular road taking him away from the spiritual place they had just visited. He drifted back into his thoughts as he admired the road, lined with beautiful flowering oleander trees, filled with blossoms in brilliant colors of magenta, pink, and white flowers he had overlooked on the trip up the hill.

As they meandered along Via Giramonte, behind the Basilica di San

Miniato al Monte, Noble dwelled on his conversations with Hamilton and tried to identify what he might have missed. He paused shortly, then resumed taking in the beauty of the moment, knowing that he would continue to roll over that conversation in his mind for some time to come.

—

When they returned to the villa, Aldo was waiting at the door. He immediately took over the wheelchair and pushed Hamilton to his bedroom, to prepare him for his afternoon nap.

Noble walked to his room and sat in the corner looking out toward the Duomo in the distance, as the sun hovered low, giving the cathedral a golden glow. As he stared out the window, he recognized that his life had changed forever, but he hoped he would not face the same emptiness that Hamilton experienced.

Hamilton's expression when he responded to his last question was etched in his mind indelibly. Grinning to himself, Noble recalled, *Hamilton always answered a question with a question.*

He finally conceded he was exhausted, partly because of jet lag, complicated by the new demands heaped on him. Surrendering, he decided to put his thoughts to rest and nodded off to sleep. Then there was a sharp rap on the door of Noble's bedroom, seemingly as soon as his head hit the pillow, but when he peered out the window, he could see stars in the sky and a full moon illuminating the villas dotting the countryside. Partly dazed, he saw Aldo peering through the opened door.

"Sir, would you please meet me in the living room?"

"I'll join you in a moment."

Noble freshened up, dressed, and feeling somewhat renewed, joined Aldo. Walking into the lavish room, Noble immediately recognized the grief-stricken face and knew instantly that Hamilton had passed away in his sleep.

Silence took hold of them as they shared a mutually sympathetic embrace.

Moments later, Aldo handed Noble an envelope and blubbered, "The director instructed me to give you this without delay," and left the room.

Noble sat down and was quiet, tears streaming down his face as he reminisced about all the times at the SIA, and the private times, they shared together. Eventually, he looked down at the envelope in his hand, but wasn't ready to do any more heavy lifting.

First, I need time to absorb the events of the day, a day that seemed like forever, he lamented. *There will be plenty of time later to open the envelope, but for now, I vow to sleep.*

29

DIVINE INTERVENTION

Aldo had scheduled the funeral for Wednesday.

Noble would not delay his flight to attend; he was leaving on Tuesday as planned. He felt obliged to explain to Aldo that, since his parents' death, he avoided all funerals. "I believe a person's greatness should be celebrated while they are alive."

"I understand," he replied, without expression.

However, before Noble returned to the States to carry out Hamilton's decree, he decided to use his remaining day to tour Florence. He was hoping to capture the deep love Hamilton experienced—a paradox that drew him to a foreign city to live out his life, after devoting most of his time to protect his own country. Noble concluded that a formal tour, laden with tourists huddled together, following the leader with an umbrella, was not the way to capture the essence of Hamilton's affection for Florence.

"Aldo, you must be terribly busy arranging for the funeral, but would you be able to spend a few hours with me today? I'd like to see some of the director's favorite places."

"Actually, the director made most of the arrangements for the funeral some time ago."

"Of course he did." Noble smiled, remembering Hamilton left no strings untied.

"I'd be honored to show you the director's Florence."

—

Within the hour, they ventured out of the villa and turned left onto Via della Torre del Gallo. They continued up to the top of the hill, where they viewed the twelfth-century fortified castle that belonged to the Galli

Family.

"We could take a right and continue down this hill to Via di San Leonardo, which leads straight down to the Arno and into the historic district," Aldo offered. "Another choice is to take this left, onto Via del Pian de Giullari, and walk through Arcetri, a sort of seamless suburb. It was a favorite walk of the director."

"To the left." Noble smiled.

As they began to wander, Noble viewed the vast countryside of Tuscany, and looking to the right, he eyed the Osservatorio Astrofisico.

"It means the Observatory of Astrophysics, and it is where the Galileo Galilei Institute for Theoretical Physics is located," referenced Aldo. "Ingenious minds such as Galileo made amazing discoveries there, which left permanent and positive effects on the world."

I'm reminded of another genius, the elusive Simon, who wreaked havoc and left destruction in his wake—a passing thought Noble kept to himself.

As Aldo continued his walking tour, Noble could not help but reflect on the massive decisions, affecting many lives, Hamilton had handed him to make. He viewed most options with compassion, save those involving Simon and the president, both of whom earned his disrespect and disgust.

"Are you feeling all right?" Aldo inquired, noticing the vacant expression on Noble's face.

"I'm fine. It is just that since the death of the director, I keep recalling some key aspects of the last case we worked on together," he offered apologetically. "I do appreciate your time, and I am fascinated by the history."

Noble continued to listen to Aldo, but at the same time couldn't help thinking about his brother-in-law, Paolo Salvatore, "the savior," and his sister Natalie, who were working on reconciliation. Natalie had refused to continue her relationship with Paolo as long as he worked for the White House.

At first, Paolo found it impossible to extricate himself from his role as the president's communications director, which he'd learned to love as much as writing the speeches. Illogical as it seemed, he even had aspirations of continuing his career with the next administration, the party notwithstanding.

Natalie continued to urge him to step down, or to resign, after discovering Simon's plot. She frequently mentioned her concern that if the events were uncovered, he could be convicted of defrauding the government, which would devastate their lives. Using legal semantics, she cited several other possible crimes, holding even stiffer penalties, in an emotional attempt to dissuade him from continuing his role. Despite her legal training and persuasive skills, Paolo was undeterred.

However, after suffering several months of separation, Paolo capitulated. He understood his gross misjudgment. His family was far more precious to him than his fleeting eminence in the White House. He began to devote time to repair the broken trust in their marriage. In an attempt to reconcile, he arranged for an extended, long-overdue vacation with Natalie and Mario. Fortunately, he had been able to accumulate significant savings over the years for this venture.

Simon had paid him well.

Simon had paid everyone well.

Paolo dipped into his funds, and the three of them departed on a month-long cruise along the western coast of Italy. Upon his return, he established a consultancy, specializing in speechwriting and public relations, for the movers and shakers in the private sector. Once again, the revamped Paolo was thriving in a successful career, supported by a blissful family life. In many ways, his Italian family roots wrote the script for him.

Recovering from his reverie, Noble heard Aldo say, "On our right was once the country home of Galileo. Actually, it was the home where he endured eleven years of forced exile."

"You caught me, Aldo. Sorry! I was thinking about my family, which includes an Italian, I might add. That is no excuse," Noble said remorsefully. "You were speaking of Galileo's exile, yes?"

"Yes." Aldo smiled.

"Not a bad alternative, considering the Church of Rome almost tried him for heresy for his sun-oriented theory of the universe," Noble recalled, noting the size of the villa located on the edge of Florence.

"I quite agree. We are now walking on Via di San Matteo in Arcetri and on your left is an elementary school, named after, of course, Galileo Galilei." A few moments later they walked passed a convent where the daughters of Galileo lived out their lives.

Noble continued to listen with interest to the history lessons Aldo was imparting as they meandered down a long, winding road, when thoughts of Seymour crept into his wandering mind.

Seymour was in the same relative position as Paolo. Apparently, he had worn out his welcome when his tactics were exposed, and he had become persona non grata in the political world, for reasons that were not clear. Seymour eventually took Hamilton's advice and extricated himself from the White House without adieu. He wrapped up the last of his projects and then headed to L.A.

When the president encountered resistance, Hank attempted to induce Seymour to create a few political ads. However, Seymour always refused, replying with the excuse, "I don't have the time to commit to another project." Hank realized there were other deeper reasons.

Finally, Seymour produced his epic film, *The Framework*, based on the lives of the Founding Fathers and their contributions in the drafting of the Constitution. The theme of the film delved into the collective thinking that led to a durable construct of government incorporating common values. The film was a smashing success at the box offices and Seymour was riding high.

Just as Noble tried to shake his thoughts away from La Fratellanza, they walked around a bend to be presented with the most breathtaking view that caught him short. "What is that large structure off in the distance?" Noble asked, attempting to refocus.

"It is the monastery at Certosa. The monastery was built in the fourteenth century, originally for the Carthusian Order, and has a fascinating history."

I'm truly trying to stay focused on the present, he counseled himself, *but the shock of Hank, being the complete converse of a monk, overwhelms me.*

Noble's empathy for Hank was slight. Predictably, he did not heed Hamilton's advice, but was drawn to the side of the president. His loyalty shifted smoothly and undetectably from Simon to Abner Baari. His organization, the Chestnut Foundation, continued to be under investigation, at present for voter fraud.

Perhaps it was another mysterious leak? Noble asked himself. Naturally, Simon had popped into his head momentarily. *As I reflect on the mysterious disclosures of information that continue to plague the gang of four, Simon always comes to mind, and although fleeting, it is disturbing,* Noble wondered. *It seems like more than a mere coincidence.*

Aldo, recognizing he had lost Noble's complete attention once again, simply smiled and proceeded, but this time with a slightly elevated voice. "This is the entrance to the Istituto di Fisica, meaning Institute of Physics, which leads back up to the observatory we passed when we started our walk. We are now on Via di San Leonardo and at the corner, just up ahead, is the Viale Galileo Galilei. A *viale* is considered larger than a *via*. I know our language, and many of our expressions, can be somewhat confusing."

"Yes, a lot is confusing, but it is a melodic language, so beautiful to the ear."

"Thank you. May I suggest we cross over and continue to walk down the rest of Via San di Leonardo to the Arno?"

"Absolutely! By the way, that was a marvelous walk through the countryside. I can understand why it was a favorite of the director."

"Now are you ready for the busy streets of Florence?"

"Lead on, my friend."

Odd, Aldo feels like my friend, and even stranger, he reminds me somewhat of Chase, he reflected.

Chase was honest and decent to the core, except for his slavish loyalty to Simon. Whether it was a character flaw or an irrational devotion, Chase's fate was about to be sealed. Another suspicious leak of information led his bank to be under investigation, for falsifying reports sent to the Securities and Exchange Commission.

Knowing Chase, I suspect it is not true, but I suppose it is painful for him nonetheless, Noble concluded.

Chase continued to function in his dream job in New York, even with the cloud of the SEC overhead. He was always confident he'd be exonerated in the end. That aside, he continued to enjoy his family life in Connecticut—he never contacted any of La Fratellanza again.

Simon manipulated all of them, and perhaps, his manipulation persists in the form of unexplained leaks that continue to afflict each of them, a feeling he could not keep at bay. *Unfortunately, I can't share any of these thoughts with Aldo, or with anyone. There was a time when I could share them with Hamilton,* he thought wistfully.

Attempting to engage, he said, "I read in the guidebooks that the Florentine's call Via di San Leonardo one of the most beautiful streets in Florence."

"Yes, and I think you will agree."

They ambled down the twisting cobblestone road, lined with stone walls surrounding elegant villas, with an occasional open gate exposing lush views of the countryside.

"I am beginning to get a sense of what drew the director out of his beloved country to that of another," Noble acknowledged.

Aldo turned his head toward Noble and smiled.

They approached the arch leading to Costa di San Giorgio. *Costa* meaning a street with a slope, which they passed through, and soon thereafter, past the once "city" home of Galileo, a scant two miles from his "home in exile."

"I'm starting to feel as though I have been walking in the footsteps of Galileo."

"You have been, along with many other extraordinary people," Aldo confirmed.

Suddenly, another observation crossed Noble's mind, as he remembered the charges of heresy against Galileo and was gripped by the fear that he could be facing serious charges for his part in the entire scheme. Noble agonized silently. He felt he was in a whirlwind with his head spinning, not being able to control his thoughts, stray thoughts about his friends, his family, his career, and most of all, his country. Passing through the ancient street with its stone walls, he couldn't help but ponder, *If these walls could talk, I wonder what they would say.* He imagined walking behind Lorenzo "the Magnificent" de Medici, perhaps the greatest patron of the

Renaissance artists and scholars. He could almost hear him offering and receiving advice from those that followed him.

"The Medici court included such greats as Pico della Mirandola, Niccolò Machiavelli, and Leonardo da Vinci, to name a few," Aldo injected.

I wonder what counsel they would give me, Noble contemplated silently.

"I would have loved to hear from Machiavelli!"

"Why Machiavelli?" Aldo asked.

"While there are those who think his political manipulation was for evil, I believe his 'trickery' was to control the politician for the good of the people."

"Interesting theory."

"If only these walls could talk," Noble repeated, this time aloud.

Quickly snapping back to reality, they walked through the arch at the end of Costa de' Magnoli, leaving the walls behind with the Arno River in front of them.

"Just up ahead we'll make a right where we will cross the Arno on the Ponte Vecchio."

"I understand it was the only bridge not destroyed during World War II," Noble said, displaying his prowess.

"That is true. It was considered an architectural wonder and was spared by a Nazi German officer. Out of the six bridges, only the Ponte Vecchio survived solely due to a German officer simply feeling 'it was too beautiful to blow up.'" Aldo beamed.

"I must admit, after having studied all those travel books over the years and now actually being in this beautiful city, I'm starting to feel at home."

"The director would have liked that."

At the mention of the director, Noble tried to resist the thought, unsuccessfully, of Hamilton and Simon in the Vasari Corridor, the famous structure above the goldsmith shops, on the east side of the pedestrian walk on the Ponte Vecchio. They apparently had been standing only several feet apart from each other. Hamilton had come within a hair of capturing a world terrorist, once considered Noble's friend.

They entered the busy, narrow streets of Florence, and spent the next hour winding in and out of those pathways in the historic center of town.

"Many times the director would describe the city to me as 'a walking museum.' It truly is as we pass the statues, tabernacles, palaces, and palazzos, which appear in abundance."

"Yes, he was correct," Aldo said, then added with regret, "I'm sorry, but at this point, I must leave you and return to the villa to manage a few affairs. Will you be comfortable roaming on your own?"

"Yes, and thank you. I appreciate your time and the tour. I'm sure I can find my way back easily."

Aldo headed up the hill to La Piazzola degli Uganelli and Noble wandered toward the Duomo.

Only a short time had passed when Noble, feeling a lull coming on, headed toward a café for one of those energy-producing espressos. However, as he passed the beautiful church, Orsanmichele, he noticed the small street Via Tavolini. He remembered that earlier, Aldo had recommended a restaurant at the end of the street in the small piazza, a favorite of Hamilton's. So, Noble decided to look for the Ristorante Birreria Centrale, in the Piazza Cimatori. Within a five-minute walk, he stumbled into the small restaurant, described by some as an old Tyrolean tavern. Evidently, its Austrian neighbor influenced the cuisine of the northern region of Italy.

A tall, balding man with a very gentle face and with smiling eyes greeted him at the entrance.

Noble asked for a table, mentioning the restaurant was a recommendation by an acquaintance, Aldo Tancredi.

Oddly, this gentle giant asked, "Are you a friend of the director?"

Stunned he replied, "Yes, he was my dearest friend."

The restaurateur quickly ushered Noble to the inside table directly behind the entrance door, where Noble sat down, and so did the restaurateur.

"My name is Alessandro." He explained they were sitting at the director's table, the place where he sat most Friday nights.

Noble could sense he was not fluent in English, but was doing quite well.

"I am deeply sorry to hear about the death of the director. He was also my dear friend," he offered, clearly with a heavy heart.

Noble heard Florence was truly a small town, despite its size, and that the Florentines communicate the old-fashioned way, by speaking to one another. Without the use of the Internet or texting, they were still able to convey rumors and news to one another at warp speed. Within less than twenty-four hours, anyone who knew Hamilton received notice of his death.

Noble, going from a slight lull to being famished, asked if he could see a menu.

Alessandro insisted he leave the ordering to him, and for the next two hours, he lavished Noble with some of the best Italian food he had ever tasted.

Noble also discovered that if you are a friend of someone the Italians respect, then you are likely to become their friend, as well. During the lunch, and for another hour after, Alessandro introduced many of the restaurant's regulars to him, who were also friends of Hamilton.

Noble met Alessandro's brother, Massimiliano, who was operating their other restaurant near the Duomo, called Antico Ristorante il Sasso di Dante. Amazed by the coincidence, he thought, *I believe this is the very same restaurant where Hank and Hussein had shared many dinners.*

Then Alessandro introduced Noble to an art instructor from the Florence Academy of Art. Again, with a sense of déjà vu, he thought, *That is the same school where Professoressa Ducale was an instructor.* Fortunately, for Noble, the art instructor spoke English, so he asked him if he knew the professoressa.

"I vaguely remember she resigned shortly after an incident with the police, but I wasn't familiar with the details," was all he had to say.

Of course, Noble had total recall.

More introductions followed, and he met Eugenio Bresciani, the curator at the Uffizi, the same guide Hamilton had detained after Simon's escape, and then later befriended.

"My sincerest condolences, he was a kind man," Eugenio offered.

As touched as Noble was with all the outpouring of affection for Hamilton, it was close to four o'clock, long past the restaurant's closing time for lunch. He didn't want to overstay his welcome, so he politely disengaged from the conversation and asked for the check.

Alessandro immediately waved his hand, signaling no check, and in his best English said, "It is my pleasure."

Another attempt to pay was futile, so he thanked Alessandro for his hospitality and generosity before departing. As he was about to bid his final adieus, he noticed Alessandro had poured him a grappa. Moreover, not just for him, but for all those present, including the wait and kitchen staff.

With everybody standing, Alessandro proposed a toast. "To the Direttore."

With tears flowing freely, and sorrow in their hearts, they downed the grappa, at the same table where the director had also enjoyed many a grappa.

Hamilton must be smiling at the sight of us all together. Noble smiled along at the thought.

After more hugs, and kisses cheek to cheek, Noble departed en route to the villa.

He was sure that after the long lunch, hearty wine, a hint of jet lag, and of course, the grappa, it would be impossible for him to maneuver back up the two torturous hills he had previously walked. However, he resisted the temptation to hail a taxi and ventured toward the Arno.

During the trek, a sudden insight gave him one of the reasons Hamilton never returned to the States, an answer that had eluded him. Pausing in observation, he realized something. *It was about the small restaurant in the corner of a small piazza, where I just met Hamilton's family. His life was not as empty as I had imagined. Now I understand one reason why Hamilton loved Florence so much and remained here until his death*, he concluded, with a consoling smile.

Actually, he was so lost in his thoughts that he did not recall the hills he climbed. He was surprised to find himself standing at the front door of Hamilton's home so soon.

—

As Noble opened the door to the villa and inhaled the aroma, his heart sank as he deduced Aldo was in the process of preparing dinner. He was still full from lunch, and had hoped that in the next few hours he'd feel less sated. At eight, dinner was announced and Noble, without an appetite and embarrassed, nibbled enough so he wouldn't offend.

After dinner, Aldo presented him with his second grappa of the day. This time it first burned his throat, then transformed into a pleasantly warm and soothing sensation. On the second sip, it worked its way effortlessly into the digestive system, making peace with all the foods he had consumed. Surprisingly, he felt as though he had not overeaten, but was just pleasantly sated. Now he understood why Italians love their *digestivo*, a lesson he would not forget.

Noble had invited Aldo to join him for a nightcap, which he did. Their conversation started with pleasantries, and then Aldo opened up with more information about the director's life in Florence, in affectionate terms. Noble could easily see what a devoted servant and friend he had been.

"The director has made provisions for me to return to Veneto, northeast of Florence, where my sister and her family live. He was a very generous man and made it possible for me to retire. However, I must close the villa and dispose of the director's possessions according to his wishes," he reported with immense sadness.

They continued their chat until Noble surrendered to his persistently closing eyelids. He thanked Aldo for his service to Hamilton, thanked him for his hospitality, and bade him a good night.

—

Noble returned to his room thoroughly spent, but his mind kept drifting to Hamilton, which kept him awake. *I know Hamilton loved his country. He was a true patriot and devoted his life fighting to keep the U.S. safe. Despite his passion, he never returned.* "Something I don't understand," he said, speaking to the air. He met his Florentine family, which explained only part of the quandary, but not all. It only suggested that he had deep roots in the community.

I believed initially he had compunctions about not exposing the president sooner, which he considered part of his sacred duty to his country. With great trepidation, Noble squirmed a bit, as he took into account that he now wore the mantle.

Or perhaps it was the retirement benefits that came his way, compliments of Simon. I was thunderstruck when he indirectly confirmed that he had helped himself to a share of the illicit pie.

Questions kept invading his sleep. *Perhaps Hamilton preferred isolation to the constant reminders he would have encountered from the newscasts, newspaper headlines, and gossip at the water cooler.*

"Hamilton knew he had the power to change it all, to stop everything, and at the same time, he knew he couldn't bring himself to do it," he mumbled, half awake.

Finally, unable to continue the fight against the sleep that was enveloping him, he gave in with the words, "It really isn't important to know his rationale—anymore." He hoped to take solace in believing Hamilton wanted to live out the rest of his life with his compromises, but wondered if he'd truly been at peace.

However, Noble's eyes were wide open to the tremendous burdens he was undertaking. Despite the weight of many obstacles, he felt ready to take on the challenges. Fate brought him to this juncture, but he conceded it would take fortitude and dedication to achieve success.

—

The next morning, while seated in a taxi, he asked the driver to make one quick stop before he headed to the airport. He couldn't resist the desire to visit Hamilton's favorite spot in the piazza of the church of San Miniato al Monte.

Noble had abandoned his religious beliefs shortly after the loss of his parents. He had refused to accept their sudden deaths, as it would require an act of faith. However, at San Miniato, while spending those few precious hours with Hamilton, a sense of spirituality that he thought he had lost forever, overcame him. It was unexpected, but all consuming.

I suppose I want to confirm the validity of my earlier experience before leaving Florence, he conceded.

The driver stopped the taxi at the arch entering the piazza, and Noble proceeded to the wall under the cypress. As he sat there looking out over the beautiful city spread before him, a hand touched his shoulder. Startled, he turned around to find a monk, with a glowing smile, in a long flowing white robe. The sunlight encircled his face almost like an aura.

"My name is Angelo," he said, introducing himself in a soft, pleasing voice. "May I sit down beside you?" Before Noble could respond, he took Noble's hand in his and, with his halting English and melodious accent, proceeded to stun Noble. "I saw you sitting with the director yesterday and I know he considered you a son." Noble sighed as the monk continued, "The director had many conversations with me over the years and shared many of the decisions he made that tormented him."

Angelo did not expose the details of those conversations with Noble, but he was comfortable that they were secret and safe. It struck Noble as the moral equivalent of a Roman Catholic confession.

"Before the director died, God visited him, and he was forgiven for all his sins," Angelo assured him. "When Hamilton walked through the Gate to Heaven, he was at peace." Still clasping Noble's hand between his, he continued. "I suspect there are terrible burdens placed on you with the director's death, but he died having complete faith that you will always do *the noble thing*."

Angelo may not have expected Noble to smile, but Noble was remembering the times Hamilton said those exact words to him, whenever he faced a dilemma. *I wasn't sure if Angelo knew my name or its relevance, but it was of no significance except to me,* he later reflected.

As Angelo spoke of the burdens, Noble faced a strange sensation that came over him, much like his experience during his first visit to San Miniato. *I feel as though this kind monk, with the glowing face, is absorbing my pain, and in return transmitting an enormous sense of peace, one of clarity and enlightenment*—an awesome sensation Noble never forgot.

Then as quickly as Father Angelo arrived, he was gone.

Noble turned to see this spiritual man walk away, with his long white robe flowing in the breeze, against the stunning facade of San Miniato as a backdrop.

He took one last look at the beautiful city that lay below, as he thought, *If there truly is a heaven on earth, this must be the place—a place where I'm beginning to feel a divine intervention has just occurred.*

Noble walked back through the arch, this time with a lighter step, and returned to the taxi to begin his long journey home.

—

Sitting in the Peretola Airport, waiting to board his flight, reality set in regarding the path of life-changing decisions he could not escape. He returned to the time the president appointed him interim director, and then his confirmation as director of the SIA, remembering it was not a welcome moment. He was well suited for his position as a research analyst and recognized he was relatively inexperienced to manage the agency. Besides, he always preferred to work alone. However, in April 2009, he had had no choice but to accept. At that time, Noble was deeply entrenched in the Simon case and was certain the president was aware of his role as the assistant to Director Scott. So unwillingly, he had become the caretaker of the SIA, expected to carry out all of its responsibilities—except exposing the president.

He blithely assumed Hamilton would always take the lead when that day arrived.

Unfortunately, his death changed the metrics radically.

Hours before he passed away, Hamilton decided the time had arrived to expose the president and take steps to prevent a repetition. To have the desired effect, he concluded, the American people were entitled to the disclosure of the elaborate plot before they voted in the upcoming election—now the onus was on Noble to end the entire conspiracy.

It is strange how dramatically circumstances can change, he reminded himself.

As he started to deliberate on a number of issues, he heard his flight called and headed for his gate. Once settled into his seat, his mind began to race for answers. During the seven-hour flight back to Washington, he was compelled to review the plan he would then have to execute, all the while feeling the enormous weight on his shoulders.

As visions of Hamilton passed before him, so did those of Father Angelo. Those images renewed his confidence and resolve as he prepared to take the final vital steps. He decided to run through the pros and cons, knowing all the while the pros would win. Ultimately, the means by which he would execute the plan would become critical.

As he reached into his briefcase for his iPad, he latched on to the envelope Aldo presented him before he left Hamilton's home. He held the packet for some time, staring at his name written in scrawled handwriting by Hamilton's shaky hand. Sensing he was now prepared for his words of wisdom, he proceeded to open the envelope, and removed the single white sheet of paper. However, to his surprise, there were no words of wisdom, only another mystery to unravel.

Written on the paper was simply "National Depositors Trust Bank, Wisconsin Avenue, Georgetown. Use it wisely." In the envelope, there was also a key—obviously a safe-deposit-box key.

30

A NOBLE THING

Noble sat back in his office chair with his feet on the desk and his hands clasped behind his head. He was reflecting on his Florence trip and the events that unfolded.

He was sitting just a stairway from the president.

During the flight home, he repeatedly reviewed the steps he needed to take to finalize Hamilton's plan, which was now his to execute. All the while, the knot in his stomach was unyielding; he was not able to shake off the tension that had been building up. Although, after a night of sound sleep he was more at ease, confident, and ready to face the enormous challenges that confronted him.

Noble knew he was about to jeopardize his position as director, and more important, his personal life, for the actions he and Hamilton had taken, which would be put into question. To start, there was the fact that he had provided immunity to the members of La Fratellanza further complicated by the means they undertook to track down Simon. Both actions could be a legal nightmare, and not having shared this vital information with other national security agencies exacerbated that complication.

Then, of course, there was SAVIOR.

Most significant, he and Hamilton had knowledge of an ongoing crime that continued for years—now the time had arrived to begin unraveling the complex plot.

Noble's first order of business, when he arrived at his office, was to consult the in-house attorney. He created a hypothetical case involving the rules and restrictions to grant immunity. He was able to confirm his own belief that their course of action would stand up in court.

Next, Noble sorted through the cast of characters, as he reviewed the roles of the key players.

He knew Hank's involvement had been questionable for years. He and his foundation were already under investigation, and while not directly related to his activities with the president, it appeared it would keep him embroiled in legal entanglements for years.

Chase's efforts, considered by some to be tantamount to shouting, "Fire!" in a theater, would be complicated to prove. The distribution of his white paper showed no direct correlation to the crisis, even though his prediction had been accurate. Chase did allow Simon access to his banking system, and if revealed, it most probably would cost him his job, but it did not rise to a federal crime. As of the moment, he still faced legal battles with the Securities and Exchange Commission.

Paolo and Seymour had always worked on behalf of the senator and then the president, and while their methods were dubious, they did not commit a crime per se.

The only concrete evidence Noble had on La Fratellanza was their video-recorded testimonies. However, they had already received conditional immunity in exchange for their statements, which was uppermost in Noble's mind. He also believed the gang of four had no real knowledge of Simon's ulterior motives, but only harbored their suspicions. Consequently, the only provable evidence of a crime was the events that linked directly to Simon. Of especial import was Simon's falsification of the president's identity.

No matter, Simon had vanished.

In the final analysis, it was Noble's responsibility to close the book on the entire multifaceted conspiracy. According to plan, it would be a way to minimize the damage to the country, and square it with the American people.

At the time the plot had unraveled, Hamilton and Noble felt bound by their patriotic duty, but recognized they would be the targets of critics, and possibly face court trials and lawsuits; no doubt, it would have provided fertile ground for congressional investigative committees, ad nauseam. In the end, they considered it a small price to pay to protect the United States.

Now—all the risks aside—Hamilton had determined the decisive moment had arrived.

Noble was committed to honoring his decision.

—

Noble took a moment to call Paolo to see how he and Natalie were doing and to tell him about Hamilton's death. "I also want you to know about a decision I have made," he announced, with noticeable sadness in his voice. He trusted Paolo, who was pivotal in upending Simon's original plot, and wanted him to prepare Natalie for any fallout. Noble informed him that he was going to expose the president, but would try to protect La Fratellanza within legal limits in the process.

Paolo was equally dismayed to learn about Hamilton, but was even more sympathetic toward Noble, knowing what he was facing, and the steps he was about to take. However, hearing about Hamilton caused Paolo to recollect an unusual conversation, which had taken place between the president and Hank a short time after Hamilton left for Florence in 2009.

"I have some information that may be of importance. I'm just sorry I had forgotten about it until now," he said hesitatingly. "Hank acquainted me with a conversation, but at the time I wasn't focused and was trying to deal with my own problems at home."

Paolo explained that according to Hank, the president confronted him, telling him the director of the SIA had discovered his identity, and then asked him what he knew about Simon Hall.

"Hank said, 'I feigned shock and decided offering half-truths is better than no truth.'"

Hank told the president Simon was a classmate at Harvard and contacted him in 2002, asking for his help. Hank's fabrication was that Simon was the person who had informed him that a team of powerful men had identified a brilliant young man living in Italy. Simon claimed this powerful group wanted Hank to take whatever measures were necessary to have the Chosen One elected president of the United States, with their full support and total financial backing.

"You know Hank can be quite full of himself, and as he relayed his version, when speaking with the president, he puffed up and declared—'Now the SIA knows that young man is you.'"

"How did the president react?" Noble asked.

"Evidently, the president asked Hank if he had disclosed the information about his identity."

"I surmise Hank denied it and said the leak must have come from either Simon or the group of supporters, whose identity of course had remained anonymous."

"Exactly, you've got his number."

"Did the president accept his explanation?"

"Yes. Without further inquiry into Hank's involvement, the president told Hank that Simon Hall had stolen funds from his TSAR account, the funds which had been set aside for his social programs. The president then suddenly erupted, 'All of it, over five hundred billion dollars, is gone!' Hank told me he was shocked, and this time it was genuine. I must admit I was even more surprised. We had suspected Simon was up to something, but I never imagined to such a degree," Paolo commented.

"It's a far cry from the alleged game," Noble admitted.

"Noble, you'll love this. Hank told me he almost fell off his chair when the president announced he wanted him to gear up for his reelection campaign for a second term. Hank, unfazed, said, 'At one time I was concerned with the president's arrogance and guile, but I am no longer concerned because now I find it an appealing asset that will win over the public,'" Paolo conveyed with disgust.

Noble could hear Paolo mutter, "The guy is unbelievable!"

In a short time, the president had lost his ill-gotten social programs funds, his phenomenal source of political contributions, his communications director, and Seymour, the man who created and maintained his image in the media. Of particular importance, the president had squandered his precious political capital on a variety of dead-end issues. And even with the prospect that Director Scott would one day reveal his identity, Baari forged ahead. Ignoring the impossible headwinds, he enlisted the help of Hank, who was quick to climb on board, to win a second term.

"Obviously, unbeknownst to the president, he had no idea of the extraordinary talent he'd lost, with the disappearance of Simon." Noble scoffed.

"Hank was quick to report the president's last comment." Paolo sneered, "Power is not only what you have but what the enemy thinks you have."

Hank knew the quote well; it was Saul Alinsky's.

"After relating his conversation with the president, Hank blurted out, 'I feel more like Dr. Frankenstein than Henry Higgins,' whom he used to boast about comparing his resemblance to the *My Fair Lady* character."

"Hank may have thoughtlessly created a monster, but evidently, he still feels responsible for the care and feeding of that monster." Noble teased.

Hank decided to ride the wave with the president for as long as circumstances allowed. He had not given up on his original agenda and wanted to ram through as many social programs as possible while they had control of the Oval Office.

"According to Hank, 'He'd find the funding later.'"

Meanwhile, Hank's Chestnut Foundation continued to be plagued with investigations, the president's influence notwithstanding.

Hamilton had warned the president years ago that the day of reckoning would come. The president, having no choice, lived up to his word more or less. He halted some of the spending and made moderate efforts to reduce the huge deficit. Without his $500 billion slush fund, he had no choice but to unwind some of his social programs, and much to Hank's chagrin, prevented Congress from imposing others.

"I guess I feel a whisper of sympathy for Hank, Chase, and Seymour, and would be deeply saddened if my actions affect you and Natalie. However,

I hope you understand that, feelings aside, there could be another puppet waiting in the wings to step into the president's role, and the prospect of that happening again trumps any feeling of regret I may have."

"I understand what is at stake, and I know America can't afford to have this happen again. You have my full support," Paolo avowed.

"Thank you, my friend, this means a lot, because when I meet with the president I will explain to him that the wheels are in irreversible motion. He has had years to prepare for this moment. I'm giving the president sufficient notice to carry out his plan in response to the exposé. At that time, I will disclose his citizenship to the media, followed by a press conference."

"I gather you will strongly encourage him to step down immediately?" Paolo inquired.

"Most certainly. He will have no choice, or I will implicate him in the Treasury scandal as well, especially with regard to his manipulation of TSAR."

Noble also shared his belief with Paolo that it was best to identify the mastermind of the plot as Simon Hall. Others were involved to varying degrees, but he was blatantly guilty of committing numerous felonies. Exposing Mohammed al-Fadl at this time was an issue Noble would wrestle with for some time.

What would be the consequences? He would repeatedly ask himself.

Since Simon was still at large, he reasoned the revelation would have a large-scale negative effect on the American people, heightening their terrorist paranoia. Besides, Noble was never able to determine Simon's underlying motives. He could only assume the money siphoned from TSAR would have been used for more deadly events, even worse than those he had committed in the past. Since Simon's escape in April 2009, Interpol had been relentlessly hunting him down, to no avail. After mulling over the pros and cons almost incessantly, Noble had concluded it was a battle to be fought another day. For the present, Simon's true identity would not be exposed.

"There will be no legal or political need to implicate the rest of the La Fratellanza, so long as they live up to their vow of silence," Noble assured Paolo. "Baari may ultimately choose to implicate Hank for his role, but there is no advantage for Hank to expose La Fratellanza, unless he is forced to by events beyond his control," he added. "I'm sure I don't need to remind you of the conditions of immunity."

"No, I remember vividly—one of us talks, we all go down."

"Don't hesitate to jog the memories of your brethren."

"No need to worry about Chase and Seymour, but Hank could be a problem."

"There is no advantage to Hank. I'm confident he'll remain silent, knowing the consequences. Besides if he did talk, I'm sure he would take all the credit for the care and feeding of his monster," Noble joked, even though it wasn't far from the truth.

He could hear Paolo chuckle from the other end of the line.

"Paolo, with all seriousness, the main purpose of this call is to make you aware of what is about to happen. I trust you and Natalie will remain silent, as well. Give my love to Natalie and Mario, and I'll see you both soon."

—

Left alone with his thoughts, Noble began to ponder how he would broach the conversation with the president and how he would deal with the media.

His first priority was to inform the vice president that he would be stepping into the breach in accordance with the president's plan, and to caution him that, in the interest of national security, he must remain silent on the matter until he was specifically released from his pledge of secrecy. There were only a few months before the election, and Noble believed the vice president could be kept under control during that time—in fact, his own party, having to defend his gaffes continuously— would see to it.

Second, and equally vital, Noble began to sort through his options. He needed to determine the degree of information that would need to be divulged, producing the least amount of backlash.

Of course, the president knew Paolo, Seymour, and Chase, but only as legitimate staff members during his presidential campaign in 2007, who he retained during his administration. He had no knowledge of their involvement in the master plot or that they were aware of his identity. He only knew they had resigned from their positions for personal reasons, which he accepted. Noble was confident their roles in the plot would remain confidential.

However, there were other factors in play. He knew he would have to take careful measures when describing Hamilton and his unorthodox methods to expose the entire conspiracy—placing himself at greater risk.

Word had leaked, from an unknown source, about the missing funds, so Noble would adeptly diminish the role of the Treasury secretary by simply stating that he hired Simon as a consultant, based on his impeccable qualifications, to design TSAR, as a system to manage the accounting of the TAP fund. He would make clear that the Treasury secretary had no idea of Simon's ultimate plot to steal those funds. Once again, all evidence pointed to Simon—he alone siphoned off the money—a point that would be stressed nonstop.

Noble would illustrate how he and former Director Hamilton Scott uncovered Simon's plot to defraud the United States and how they traced some of the stolen funds to a bank account in Florence, Italy. He would explain how the president sent the former director to Florence to oversee a sting operation in conjunction with Interpol. Unfortunately, he would report that Simon escaped before they could retrieve the money.

There would be no mention of setting up the Zurich accounts—or the transfer of funds for safekeeping—which the director deliberately left out of his briefing on the amended flash drive. At the time, Hamilton determined that if they transferred the recovered funds back to the Treasury, there would still be opportunities for the administration to squander the money unless he maintained control of the funds.

In keeping with Hamilton's instructions, Noble would escrow those funds and transfer them into the TSAR holding account on January 19, 2017, the eve of the swearing in of the new president, whoever that might be.

With every new administration, the General Accountability Office reruns the numbers and the new president inevitably discovers an inherited surplus or a deficit, a ritual on which Noble relied.

To be exact, this new administration would discover a surplus of $479,848,376,702.00.

—

Before Noble arrived at his office that morning, he had stopped at the National Depositors Trust Bank in Georgetown. He wanted to be absolutely certain he left no stone unturned. Not knowing the contents of the safe-deposit box, he felt it imperative to pursue what could be another lead.

Noble met with the bank manager and asked for access to safe-deposit box #698. Using the key Noble had found in the envelope Aldo had given him, the bank manager was able to retrieve a large, square metal box. He left Noble alone in the room, with a guard posted outside the door.

With some uneasiness, he opened the box slowly, as if expecting a shock of some kind, even knowing it was from Hamilton. Taking a deep breath, he lifted the lid and noticed two envelopes. Noble opened a small gray envelope first. This envelope contained the flash drive, no surprise to him. He clasped it tightly, realizing he literally held the president's future in his hands. *I can hear Hamilton now, as he describes the masterful plot orchestrated by Simon Hall,* he contemplated. This same envelope also contained a set of the six memory sticks holding the video-recorded interrogations.

Noble placed both the flash drive and the memory sticks in the envelope and returned them to the metal box for safekeeping. Then he opened the smaller white envelope to find a single folded sheet of paper with an account number and, in an elegant script beneath it, the words "*Onorare il direttore*," signed by Aldo. He recognized the account number as that of a bank, and suspected it was the same bank where he was standing, but that would have to wait.

He had a crucial meeting scheduled within the hour.

—

Noble opened the meeting by informing the president that Director Hamilton Scott had died.

The president expressed perfunctory condolences.

"Before his death, Director Scott instructed me that the time had arrived to take the steps we should have taken many years ago," he said, speaking forcefully. "I feel there is no need to lay out the case for impeachment again—the same explanation that Director Scott presented to you years ago."

The president listened, and Noble was convinced he remembered the conversation vividly.

"And I am sure you will recall that we have concrete evidence to expose the appropriations you earmarked in TSAR. As has been agreed, it will continue to remain classified, unless you choose not to comply."

Noble sensed strongly that the president understood that he had already been granted a lengthy grace period to plan an exit strategy. The president showed every sign that he recognized that his time had run out.

"I still have the flash drive and the memory sticks containing all the evidence, and there are other strategically placed copies." Noble looked directly into the president's eyes and warned him. "I have made the same arrangement as Director Scott, in the event I encounter any suspicious, unexplainable events in my life."

The entire time Noble was speaking, the president listened intently and without interruption, especially when Noble informed him about revealing his identity to the media, followed by a scheduled press conference.

When Noble finished making his case, the president tilted his head back, never losing eye contact. He knew what was about to come next.

He had a retort ready, but out of respect for the office of the presidency, he refrained and sat back while the president said, "I get it."

Noble stood up, thanked him for his time, and left.

—

Somewhat shaken by all that had just occurred, he felt enormously relieved at the same time, as he walked down the stairway back to his office. With the door closed behind him, Noble sat at his desk, tilted his head back, clasped his hands over his chest, and closed his eyes.

He began to contemplate his future.

"After my statement to the press, my prospects may be bleak," he bemoaned.

On occasion, he thought about his cubicle buried in the bowels of the CIA with fondness—he didn't long for a cubicle with bars. Even without knowing what his future held, the weight on his shoulders began to dissipate. He was more convinced than ever that he and Hamilton had made the honorable choices.

"Damn it, Hamilton," he admonished himself. "You are forcing me to hack 'unofficially' into another banking system once again. I swear this will be the last time!" he fumed.

Noble managed to locate the online account at the National Depositors Trust Bank from the account number Aldo had written on the piece of paper. As he clicked on the Account Summary tab, the account balance took him aback. Taken aback was an understatement—shocked more aptly described his feelings. As he regained his composure, he noticed the words Aldo had written, "*Onorare il direttore.*"

Of course, Hamilton knew I'd do the noble thing.

Although he cursed Hamilton mildly once again for placing another burden on his shoulders, he sat back and began to explore his options. He started to think of the many worthwhile programs that had their funding cut from the federal budget recently. After some careful thought, he gave a lot of consideration to the No Child Left Behind program, feeling it was worthy of continuation. He remembered Baari reduced the funding in favor of the Inner City Youth Core Training program set up to teach community organizing. It was one of Baari's pet projects to spawn more advocates of his beliefs.

"That really infuriated me. I always thought the 'no child', meant all children," he spoke out. "Perhaps it would be best to leave that one alone."

Then there were cuts to other affected school programs with 95 percent success rates, cuts to NASA, cuts in Transit Security, cuts to Medicare, and the list of worthwhile programs continued.

Hamilton warned me we shouldn't tinker with history too much, he recalled. *Maybe I wouldn't be tinkering to any extent if I donated my largess to an institution like the Mayo Clinic, in Hamilton's memory, specifically for the purposes of medical research.*

Noble sat up in his chair, finding it an interesting exercise of wishful thinking, but in the end they weren't choices open to him. The only acceptable course of action was to return the $51,573,298.00 Hamilton generously set aside for him—to its source—the U.S. Treasury coffers.

Noble did not hesitate to transfer the funds. He hit the enter key confidently.

Almost instantly, he felt relieved. His sense of relief was unmatched by any previous experience in his life. He leaned back in his chair once again, completely satisfied with his decision, and smiled as he recollected his time with Hamilton at the SIA and in Florence. He thought about Aldo and so many other friends he had amassed, hoping perhaps that he would reconnect with them one day. Then his ruminations brought him back to the case.

It's unbelievable that a guy from a small town would be swept into an adventure of such enormous proportions.

I'm certainly not in Kansas anymore. He smiled.

To this day, there has never been a case so mind-boggling. Certainly, no fiction writer could spin such an intricate tale, one that defies the imagination, he envisioned in wonderment.

Noble, intoxicated by his reverie, was caught off guard when suddenly, that familiar beep from the computer signaling a message, invaded his thoughts.

He turned to view the incoming e-mail, which read,

Congratulations on doing the noble thing.
Your brother, Simon ☪

ACKNOWLEDGMENTS

Special thanks go to Alessandro and Massimiliano Galli, the restaurateurs of Ristorante Birreria Centrale and Antico Ristorante il Sasso di Dante, who have been great supporters; to Massimo Pivetti, for his time to conduct a private tour through the awesome Vasari Corridor and for his drawings introducing Part One and Part Two of this book; and to my friends Andrea Prestani, Moreno Chiarantini, Flavio Benvenuti, Simone Lavecchia and Sania Kaedum at Perini's Gastronomia in the Mercato Centrale, who have always been incredibly generous. Additionally, much gratitude goes to Dottore Franco Delle Piane, David and Catherine Gardner, Tony and Laura Sasa, Suzanne Pitcher, Francesca Achenza, Maria Grazia Chiappi, and Priscilla Morss Bayard for their continued encouragement and support—all of them have helped me learn the magic of living like an Italian.

One very special thanks goes to the compassionate monk from San Miniato al Monte, who not only gave me inspiration for part of my story but also gives me inspiration every day as I sit under my favorite cypress with extraordinary views of Florence. Much of the story unfolded during my moments of contemplation on the wall at San Miniato.

A special acknowledgment goes to Nellie Newton who read my original fifty-page concept, offered thoughtful suggestions, and encouraged me to take it to fruition—and to David and Alma, dear friends and longtime residents of Florence, who generously gave of their time and volunteered to read my manuscript, help authenticate my historical references, and most important, correct my improper use of Italian.

I am eternally grateful to Cherie Eliz, for applying her own writing skills diligently to read and edit my tome, along with heartfelt thanks to Donna and Lee, and Mary V and Ray Fernandez for agreeing to proofread and critique my novel—to each of them for their undying support and for fulfilling their promise to provide honest feedback.

I cannot overlook another group of special friends who never let a conversation pass without asking with great interest about the progress of my book and for continually cheering me on: Philip Claypool, Bella Donna, Rob, David and Ginny Freeman, Alixe Lischett, Michael Peel, Lisa Schreiber, Aabi Shapoorian, and Gary Vonk.

Love and appreciation goes to Dr. Patricia Ames, not only a very special aunt, but also my high school history teacher who first turned me onto politics, and helped to shape my analytical thought process.

Lastly, I am indebted to all of my American, Italian and other friends from around the world, too numerous to mention, for all the love and support they have given me throughout this endeavor.

ABOUT THE AUTHOR

Sally Fernandez's career background is project management, business planning, and technology, with additional experience in technical and business writing. Her books of fiction are based on knowledge garnered from careers in banking, computer technology, and business consulting, while living in New York City, San Francisco, and Hong Kong.

Fernandez's foray into fiction writing began in 2007 when the 2008 presidential election cycle was in full swing. The overwhelming political spin by the media compelled her to question the frightening possibilities the political scene could provoke. Fernandez, a confirmed political junkie, took to the keyboard armed with the current events and the need to unleash her story. Eighty-six-thousand words later, she had written a novel and discovered a new and exciting career. She had expertly weaved seemingly disparate events into a cohesive whole including a shocking, shattering climax. Fernandez is currently developing a sequel to her first novel "Brotherhood Beyond the Yard."

A world traveler, the author, and her husband split time between their homes in the United States and Italy.